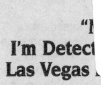

I'm Detect
Las Vegas

"Yes?" she whispered.

He flashed his identification in front of her. She could see he resembled his picture—he was an exceptionally attractive man. "I've been working on a missing person's case," he began.

No… A wave of fear washed over her. "Why are you asking *me* for help?"

He studied her for an uncomfortably long moment. "Brett?" he called over his shoulder.

Within seconds, a blond boy, probably junior-high age, and as tall as her five-foot-seven height, materialized at the detective's side.

"Brett," the detective said, "meet Martha Walters. Is she the woman you've been trying to find?"

"Yes, she's the one." *This boy had been searching for her*? Not until now had anyone from her past come forward.

"Have you been looking for a long time?"

"Since August twentieth of last year."

Martha had been dropped off at the women's shelter on August twenty-seventh—just one week later. Like a newborn babe, she'd arrived with no memories.

"How well do we know each other?" she asked the boy.

He eyed her solemnly. "You're my mom."

Dear Reader,

I loved books from a very young age and turned into a voracious reader. One story that made a deep impression on me was *Random Harvest*. I think I first read it when I was a teenager. The title meant little to me, but my mother (who read everything) told me I wouldn't be able to put it down because it was a story about a soldier with amnesia and the woman who loved him.

Needless to say, Mother was right! I couldn't put it down and have reread it many times over the years.

I have no doubts that the amnesia story I've written here, titled *She's My Mom*, was inspired by the novel I read so long ago. To be honest, I shed a lot of tears as I wrote about the love the hero and his son have for their wife and mother, who suffers from amnesia. It's my hope that this will be a satisfying and emotional read for you.

Rebecca Winters

P.S. If you have access to the Internet, please check out my Web site at http://www.rebeccawinters-author.com

Books by Rebecca Winters

HARLEQUIN SUPERROMANCE

She's My Mom
Rebecca Winters

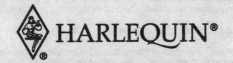

HARLEQUIN®

TORONTO • NEW YORK • LONDON
AMSTERDAM • PARIS • SYDNEY • HAMBURG
STOCKHOLM • ATHENS • TOKYO • MILAN • MADRID
PRAGUE • WARSAW • BUDAPEST • AUCKLAND

ISBN 0-373-71065-8

SHE'S MY MOM

Visit us at www.eHarlequin.com

Printed in U.S.A.

She's My Mom

CHAPTER ONE

"WHAT DO YOU THINK of this place now that it's finished, Brett?" Mr. Stevens owned the construction company that had built the Etoile, the newest hotel-casino in Las Vegas, Nevada. The hotel was shaped like the l'Arc de Triomphe located in Paris at the place de l'Etoile, the place of the star. From the restaurant window, Brett Corbitt could see half the city.

Twenty-five stories above the ground, it felt as if he was on top of a giant Ferris wheel suspended over the carnival below. But Brett had always lived in Las Vegas so it wasn't that big a deal. Since the death of his mother six months ago, nothing mattered, anyway.

"I like it a lot, Mr. Stevens. Thanks for the dinner," he added at the last second, almost forgetting his manners.

"You're welcome." He turned to his son Mike. "What have you two decided to do now?"

"Will you take us to Brett's? We're going to watch videos and then pitch a tent in his backyard."

Mr. Stevens glanced at Brett. "Your dad's not on duty tonight?"

"No."

"I thought he told me he was, and that's why he

couldn't come to dinner with us. I guess I was mistaken.''

"Dad doesn't like going places anymore, not without Mom," he murmured.

"I've noticed. He hasn't come to any parties at our house. Ellen and I have missed him. What a shame. It must be tough on you."

Brett didn't say anything. For a long time now, he wished his dad would just stay at the police station after he got off work. When he was home, all he did was read the paper with the television on, but Brett suspected his father's spirit was somewhere else. Most of the time when he looked at Brett, it was like he was staring right through him. Like he didn't exist…

"Maybe you guys should sleep over at our place," Mike's father said.

"It's okay, Mr. Stevens. Dad wants Mike to come. It's just that when he gets home from work, he doesn't feel like leaving the house again."

The older man nodded. "Eventually, that'll change." He pushed himself away from the table and got up. "I have to talk to the hotel manager on my way out. I'll only be a few minutes. Why don't I meet you guys down at the van?"

"Okay." They left the restaurant.

"Man, I can hardly wait until we're old enough to come in here and play the slot machines," Mike muttered to Brett as they entered the hallway.

Once Brett couldn't wait to do that either. But without his mom around, he couldn't care less about being in a casino. Her death had changed everything. It had especially changed his dad.

He never talked anymore. The pain in his eyes made Brett afraid to ask him personal things, let alone talk to him about *her*.

Mike reached the elevators before Brett did. There were six elevators, one for each leg of the arch. Four on the outside, two inside. At eight o'clock in the evening, all of them were packed.

His friend grew impatient. "Come on. Let's take the stairs."

That was fine with Brett. He hated the tourists who flocked to Las Vegas. Most of them were families with a father *and* a mother. Everyone looked happy. Brett had forgotten what that word meant. Tears stung his eyes as he raced down the steps behind his best friend.

Halfway down to the lobby, he saw a maid enter the eleventh-floor door and start up the stairs carrying a stack of towels. He flattened himself against the railing to make room.

She lifted her head to thank him before moving past.

"Mom?" he said without conscious thought.

But there'd been no recognition in her eyes. She kept on going as if she hadn't heard him. He stared after her until she disappeared behind the door opening on to the twelfth. She never looked back.

He'd just seen his mother!

It was her face and body. Her voice.

His mom wasn't dead.

"Hey, Brett? What's taking you so long?" Mike called from several flights below.

"I'm coming," he shouted back, torn between catching up with his friend and running after the woman who *had* to be his mother.

Brett was so traumatized by the experience he felt sick to his stomach. It was a good thing Mike's dad wasn't long in joining them in the hotel parking lot. Brett managed to pretend everything was fine until they'd driven him to his house in Green Valley.

After he'd told Mike to go to the den and choose a video, he bolted upstairs for his own bathroom. Up came the steak dinner Mr. Stevens had bought him.

When his stomach was emptied, he rinsed his mouth and brushed his teeth. Turning off the light, he left the bathroom only to discover his father standing in the middle of the bedroom, hands on his hips.

His eyes searched Brett's face. "How long have you been ill?"

Brett's pulse rate shot up. "I—I was fine until I had dessert. Mike's dad ordered this nasty banana thing. It had alcohol in it and made me sick."

"You're unnaturally pale. I want you to go to bed."

"I'm feeling better now. Mike and I were planning to watch videos."

"Not tonight. I'll run him home. When I return, I expect to find you under the covers. I'll be right back."

Surprised that his father had been aware anything was wrong, he wandered over to his dresser and pulled out a neatly folded pair of pajamas. His dad had hired a housekeeper who came in Monday through Friday to clean and cook.

Mrs. Harmon was nice enough, but Brett still hadn't gotten used to her presence. Until last year when his mother had taken a job, she'd been a stay-at-home mom. He resented anyone else invading his house.

When the woman first came to work right after his grandma went back to California, Brett complained to his father about it. In fact he was still angry at him over so many things, he couldn't wait until he turned eighteen. That was the day he planned to leave home.

Using his pajama sleeve to brush away the tears, he turned off his bedroom light and climbed under the quilt.

His mom's family lived in Oceanside, California. Brett could stay with them till he found a job. His uncle Todd owned a computer company and was a laid-back kind of guy who was a lot of fun, just like Brett's mom.

She and his uncle were only fifteen months apart and looked like each other. They both had blond hair and sunny blue eyes.

The maid had those same eyes.

"Mom…" He sobbed in the darkness. "It *was* you. I *know* it was."

GRADY CORBITT PULLED UP in the circular drive of the Stevenses' estate and stopped at the walkway, which led to the front door. Jim kept the place lit like a Christmas tree.

It was one of the residential showplaces of Las Vegas, befitting a contractor whose success had recently landed him the job of building a new community south of Las Vegas.

Jim and Ellen were a great couple, with two children. They'd lived a few doors down from the Corbitts until about thirteen months ago. Mike and Brett were still best friends, but the move had been hard on both of them. It meant riding their bikes to each other's houses, attending different schools, not getting together as often as they would've liked.

The Stevenses entertained a lot these days, opening their home to everyone. Their son Mike was equally hospitable and generous. Of all Brett's friends, he was the nicest to have around.

"Sorry about this, Mike. Maybe you boys can do something tomorrow night when Brett's over his stomachache."

"I didn't even know he was sick. He ate all his chocolate ice cream."

Mike's comment underlined Grady's suspicion that something besides food was the reason his son had come home so ill—particularly since the accounts of *what* they'd eaten didn't jibe. "Sometimes those things happen fast. He'll call you tomorrow."

"Okay." A disappointed Mike got out of the car. "Thanks for the ride, Mr. Corbitt."

"You're welcome. Do me a favor and thank your dad for me. Next time it'll be my treat."

"Okay." The boy waved goodbye, then hurried up the path to the front door. The moment he'd disappeared inside, Grady took off for home, anxious to check on his son.

Once he arrived, he let himself into the house from the garage and took the stairs three at a time. Even before he reached his son's room, he heard noises coming from inside. If he didn't know better, he'd think Brett was hallucinating.

He put his ear to the door. With every sob a torrent of words escaped. He couldn't quite make them out— except one.

Mom.

Grady felt his gut twist a little more. Something was wrong with both of them. They weren't getting over their grief. Time was supposed to be the great healer, but that was a lie.

Susan had been gone six months, yet they seemed to be sinking deeper and deeper into an abyss of sorrow and depression, a dark place where no light could reach them. Grady needed to do something quickly before he lost his son, too.

Opening the door, he walked over to the bed and sat down. The mattress shook from his son's heaving body.

"Brett?"

The boy lifted his head. "Yes?"

"Will you look at me so we can talk?"

"What about?"

He squeezed his son's shoulder. "Your mother."

Brett's breath caught. "I thought you didn't like talking about her."

Grady realized his silence had done a lot of damage. "I was wrong to keep everything bottled up inside," he said frankly. "When I heard you in the bathroom, I knew it was the pain of losing her that had made you so sick. I can't tell you the number of times I've been sick during the night, just like you.''

"You have?" Brett turned over and sat up against the headboard.

"I'm afraid so. When your mom and I met, we knew we wanted to be together forever. We got married, worked hard and finally had you four years later. She was such an integral part of both our lives, it never occurred to me that she wouldn't always be with us.''

"Me, neither," Brett whispered in a tearful voice.

"Forgive me for being such an inadequate father to you through this period. I'm going to try to do better. Since it's the beginning of your spring vacation, what do you say we pack up in the morning and take a trip? I've been thinking Disney World in Florida. We could even take one of those cruises around the Caribbean and do some snorkeling.''

"You mean you can get away?"

Brett's incredulity deepened Grady's guilt over his own blindness toward his son's grief.

"Yes. It's long past time."

He felt, heard Brett's hesitation. "Could we go the day after tomorrow?"

"What's so important about tomorrow?"

"Promise you won't get mad?"

Shaking his head sadly, he asked, "Is that what I do?" His sense of guilt kept mounting; not only had he been no support to his son, he'd caused him additional pain.

Brett averted his eyes. "Not exactly."

Grady reached out and hugged him. "I'm sorry

I've been so unapproachable, Brett. You must know how much I love you.''

"I love you, too, Dad.''

After more tears had been shed, Grady sat back again. "Then let's decide where we want to vacation. I'll make plane reservations tonight.''

"I'd rather visit Grandma and Uncle Todd.''

Grady should've seen that one coming. Todd was a strong physical reminder of Susan. But Grady wasn't ready for that experience. Maybe by Christmas.

"It might not be a convenient time for him and his family to have visitors, even if we are relatives. I was thinking we should go to a place where we could make some new memories.''

"Can we at least call him and see?'' Brett persisted. "Maybe they could come to Florida with us. Grandma, too. If we don't leave till Sunday or Monday, it might give them enough time to make plans.''

What was going on with his son?

"It'll probably take them longer than a few days to get ready for a trip like that. Don't forget Lizzy's still having problems since her best friend was kidnapped.''

"I don't see why. Her friend got rescued from the kidnapper and he's in jail and now she's home safe again.''

"But it frightened Lizzy to think her friend was kidnapped at the park. She's still afraid to go outside or be left alone. Until her nightmares stop and she feels a lot better, their family's not going anywhere. What mystifies me is why you don't want to leave

Las Vegas as soon as possible to take advantage of
your vacation.''

Brett's head was bowed. ''There's something I
have to do first.''

''It can't wait until we get back from our trip?''

''No.''

Grady was trying to understand Brett without further upsetting him. ''Does this have to do with swim-
team tryouts? I thought they were going on all month,
so you'll still have time to do it after we get back.''

When there was no reply, Grady grew alarmed. He
tousled his son's blond hair. ''Are you in some kind
of trouble? Don't you know I'd help you with anything?''

''Yes'' came the quiet admission. ''But I don't
know how you're going to react when I tell you this.''

Grady's body tautened. ''I promise I'll handle
whatever it is.''

After a tense interval, Brett raised his head. There
was enough light coming from the hallway for Grady
to see his son's haunted expression, and it frightened
him.

''You said Mom and Mr. LeBaron were blown up
in the bomb blast, so that's why there couldn't be a
burial.''

The blood chilled in Grady's veins. ''That's right.''

''Dad…you're probably not going to believe me,
but she didn't die in the explosion.''

He stared at his son. Maybe it was time to get some
professional help for Brett. Instead of making airline
reservations, Grady ought to be seeking out the best
psychiatrist he could find.

His hand went to Brett's shoulder again. "We've been over this ground too often already."

"You said you never found their bodies," he said in a quiet voice. "I remember you telling me that when you're investigating a bombing, the body's the definitive proof."

Grady promised his son that he'd handle whatever revelation Brett shared with him. Trying to be patient, he said, "There was enough evidence, including parts of their cars gathered at the explosion site, to put our questions to rest."

"Maybe someone planted the evidence to make it look like they died in the explosion. I've seen that in movies."

Brett hadn't been this distraught—or this insistent—since the memorial service, when he'd blurted, "Couldn't the blast have thrown her body the way a tornado does, and she landed someplace where no one would think to look for her?"

Full of fresh anguish, Grady said, "Something happened at dinner to disturb you. Tell me what it is."

Brett bit his lower lip. "I saw Mom tonight, Dad. I even called her Mom."

Grady exhaled a relieved sigh. So that was what had thrown him into such turmoil. At least *this* was something they could talk about and deal with. Then they could plan their trip.

"Do you know I can't count the number of times I've been in a crowd and thought I saw the back of her head? In the beginning, I used to wait until I could see the woman's face to prove myself wrong. You and I will probably go on doing that for a long time."

"You don't understand. It *was* Mom. But she didn't recognize me."

A groan escaped Grady's throat. "That's impossible. You just saw a woman who reminded you of your mother. You want her to be alive so badly, you've talked yourself into believing something that isn't true."

"No. I *knew* you wouldn't believe me." He slid out the other side of the bed and stood up. Fists clenched, he said, "I know what I saw. She's had her hair cut shorter and dyed brown. All the way home from the hotel, I kept telling myself it was just a lady who looked like her.

"But the more I thought about it, the more I'm positive no woman could look like that and *not* be my mom. I got sick because…because she pretended not to know me and didn't answer me."

"Son—"

"Then I remembered seeing a World War II documentary in my history class. It was about some soldiers who got wounded in battle and suffered amnesia. They didn't recognize their families after they got home. Except for one of them, the rest couldn't cope with it and went to live somewhere else."

Grady desperately needed some inspiration. If he didn't respond to this in the right way, there would be no sleep for either of them tonight.

"Where did you see this woman?"

"Coming up the stairs."

"You mean outside the entrance to the Etoile?"

"No. After dinner in the restaurant, the elevators

in the southeast leg were too crowded. So Mike and I decided to go down the stairs to Mr. Stevens's van.''

All twenty-five flights? "Did Mike see her, too?"

"No. He'd already passed the eleventh floor when this maid with brown hair opened the door and started up the stairs with a stack of towels. As she passed me, we looked at each other.''

Grady noticed the boy's throat working.

"I swear to you, she's my mom!"

"Is that what you told Mike?"

"No. He would've told me I was crazy, but I'm not!"

Brett's voice rang with conviction, and Grady broke out in a cold sweat. The reason his son didn't want to leave town immediately was beginning to make a strange kind of sense.

Forcing himself to calm down, he said, "If this woman looked so much like your mother that you even called her Mom, I wouldn't blame you if you wanted to see her again."

He blinked. "Then you believe me?"

"I believe that you believe it. Why don't you get dressed and we'll drive over to the hotel. She's probably still on duty. We'll find out who she is and talk to her."

Just as Grady had predicted, the second he suggested they meet the woman in question, Brett's expression wasn't quite as certain as before. He fiddled with the buttons of his pajamas, proving his nervousness.

"Dad?"

"I'll understand if you don't feel well enough to

go tonight," Grady said reassuringly. "We can always visit her tomorrow."

"It's not that."

"Then what's wrong?"

"I'm afraid," he whispered.

"Of what?"

"That when you see her, you might die of shock or something."

The combination of love and fear in his son's eyes shook Grady to his very foundation.

"Don't worry. I just had my department physical and passed without a single problem."

"Honest?"

"Brett," he said in exasperation. "I wouldn't lie to you. Nothing's going to happen to me. Now hurry up and get dressed."

"Okay. I'll be out in a minute."

Grady left for the master bedroom. It was automatic to put on his shoulder holster first. He never went anywhere without his weapon, whether he was on duty or not.

To his surprise, his hands were trembling by the time he pulled his suit jacket from the closet and shrugged into it. He hadn't eaten since lunch. What he needed was food.

Heading for the kitchen, he made himself a bologna and cheese sandwich. He'd just finished it off with a glass of milk and a banana when Brett joined him. He held something in his hand.

"What have you got there?"

"It's a close-up of Mom with her hair swept back from her face. I've got to fix it so the person at the hotel will know which maid we're talking about.'' He opened the junk drawer and pulled out a brown marker.

Grady watched his son in guarded fascination. Brett drew on the color photo, turning their beautiful blond wife and mother into a brunette with hair to her jawline rather than her shoulders.

When he'd completed his alterations he put the marker back. ''Okay. I'm ready.'' He handed the picture to his father. ''Let's go.''

They went out the back door to the car and drove toward the Strip. Maybe it was wrong to indulge Brett like this, but until the matter was settled in his son's mind, a vacation was out of the question.

When they met the woman, Brett would realize his mistake and that would be the end of it, thank God. It was time for both of them to move on. A trip to some new place, someplace not associated with Susan, was exactly what they needed.

As the Etoile came into view, Brett turned to him. ''What will we say when they ask why we want to talk to her?''

Grady had already anticipated his son's question. ''I'll tell the manager I'm working on a missing-person case.''

''That's good, Dad. Especially because it's not a lie.''

The change in Brett since he'd come back from dinner made Grady nervous as hell. His son was riding for a fall. First thing in the morning, they were leaving Las Vegas, regardless of Brett's state of mind.

After Grady had parked in a ''police only'' zone

near one leg of the arch, he removed his official tag from the glove compartment and hung it on the rear-view mirror.

There was no point in saying "Let's go." Brett had already climbed out of the car and was halfway up the steps to the southwest entrance. Grady set the lock with his remote and started after him.

The familiar sounds of a casino alive with people and slot machines met his ears. "The floor manager's door is over there on the left," his son informed him in a loud voice.

Brett and Mike had been over here a lot visiting Jim while the hotel was under construction. They knew their way around.

No longer taking the initiative, his son fell into step beside Grady, who maneuvered through the crowd to knock on the manager's door.

"Come in."

A man seated in front of a computer glanced up at them. "I'm Ken Adair. What can I do for you?"

"I'm Lieutenant Corbitt with the Las Vegas specialized detectives' division. This is my son, Brett." They all shook hands.

Grady pulled out his official ID and showed it to the manager. "I'm following up on a lead in a missing-person case. Earlier tonight Brett saw one of the maids working here who might be the person I'm looking for.

"He saw her on the stairs between the eleventh and twelfth floors of the southeast leg at approximately 8:00 p.m., carrying some towels."

Grady took the picture from his pocket and handed it to the manager. "Do you recognize her?"

The man studied the photograph for a moment. "No." He shook his head. "But that isn't surprising. With four thousand rooms, we have a huge staff. I'll scan this photo into the computer and send it over to the night manager of housekeeping. He'll know who she is."

"Thank you. If I could talk to this woman tonight, it would only take me a minute to ask her a couple of questions. I don't want to interfere with her work schedule."

"We'll see what we can do. Sit down. Depending on her location, this may take some time. If she's already gone off duty, then I'll get you some information on her."

Brett flashed Grady a look of gratitude as they found chairs in front of a long rectangular coffee table loaded with magazines. Neither of them reached for one. It was obvious his son was too intent on their mission to concentrate on anything else. As for Grady, he just wanted this whole thing to go away.

They both watched various employees file in and out of the office. Ten minutes went by before the manager called Grady to his desk.

"The assistant housekeeping manager is on his way to my office. Hopefully he'll be able to help you. Before I forget, let me give you back the photo."

Grady pocketed it once more, then walked over to Brett to convey the message. His son stood up, looking anxious.

"Do you think he'll be bringing Mo—the maid with him?"

Brett's slip of the tongue revealed his absolute certainty that Susan was alive. When his son met the strange woman face-to-face and discovered it wasn't his mother, Grady didn't know if he'd be able to comfort him.

"He will if he can," Grady murmured.

More employees swept in and out of the office. Each time the door opened, a light appeared in Brett's eyes, only to be extinguished when the person who came in wasn't the person he was hoping to see.

Finally a man entered the room. He chatted with Mr. Adair, then turned toward Grady and Brett. He'd come alone.

"Lieutenant? I'm Carlos from Housekeeping personnel. I recognized Martha Walters from your photo. I understand she might be the missing person you're looking for."

Grady froze.

He hadn't doubted that Brett had seen a woman who resembled Susan. But for this man to be so definite about a match...

"She's a very attractive woman," the assistant manager continued in a confiding voice. "I've never been able to figure out why she wanted a maid's job when she could be a showgirl. She's really built and has these long legs that go on forever. You know what I mean?"

Grady had heard enough of the man's personal opinions. "Did you tell her I wanted to ask her a few questions?"

"I would have, but she works the one-to-nine shift. By the time my boss caught up with me, she'd already checked in her time card and couldn't be located. I presume she's left the hotel. According to the schedule, she won't be working again until Monday."

Tonight was Friday. There was a whole weekend to get through. One glance at Brett, and Grady could tell his son was close to tears.

"Thanks for your help."

"You're welcome. Mr. Adair told me to print off the information from her employment application and give it to you."

He reached in the pocket of his uniform and pulled out a folded sheet.

Maybe all wasn't lost.

"Thank you again." Grady put the paper in his pocket before shaking the other man's hand. On the way out of the office, he murmured his thanks to Mr. Adair.

"Come on, Brett. Let's go."

His son needed no urging. They walked slowly through the crowds to the parking area. As soon as he backed out of the space and headed for the exit, Brett said, "Let's drive to wherever she lives. Maybe she'll be outside."

Grady had started this by offering to take his son to the hotel to meet the woman who looked like Susan. If he wanted any peace, then he had little choice but to see this through.

He felt in his pocket and handed Brett the paper. "What's her address?"

His son reached for it with too much eagerness.

After he'd scanned it he said, "She lives at 312 Meadow, apartment five." He raised his head, frowning. "I've never heard of that street."

"I'm not surprised," Grady murmured as he turned in that direction.

"Why?"

"Because it's in a lower-income neighborhood at the north end of the Maryland Parkway near the Cashman Center. Beyond the embankment are some rundown apartments. They're in bad shape, with broken windows and peeling paint."

At this point Grady wasn't opposed to painting a reality picture for his son. Anything to dampen his hopes about a situation that could only end in more grief and pain.

But when he glanced at Brett for a reaction, his son was poring over the application and probably hadn't even heard him.

"Dad!" he cried out unexpectedly. "Listen to this! She made out this application three weeks after the explos—"

"Why don't you give me the paper," Grady interrupted, trying not to reveal the depth of his frustration. This whole thing was a mistake. So much for parental psychology.

What he wanted to do was crush the sheet into a wad and toss it out the window. But he couldn't lose his temper like that in front of Brett. Calling on his last vestige of self-control, he stashed the paper above his sun visor.

They drove another couple of miles to the rolling curves at the end of the parkway. Grady took the first exit leading to Meadow. If he remembered from his early days as a patrol officer, it was the next street on his left.

Brett stared out the passenger window. "It's weird how we've lived here all our lives and I've never been in this part of town."

Grady found Meadow where it was supposed to be and drove to the three-hundred block.

By now Brett's expression had sobered. "I thought people who worked in hotels like the Etoile earned good money. Mike's older brother, Randy, has a job at the Sahara. He just bought a new twenty-thousand-dollar Ducati 996R."

"Randy Stevens still lives at home in a Las Vegas Lake mansion. Jim is a millionaire several times over. People like Martha Walters have to survive at the other end of the spectrum. It isn't easy."

"That's not her real name, Dad."

Grady's hands tightened on the steering wheel. His son was too far gone to listen to reason. If fate was kind, they'd find the woman home, she'd be exactly who she said she was, and this nightmare would stop.

"If you don't believe me, check the handwriting on her application. You know how you always teased her that she writes like a little girl because the letters are so far apart and she always makes a circle instead of a dot over the *I*'s? Well, look at this!"

CHAPTER TWO

ANXIOUS TO END THIS once and for all, Grady came to an abrupt halt in front of a small two-story apartment building. If there'd been any landscaping done at the outset, all traces of it had disappeared long ago.

He shut off the motor and reached for the paper stuck in the visor. After unfolding it, he turned on the map light to see the handwriting for himself. Once he'd proved it only resembled Susan's, there would be no further need for discussion on the subject.

But Grady never did get to the written part because the photo in the top-left-hand corner drew his gaze. He looked more closely. Then his world stood still.

Staring back at him were the eyes and face of the woman he'd loved more than life itself.

His body quaked.

It didn't matter about the hair. Because only an identical twin or a clone could be such a perfect match.

"Susan—"

In the background he could hear his son calling to him in a frightened voice, but Grady couldn't move, couldn't breathe.

Dear Lord.

His wife was *alive!*

He buried his face in his hands, terrified that this was a dream and Brett was telling him to wake up.

"Dad?" His son sounded frantic. "Are you having a heart attack? Dad? Answer me!"

When Grady felt his son grab his arm and shake him, he finally lifted his head. He was still sitting in his car. They were still parked in front of the apartment. This was no dream.

He threw his arm around Brett, practically crushing him in the process.

"You believe me now, don't you, Dad?"

"Brett…" His voice shook. "Son…" He hugged him harder, unable to find words.

"I *knew* it was Mom. Something must've happened to her and she doesn't remember us or anything. Let's go get her and take her home."

Still deep in shock, Grady didn't realize Brett was already out of the car until he heard the passenger door slam. The sound brought him back to some semblance of reality.

He leaped from the driver's seat and ran after him. "Don't go in there yet!"

Brett paused outside the building door until Grady caught up to him. "Why not?"

Because Grady was no longer simply a grieving husband who'd suddenly found out his wife wasn't dead.

The detective part of him had just kicked in, raising dozens of questions for which he had no answers. He didn't dare make a wrong move. If she was inside, he could only hope her apartment didn't have a view of the street. And if she hadn't returned from work yet, he didn't want her to find them there on her doorstep.

"We have to talk first. Come on back to the car."

"But, Dad—"

"Please, Brett," he said quietly. "I have my reasons. Just do as I say. Quickly."

The hurt in his son's eyes devastated Grady. When he got to the car, Brett was already inside, sobbing brokenly.

Grady started the engine and drove to the next block. After he'd turned the corner, he pulled over to the side of the street behind a parked car whose body had rusted out.

"Brett—listen to me. As soon as I saw that picture and realized you'd been telling me the truth, I wanted to run in there and throw my arms around your mother as badly as you did," he began. "Don't you know that?"

His son stared at him with a wet face. "Then what stopped you?"

For one thing, she might be living with a man.

"Tell me one more time *exactly* what happened when the maid started up the stairs."

It took Brett a minute to compose himself enough to relate the incident. His story didn't change.

Lord… What to tell Brett?

There were only two explanations that made sense. Either Susan had true amnesia, or she'd pretended not to know her son.

Grady could suggest several chilling reasons for the latter possibility, but he didn't think Brett would be able to deal with them right now. Grady wasn't sure *he* could.

No bodies had been found after the explosion, but the police had discovered fragments of both her car and Geoffrey LeBaron's. That meant evidence had been planted for the police to find.

Before tonight, Grady hadn't known what to think. His colleagues had believed LeBaron was guilty of tax fraud and had committed murder-suicide because he knew the IRS was going to audit his books. They maintained that he didn't want Susan—who'd been assigned by the Lytie Group CPA firm to work on his accounts—to give expert testimony against him in court.

But Grady could throw that scenario out the window because she was alive!

That was definitely her picture on the copy of her job application. Her handwriting. The dates fit. More important, Brett had seen his mother on the stairs. He'd been an eyewitness.

Now Grady's mind was grappling with the possibility that she'd had a relationship with LeBaron socially before she'd ever thought of looking for a job.

If they'd become romantically involved, LeBaron might have been the reason she'd chosen to work for the Lytie firm. That way she had a legitimate excuse to see him while she worked on his books. No one would be suspicious of the time they spent together.

If Grady was right, then it explained why he'd felt distanced from her during the last seven months of their marriage.

Taking it another step, he imagined that when she

and LeBaron weren't satisfied leading double lives and wanted to run off together, they faked their deaths in order to be free of their families.

Grady shook his head to think that Susan wasn't the woman he'd thought she was, that she could walk past her own son tonight without giving herself away. Yet the old adage about truth being stranger than fiction applied here.

Such an explanation wasn't palatable, yet he'd worked on similar cases in the line of duty and knew they could happen.

There could be another explanation, aside from amnesia—the kind of scenario that had happened to a judge in Reno a few years back. A prison escapee had taken revenge on the judge, who'd sent him to prison for life. The criminal had murdered his whole family.

Perhaps some felon who'd done time in prison because of Grady had been released. Maybe it was a criminal with Mafia ties who'd decided to find a creative way to pay Grady back.

What better method than to plan a diversion that made everyone believe Susan had died in the explosion?

With no one the wiser, he could have set her up at the Etoile with a job, a new name and identity, warning her she would stay alive only as long as she kept her mouth shut. The moment she didn't cooperate, she could watch the TV news about the brutal deaths of her husband and son.

Yet Grady still couldn't imagine the wife he'd loved for so many years being able to ignore her own child on that stairway.

He ran trembling hands through his hair, trying to deal with the shock. All this time, she'd been alive in the same city, only a few miles from their home.

Was he letting his imagination run riot? Grady was no stranger to the bizarre. He knew that anything was possible.

Maybe she *was* suffering from amnesia; in that case, she might have been an accidental victim in the bomb blast.

Or its target.

But right this minute, Brett didn't need to know everything Grady was considering.

"Son?" He turned to him. "Let's suppose for a moment your mother has amnesia, the kind you heard about in that documentary."

"Yeah?"

"We're going to be total strangers to her. When she answers the door, she might not even remember seeing you on the stairs. You'll have to be prepared for that."

"I am. Does that mean we can go over there now?"

Seeing his mother was all Brett could think about.

Seeing his wife was all Grady could think about.

However, he had to try to prepare his son for more pain. Something told him the agony they'd suffered up until this point was only a small portion of what was still to come.

"Yes. Just remember we might make her nervous. She could ask us to leave."

"Mom won't do that when we tell her we're her family!"

The faith of a child was still alive inside his thir-teen-year-old son.

"Maybe. Maybe not."

"Then we'll come up with a plan so she'll want to live with us again, won't we, Dad?"

"Brett, she's been away from us for six months. If she's got no memory of her past, it's possible she could be involved with another man."

If, God forbid, she was the prisoner of an ex-felon, then Grady needed to ascertain that before any attempt at contact was made.

"So what? When we tell her who we are, she'll *want* to let us in."

"Not necessarily." *Not if she was only pretending with you.*

"Dad, if you had amnesia, wouldn't you want to find out about your past?"

He couldn't hold out against the hope in his son's soulful eyes. "Yes, of course I would. But we're not your mom. We don't have a clue what's going on inside her."

"I know one thing we can do." Brett sounded brighter than before. "Let's go back to the house and get our photo albums. She'll *have* to believe us then!"

"That's an excellent idea, but she still won't have any feelings for us." *That is, if she truly has amnesia.*

According to what he'd heard from experts in the police department, amnesia was virtually impossible to fake in front of a loved one.

Grady had seen car accident victims who suffered from temporary memory loss. Their families went through anguish waiting for the trauma to pass.

Brett might understand it on an intellectual level, but emotionally he'd have a difficult time accepting the fact that he was a stranger to his own mother.

"I don't care. If I knew I belonged to a family that loved me, I'd try to get to know them again. Let's not tell her about the explosion. Why don't we just say that one day six months ago she disappeared and we've been looking for her ever since. Maybe being around us will make her memory come back."

He didn't want to raise his son's expectations. "According to the documentary you saw, it doesn't sound very likely." Especially if there was another man.

Lord—the thought of anyone else touching Susan...of her responding to someone other than Grady...

"Then we'll have to get her to love us all over again," Brett said in a quiet, determined voice.

Oh, Brett. Grady had never loved his son more than he did at this moment.

"All right. Tell you what. There's a house next door to the apartment. I'm going to park in front of it and leave you in the car with the doors locked. While you wait, I'll have a little talk with the manager of her building. Our next move will depend on what I find out. Okay?"

"Okay," he muttered.

Grady started the car and made a U-turn. Within seconds he'd pulled up to the house and shut off the engine.

"I've set the lock. I'll be right back."

Fresh tears of pain and anger gushed from Brett's

eyes as he watched his dad disappear inside the apartment house. Defeated for the moment, he rested his head against the window.

He'd grown up with a father who was far more cautious than all the other fathers he knew. His mom had told him it was because of his profession; his father was instinctively protective, and being a cop, with everything a cop knew and saw, made him much more so.

Though it was hard, Brett had learned to live with it. But tonight was different.

Anyone else who'd just found out his wife was alive wouldn't have been able to wait to see her. Except for *his* dad. No, his dad had to talk to the landlord first and wouldn't let Brett go with him.

More and more he resented being treated like a baby. That was why he liked his uncle Todd, who was open and talked about things as if Brett were a grown-up. Even Mr. Stevens didn't make him feel like he was still in grade school.

If Brett's father had been the one taking them to dinner tonight, he would've walked them to the elevator to make sure they got on safely.

Brett was surprised his dad hadn't chewed him out for using the hotel stairway. He could hear it now. ''Those stairs are there for the staff and for emergencies. Not only that, the stairs are often deserted and they can be dangerous. You boys can wait your turn at the elevator.'' But if he and Mike had waited, Brett would never have seen his mom.

He stared at the apartment building. She was probably in there right now.

Maybe she did have amnesia and really hadn't recognized him.

But after all the things his dad had said, Brett was starting to worry. What if her memory *had* come back after the explosion and she didn't tell anyone because she'd decided not to live with him and his dad anymore?

There were moms who left their kids. He'd heard stories about them on the news. In fact, he'd seen cop shows on TV where the mom just took off.

Did he have a mom like that? Was that why she'd gone to work in the first place? Because she didn't like him or his dad anymore?

Perhaps what Brett had once feared was really true. Prior to the accident, his parents might've been planning to get a divorce, but they'd been too nervous to tell him. That would mean his dad had lied to him earlier tonight.

Now he was being all secretive by going into the apartment by himself, playing the big detective. When he came back to the car he'd probably say, "We can't try to see your mom tonight. Before we approach her, I have to check on some more things."

Brett couldn't stand it.

He reached for the cell phone his dad had left lying on the seat. He needed to talk to his uncle Todd in California right this minute and tell him that his mom was alive. He didn't care how angry his father got.

No sooner had he dialed the area code than his father opened the car door and slid behind the wheel. Brett dropped the phone on the seat. For once his dad didn't seem to notice his furtive movement.

"I found out your mom lives with two other women who work at the Etoile with her. We'll go home and get a photo album. When we return, I'm going to let you do most of the talking." He started the car and they drove off.

Brett couldn't believe it!

His father was acting a lot more excited than before. After what he'd just said, Brett felt kind of guilty he'd had so many mean thoughts about him.

"Dad?"

"Yes?"

"Did you find out from the manager if she has a boyfriend?"

"He said he'd never seen her with one."

"That's good, huh?"

"It's very good." He reached out to squeeze Brett's shoulder.

"How long has she lived there?"

"Since she started working at the Etoile."

Euphoric that Susan wasn't an ex-con's prisoner or some man's lover, Grady found himself driving over the speed limit. It would be ten-thirty before they could get back to the building. Too late to be disturbing people, but he couldn't wait any longer to see his wife. None of this would be real until he'd done that, until he'd seen her face-to-face.

His heart slammed into his ribs as he thought about looking into her eyes again…and watching her mouth break into that smile that always took his breath away.

"KNOCK, KNOCK."

Martha lifted her head from the pillow. She was dead tired after her shift. "What is it, Tina?"

"Sorry to bother you, but there's a police officer out in the hall wanting to talk to you."

She sat straight up in bed, clutching the sheet in her hands.

"H-how do you know it's a real policeman?"

Months ago she'd been taken to a women's shelter without any memory of her former life. Several of the residents had said her head wound might have been the result of a beating from a jealous boyfriend.

With her looks, they said she could've been anything from a call girl to a showgirl or exotic dancer, even a stripper who'd somehow fallen into disfavor.

When one of the women at the shelter found out Martha had been found on an Indian reservation, she suggested Martha might've been a mob boss's girlfriend.

Apparently that was how Mafia types got rid of people who knew too much. Dump their bodies out in the desert and let the vultures take care of the rest. If she was smart, the woman had said, she'd change her hairstyle and color, just in case the guy was still looking for her.

Terrorized by the thought, Martha had followed her advice. So far she hadn't met with any trouble. Until now.

"He showed me his picture ID. The photo matches the face. Let me tell you, hon, he's the best-looking cop I ever saw. He probably saw you in the hotel, got your address and came over here to ask you out."

"That's ridiculous."

"No, it's not. Most of the guys on the staff have asked you out and you always say no. Carlos hasn't stopped begging me to set him up with you."

Tina meant well, but she was obsessed with men and couldn't understand why Martha stayed away from them.

Neither Tina nor Paquita, their other roommate, knew about Martha's amnesia. The three of them were maids who'd started work at the Etoile at the same time and had the same shift. They'd decided to share apartment expenses to save money. Tina had a car, which got them to and from the hotel. Everyone contributed to the apartment's upkeep.

The girls had no idea that Martha lived in constant fear that either someone had tried to kill her and could still be looking for her, or that she was a bad person whose past would one day catch up with her.

The possibility that she might have been a criminal herself, or had a prison record, lurked at the back of her mind. Maybe she'd been in the middle of committing a crime when she'd hurt her head.

To satisfy the girls' curiosity, Martha had said she was divorced and from Arizona and that she didn't want to talk about her problems. They didn't ask her any more questions after that.

Frightened that this police officer had come to arrest her, Martha's first impulse was to climb out the bedroom window and run away. But she was so tired of being a fugitive with no recollection of her past. Maybe it would be better to face him. At least then she'd learn something about her life, even if it was awful.

The only person who understood her torment was the priest at the church Paquita attended. Before her memory loss, Martha had no idea if she'd been religious or even went to a church. But she'd heard that a priest couldn't tell anyone the secrets people told him in the confessional, so she felt safe talking to him.

Father Salazar encouraged her to keep coming to talk to him and never to lose faith that one day she'd find out who she was and what had happened to her. Though nothing had changed yet, she found it helped to have someone who listened to her fears, someone who encouraged her to pray—and to hope.

"Martha? He's waiting."

"I'm coming. Tell him just a minute."

She slid out of bed to get ready. In addition to her jeans, she only had a couple of nice outfits. She'd been saving as much money as possible to go in with the other girls on a condo in a nice part of town. She went to the closet she shared with Tina and studied her skimpy wardrobe. If the police officer was going to take her to jail, she wanted to look as presentable as she could.

Deciding on the short-sleeved pink dress she'd bought at a discount store, she dressed quickly. After stepping into her white flats, she hurried to the bathroom to brush her hair and apply some pink lipstick.

She took a deep breath to compose herself, then walked through the small two-bedroom apartment. Tina was watching TV in the living room, sitting on the hide-a-bed couch. It was her bedroom for the month. Every month they changed rooms in order to be fair. It had worked so far, giving each of them a measure of privacy.

Tina wriggled her expressive brows, as if to say Martha was one lucky woman.

Wouldn't her roommate be shocked if it turned out the officer *had* come to take her in? Martha would die if she was hauled away from the apartment wearing handcuffs. She hoped Paquita's boyfriend wouldn't be bringing her home yet to witness her shame.

With her heart in her throat, she stepped out in the hall, pulling the door shut behind her.

In the dimly lit corridor she caught sight of a tall, well-built man, mid-thirties, dressed in a tan business suit. He had dark hair, more black than brown. As he moved closer, she caught the glint of hazel eyes fastened on her with such intensity, she felt her body break out in perspiration.

"Ms. Walters?" he asked.

"Yes?" she whispered.

"I'm Detective Corbitt from the Las Vegas Police Department."

He flashed his identification in front of her. She could see he resembled his picture. Tina was right; he was an exceptionally attractive man. However, he'd clearly come here on official business.

"H-have I done something wrong?" Better get it over with right now. She couldn't stand the suspense. Her legs were shaking so hard she didn't think they'd hold her up much longer.

His face darkened, as if her question was the last thing he'd expected to hear. "No."

"You mean it?" she cried in disbelief. "You're not here to arrest me for something?"

His searching eyes played over her features. "Not at all."

"Thank heaven." She blinked back the tears that were threatening.

"I'm sorry if my presence alarmed you. I've been working on a missing-person case."

No...

A new wave of fear washed over her.

Maybe word had gotten back to the man who'd wanted Martha out of the way that she was still alive. He could have hired this detective to track her down.

She'd heard that mob types worked out deals with the police. Was this man an honest cop? How could she trust anyone?

"Why are you asking *me* for help?" She wanted nothing but to run back inside the apartment, pack her bag and disappear.

He studied her for an uncomfortably long moment. "Brett?" he called over his shoulder.

Within seconds, a blond boy, probably junior-high age and as tall as her five-foot-seven height, materialized at the detective's side. He carried what appeared to be an album of some kind under one arm.

When he lifted his head, she blurted, "You!"

The boy nodded, then gave her a tentative smile.

Both he and the officer were staring at her so hard, she wondered if she'd suddenly grown scales or something.

"We passed each other on the stairs at the hotel earlier tonight." He broke the awkward silence first.

"Yes. You were very polite and moved aside for me."

She'd thought him appealing then, and even more so now, especially with those soulful gray-blue eyes. "Are you in Las Vegas on vacation?"

"No. I live here with my family. Earlier this evening my friend's dad took us to dinner at the top of the Etoile. The elevators were so busy, we decided to take the stairs."

"I'm sure they were faster."

He nodded.

She rubbed her damp palms against her hips. "Are you the person looking for someone?"

"Yes."

"Brett?" The detective spoke up. "Meet Martha Walters. Is she the woman you've been trying to find?"

"Yes. She's the one."

This boy had been searching for her?

After the Indian family had brought Martha into the women's shelter, Colleen Wright, one of the staff, had checked with the police to find out if she'd been listed as a missing person.

Using the resources available, she'd gone to great lengths to find out who Martha was and where she'd come from. When there were no results, speculation grew that Martha was one of those women who'd fallen through the cracks.

The entertainment scene in Las Vegas was full of showgirls and the like who flocked to the desert city to make money. Long ago Martha had come to the conclusion that she must have fit into that category and then gotten involved with some sleazy under-world criminal.

But not until now had anyone from her past come forward. She'd certainly never expected it to be a teenager. Afraid to get too excited for fear she might still learn something bad about herself, she proceeded with caution.

"Have you been looking for a long time?"

"Since August 20 of last year."

Martha had been dropped off at the women's shelter on August 27—just one week later. Like a new-born babe, she'd arrived there with no memories and no past.

"You honestly think we've met before?"

"Yes." The boy looked at the detective, who pulled a picture from his pocket and handed it to her. "Your hair's different," he explained. "You used to be blond and wore it long, but I'd know you any-where."

Her heart started to pound.

"After I saw you on the stairs, I colored in your hair with a brown marker and—"

"What Brett's trying to say," the detective inter-rupted, "is that when we showed it to the hotel man-ager, he soon matched it with your application photo. We were too late to catch you before you went off duty, so he gave me your address and we drove right over."

"I see."

Martha glanced down at the picture. To her shock it was the same face that stared back at her in the mirror every morning. "Dear God—it *is* me!"

The photo slipped out of her hands. In an instant the detective had retrieved it, but her eyes were riveted on the boy named Brett.

"Where did you get it?"

"From our family photo album. I decided to bring it with me. Do you want to see some more?"

The betraying eagerness in his voice alerted her that this was no idle question. If the police officer had brought anyone other than this vulnerable boy... It looked like she was going to *have* to trust him.

"How well do we know each other?"

He eyed her solemnly. "You're my mom."

CHAPTER THREE

MARTHA HEARD THE WORDS, but her brain couldn't seem to accept the information. This boy had just told her he was her son.

She had a son?

"So that's the reason I heard you say *mom* on the stairs?"

"Yes."

"I thought you must've been speaking to your mother who'd gone down ahead of you."

"No. That was my friend Mike. When you thanked me for moving out of the way, I hoped you'd recognize me, but you didn't."

She shook her head, unable to take any of this in. "I—I'm sorry. I—"

"It's okay."

No. It wasn't okay. She could tell that from his tremulous response, but she was feeling very strange. The words wouldn't come out right. It felt as if the floor was rising to meet her.

A strong pair of arms caught her before she fell. The next thing she knew, the detective had carried her to the stairs. He set her down and told her to put her head between her legs until the dizziness passed.

"Don't try to move yet," he cautioned when she

made an effort to stand up. He kept a hand on the back of her neck.

"I feel so foolish. I'm all right now. Really."

When the detective finally removed his hand, she sensed he'd done it with reluctance. He was probably afraid she'd topple over if he let go and she tried to stand.

Her eyes darted to the boy. "What happened to your mother?"

His anxious expression changed to one of pain. "*You're* my mom," he insisted. "Dad and I thought you died in a bomb blast, but your body was never found."

A bomb?

"Take it easy," she heard the detective whisper to him.

"Can I look at your album, please?"

"Sure."

She placed it on her knees.

"This one has the most recent pictures," he explained. "You and I put it together. Well, it was mostly you. I helped a little bit. Go ahead and look at them."

In a complete daze, she ran a trembling hand over the smooth brown leather cover. But her fingers stilled when they touched the gold lettering.

The Corbitt Family.

Corbitt. Where had she heard that name before?

Holding her breath, she opened the album. There was only one color photograph on the first page. It was a five-by-seven, a posed family photo taken at home by a professional. The three people were formally dressed.

There could be no question that it was Martha standing behind the couch with her arms around Brett and…and…

Her head flew back, and she encountered the officer's unwavering gaze. She remembered him saying, *I'm Detective Corbitt from the Las Vegas Police Department.*

As if in slow motion, she put the album aside and got to her feet. Staring at the detective, she saw the same pain in his eyes that she'd seen in his son's.

Incredulous to learn that this striking man was her husband, she scrutinized his features, looking feverishly for something familiar. Anything that could make her feel a connection to him.

"My name's Grady."

"Do you believe us now?" Brett's question shattered her concentration. She averted her eyes, unable to deal with any of their expectations just yet.

She hugged the stair railing. "W-what's my real name?"

"Susan," they said at the same time.

"And my maiden name?"

"Nilson," the detective murmured.

To find out she'd been a wife and mother rather than any of the untenable possibilities she'd been harboring in her mind over the last six months filled her with inexpressible joy.

But the revelation had brought on a new bout of weakness. She needed time to assimilate what it all meant.

"Please forgive me, but I'm feeling very tired and would like to go in now. If you'll give me your phone number, I'll get in touch with you tomorrow."

The detective didn't budge. "I have no doubt you're suffering from shock, but I'm afraid I'm going to have to ask you to come home with us."

He spoke in such an authoritative tone, Martha's head swerved around in stunned surprise.

"Brett, will you go out to the car, please? Ms. Walters and I will join you in a minute. Here are the keys."

His son took them without saying anything. After picking up the album, which she'd left lying on the stairs, he hurried out.

"Detective—"

"We can't talk here, Ms. Walters. I'm speaking as a police officer now, not as your husband.

"The fact that you're alive could mean you were the target of a murder attempt, but I don't want Brett to know about that yet. Having just found the mother he thought was dead, he's too fragile to cope with anything else tonight."

She nodded. "I understand your fear for him."

"Then you need to understand something else. I believe your life is in danger."

Martha had been convinced of it for a long time, too, yet she was almost more disturbed at the prospect of going anywhere with *him*. This man was her husband. He had needs and feelings he *hadn't* forgotten. Memories of sharing everything with her, including their bed.

"When we get home, where you'll be safe, and

you've had a good sleep, I'll tell you as much as I can. For now, you're going to have to go on faith that I'm being honest with you.

"If you don't feel comfortable spending the night with strangers, you can ask your roommate to come with us. I'd prefer if we didn't have to involve her."

"So would I," she assured him.

"Then tell her I need your help on a missing-person case and that I'm driving you downtown to look through a lot of mug shots. Tell her it might take all night."

"All right."

"The important thing is to get you out of here before word spreads that I was making inquiries about Martha Walters. It could set off a sequence of events that might cause someone to come hunting for you. You don't want to be here if that happens."

His words sent chills down her spine.

"Did no one come up to you in the last six months thinking they recognized you?"

"No. But part of me didn't want them to because I was afraid someone might hurt me again, or worse."

He grimaced in reaction. "If you're wondering whether or not I'm really a detective, you're welcome to phone the police department. I'll wait for you in the car. We're out in front." There was a pause. "You don't need to pack a bag. I never could find the right moment to part with your things."

Martha watched him disappear out the doors of the apartment building in a few long, swift strides. She didn't have to call anyone to verify that he worked in law enforcement. It was written all over him. A tough professional—on the outside, anyway.

But for just a moment he'd let her have a glimpse inside. She saw and heard a man in tremendous pain, yet he'd done everything in his power to let her know she could trust him, even to the point of telling her she could invite her friend along.

This man wasn't only aware of her fears, he was considerate. She sensed that he was an unusually decent human being.

Martha was so tired of being frightened, it sounded wonderful to know she could go to a place of safety, if only for tonight. She agreed with him that it would be best not to involve her roommates.

"Well, it's about time," Tina teased when Martha entered the apartment. "What's been going on out there?"

More than you know, Tina. More than you know.

"That detective is working on a missing-person case."

"Interesting."

"It, uh, has to do with someone who stayed in a room I cleaned. He asked a lot of questions. Now he wants me to go down to the station with him and look through some photographs. He says it might take all night."

She grinned. "You mean looking at the pictures, or getting to know you better?"

"Maybe a little of both," Martha said, playing along.

"I thought so. A guy like him doesn't show up at

your door every day. He's the kind you want to take home and keep forever.''

Her words haunted Martha. ''I have to get my purse,'' she said abruptly.

She dashed into the bedroom and pulled it from the closet shelf. Much as she wanted to bring an overnight bag, she realized she couldn't do that with Tina watching her every move.

She made a detour to the bathroom for her toothbrush, then put it in a little plastic holder and stashed it in her purse. With that accomplished, she was ready to go.

''Tina? If I don't come home tonight, you'll know why.''

''I'm hoping you don't show up until you have to report for work on Monday,'' she teased again. ''Paquita and I will expect a full report, okay?''

Tina never knew when to give up. ''Thanks for being my friend. See you later.'' She locked the door behind her and left the apartment building.

A dark blue Passat sat out in front. Before she reached the car, the man who was once her husband, who was *still* her husband despite her memory loss, got out to assist her into the passenger seat. He must have done it for her a thousand times before.

It didn't seem possible that she had no recollection of a life with him or their son. She took great care to avoid his unsettling gaze. One look and she would see his anguish. Nothing could be worse when she couldn't do anything to relieve it.

They drove in silence until they reached the parkway. "Are you hungry?" her husband asked. "We can stop for something to eat at a drive-in."

"You used to love the onion rings at Buddy's," Brett piped up from the back seat.

"Thank you for asking, but I had dinner after I got home from work. Please don't let that prevent you from eating if you want to, though."

The car continued to head south.

"How did you get the name Martha?" Brett asked.

She glanced over her shoulder at him. "Well, when I was driven to the women's shelter, not knowing who I was or where I'd come from, there wasn't much to do but watch TV."

The man at her side made some kind of tortured sound in his throat.

"The first morning I was there, some of the other residents were watching a home show hosted by a woman named Martha.

"It sounded like a nice name and I needed one, so I borrowed it. Later in the day, they watched this women's panel, and there was a journalist with the last name of Walters. I thought, why not be Martha Walters."

"Dad? Did you hear that?" He patted his father on the shoulder.

"I sure did."

Both of them appeared to be fighting smiles.

"What have I said that's so amusing?"

"You never really liked either of those shows."

"I think I still don't."

When they laughed, she couldn't help but join in. The naturalness of the moment took her by complete surprise. However, it was over just as quickly, and an uneasy silence returned.

"Do you remember when you were taken to the shelter?"

"Yes. August 27."

Out of the corner of her eye, she noticed the way her husband's strong hands tightened on the steering wheel. He wore a gold wedding band on his ring finger.

Had he never taken it off? Or had he slipped it back on tonight before driving over to her apartment? Turning her head away, she shivered with unease.

Brett leaned forward. "How did you meet the Indian family?"

"It was more a case of them finding me."

"What happened?"

"All I can remember is waking up in a clinic with such a painful headache, I wanted to die. An Indian woman named Maureen Benn sat by my bed. She told me she and her husband, Joseph, found me staggering around in a patch of wild grass with no identification. No clothes. Nothing..."

"Dear Lord," her husband whispered.

She saw his gaze dart to her hands. In the photograph at the front of the album, she'd been wearing a wedding band and a diamond. They, too, were gone.

"She said the back of my head had been bleeding, that it looked like someone had given me a direct blow. They covered me with a blanket and moved me to their truck. Then they drove me to a clinic and stayed with me all night.

"When the doctor realized I couldn't remember

anything, he suggested I see a specialist in Las Vegas as soon as I felt well enough to travel. But Las Vegas meant nothing to me and I didn't have any money.

"The Benns took me home with them for a few days and took care of me until I could walk around without falling. Finally they drove me to the women's shelter in Las Vegas where people could help me." Just remembering their kindness, she felt her throat close up. "I would have died out there if they hadn't found me."

She was aware of her husband's searching glance. "Do you remember what direction you were coming from when they brought you to Las Vegas?"

"No. But their house was in a town called Nopa or Popa. Something like that."

"Moapa!"

She lowered her head. Everything about that week was so vague. "Maybe that's it."

"The Moapa Paiute Indian Reservation starts about fifty-five miles northeast of Las Vegas. One day soon we'll drive out there and thank them."

"I've been hoping to find them again and show them my appreciation."

"Who would have done that to you, Mom?"

Mom.

She still couldn't comprehend it. None of it.

Maybe she was in the middle of a dream, except it seemed to be a dream that had no end. She closed her eyes, feeling a sense of deep weariness.

"We're home now, Brett. I think we ought to dispense with any more questions for tonight. Your mother's as exhausted as you are. It's been a long day.''

She opened her eyes in time to see them turn into the driveway of a lovely contemporary home. In the moonlight it looked a pale yellow with white trim. The landscaping included several ornamental trees and was equally beautiful.

Her husband pressed the remote attached to the sun visor, and the double garage doors opened. When they'd parked inside, she noticed there was no car in the other space.

"Did I drive before?" she couldn't help asking.

He shut off the engine. "Yes."

"Did I have my own car?"

He nodded.

"You had this Jaguar in a hunter green," Brett volunteered. "Sometimes you let me drive it around the cemetery so I'd be ready when it was time to apply for my driver's license."

"That's three years away yet. I didn't know you guys did that," his father murmured in surprise.

"Mom said that with so many bad drivers on the road, it was never too early to learn. All my friends wished they had a mom like mine!"

"Let's get your mother inside, shall we?"

Before she could blink, he'd walked around to open the door for her. Obviously the discussion about her car was a painful one.

There was no use kidding herself.

For the last six months, Grady Corbitt and his son Brett had been in a living hell.

So had she, but for different reasons.

Finding out she had a husband and a son she couldn't remember compounded that hell a thousand times.

Assuming she and this man had been in love until the moment she disappeared, she couldn't imagine how he'd even continued to function. If their positions were reversed...

Martha refused to entertain the horror of it.

Listen to me. I'm still thinking of myself as Martha Walters. But after all this time I finally have answers.

My name is Susan.

Susan Nilson Corbitt.

Mrs. Grady Corbitt.

"MOM? WOULD YOU LIKE a cola or something?"

She and Brett had followed her husband through a hallway lined with family pictures to the main foyer of the house. A huge potted tree stood to one side of the front door.

She glanced around, noting that the vaulted ceilings added an elegance and spaciousness. From the foyer, they went into a den with a desk and computer. The room had been made cozy with the addition of plantation shutters and a fireplace.

"A cola sounds fine," she said as she sank down on the deep white crewel sofa. One wall contained a built-in bookcase. Every shelf was filled. How many of those books had she read?

She studied the other pieces of furniture, the interesting watercolor of a lighthouse, the entertainment center with its television and stereo.

The light gray walls and white woodwork gave everything a fresh, clean look. If Brett and his father did all the housework, she was impressed. The hardwood floors gleamed.

Did the house reflect her taste or her husband's?

It was no use asking herself why she couldn't remember living here. The past had been erased. Any memory that could tell her she belonged under this roof, that she belonged with Grady and Brett Corbitt, was gone.

Being in this home was like attending a play. From the audience she watched the man and his son give their performance. She was a fascinated spectator, *not* the involved participant they wanted her to be. Mar— Susan couldn't join them onstage.

Instead of having to endure the piercing regard of the powerful-looking man who'd known her intimately for at least thirteen years, she wished she was back at the apartment around familiar people, familiar things.

"Here you go, Mom." Brett came in the den and handed her a tall glass of cola filled with ice.

She wished he'd stop calling her *Mom*. It made her feel so guilty she wanted to hide. The boy was crying out to be loved by the mother he'd lost. The mother he thought he'd regained. That much she *could* feel.

Susan took a long swallow. How did she tell him that the mother he adored was *still* lost, that she'd probably never be back?

One of the doctors who volunteered at the shelter had taken a look at her head wound. He'd said it was healing without problem. But the loss of memory she'd suffered was another matter. Whether it would ever come back was anyone's guess.

"If you have questions that can't wait until morning, go ahead and ask them now. Otherwise, we'll show you to the guest bedroom when you've finished your drink. Your eyelids are drooping."

"Bed would be wonderful." He had no idea how grateful she was for his sensitivity to her needs.

She finished off the rest of her cola, very much aware that he didn't want to discuss his fears for her safety in front of their son. In truth, she wasn't capable of dealing with anything like that tonight.

A crestfallen Brett took the glass from her. The comment he'd made about the early driving lessons led her to believe they'd been close as mother and son. Able to share everything. She couldn't bear to be the source of more pain for him.

When he left, she and her husband got to their feet at the same time. He had to be six foot two or three. Would Brett grow up to be as tall and hard-muscled?

"After you," he murmured.

There was an air of unreality about the whole situation. She walked out of the den to the foyer, pausing at the bottom of the stairs. "How long have we lived here?"

"If you mean in this house, eleven years."

"How did we meet?"

"In California. We were both in college. I was on a trip to the beach with my friends during spring break. You were playing volleyball with a bunch of your friends.

"I took one look at you and asked if you needed

another person on your team. You looked back at me and said yes. From that moment on, we became inseparable.''

The huskiness in his tone made her swallow hard. ''How old is Brett?''

''He just turned thirteen. We've been married seventeen years,'' he added, having anticipated her next question.

Seventeen! And she couldn't remember?

Susan had so many questions, but she didn't think she could cope with any more information tonight. Desperate to be alone, she hurried up the steps.

''The guest bedroom is the first door on your left. There's an attached bathroom. I'll bring you a nightgown and robe.''

Thankful that he didn't expect her to go into their bedroom while he picked out something for her to wear, she escaped into the guest room.

Except for the moment when he'd learned about her death, she suspected tonight was probably the hardest experience he'd ever been forced to live through.

If she were the one who had to hold back from taking him in her arms because he had no memory of her and wouldn't welcome her advances, Susan's heart would be broken by now.

His restraint gave her insight into his character. One thing she'd already learned about her husband: she hadn't married an ordinary man.

Her eyes moved from the floral-print bedspread to the cream-painted walls and matching carpet. The warmth of the room drew you in. After the dump she and the girls had been living in, this house was paradise.

"Mom?" She wheeled around to see Brett enter. He put the picture album on the table, then walked over to her. "Dad asked me to bring you these."

She let him hand her a sleeveless nightgown in pale blue and a white terry-cloth robe.

"Thank you."

After an uneasy silence, he murmured, "Is there anything I can do for you before I go to bed?"

"No, but it's very nice of you to ask."

"Okay, then. I guess I'll see you in the morning."

Susan nodded. She walked him to the door, and when he left the room, she couldn't shut it fast enough. Her son was suffering, but she couldn't bear to think about that now.

She rushed into the bathroom to change. It gave her a strange feeling to put on a nightgown she'd worn before. The faint fragrance of laundry detergent clung to the material.

While she was putting her shoes and clothes in the closet, she heard a soft rap on the door. "Susan?"

That was her name. How long would it take her to get used to being called that?

"Just a minute." She tightened the belt on her robe, then hurried to the bed. As soon as she was resting against the headboard with the covers pulled up, she told him to come in.

He entered quietly and closed the door. Her husband had an intimidating presence, and she felt her heart speed up as she watched him.

"Unless you're too tired, there are a few things I'd like to discuss with you before we say good-night."

"That's fine."

"Brett's room is next door. I'd prefer if he didn't hear us talking. Mind if I pull up a chair?"

"Of course not."

He reached for one of two ladder-back chairs placed near a small table and brought it to the side of the bed. He turned it around and straddled it, gripping the top with his hands.

The strictly masculine gesture caused his jacket to part enough for her to see he wore a shoulder holster. She felt like someone who was about to be interrogated at police headquarters.

Was he the kind of man who always brought his work home from the office, or did he simply feel more comfortable facing her like this?

Eyeing her dispassionately, he said, "I've been a detective with the arson and bomb detail for close to ten years. During that time, I've arrested a lot of criminals who will spend the rest of their lives in prison. It's no secret that in this business you make enemies.

"After discovering tonight that you didn't die in the explosion, I'm beginning to wonder if one of them hired a hit man on the outside as a way of paying me back."

"That's a horrifying thought." How had she ever tolerated that aspect of his career?

"It happens." He rubbed his jaw absently. "If I'm right, then they believe they've accomplished their objective. But even if the explosion wasn't a retaliatory act of revenge against me, someone wanted you out of the way badly enough to commit murder.''

She realized he was talking about *her,* and she gave an involuntary shudder.

''For those reasons, no one can know you're alive until I reconstruct what happened and this case is solved. For now, you're safe here at the house. But before this goes much further, I may have to arrange for you and Brett to be sent someplace to keep you safe.''

She shook her head. ''Why would someone want me dead?''

''Maybe you knew more than you should.''

''About what?''

She could tell that he was wondering how much to tell her.

''You graduated from college with a degree in accounting and got your CPA,'' he began. ''You used those accounting skills on a volunteer basis for certain charities, but you didn't earn a full-time living at it until about thirteen months ago, when you joined the Lytie Group CPA firm here in town.''

She'd been a CPA?

Did her decision to go to work so late in their marriage mean she'd always intended to do it and felt that Brett was finally old enough?

Or had there been trouble between her and her husband that had made her want to find work outside their home? It certainly didn't look as if they needed the extra income.

''When you were hired, you replaced an accountant who'd died in an automobile accident. He'd been working on two accounts." He paused. "Does the name Drummond mean anything to you?"

"No."

"You don't recall ever hearing it mentioned at work?"

She shook her head.

"Johnny Drummond owns sixty-two percent of the Etoile hotel here in Las Vegas. He's part-owner of another hotel in Reno, too."

"I didn't know."

He studied her for a moment. "What prompted you to apply at the Etoile? Do you think you remembered something about it because you'd been working on that account before the explosion?"

The hope in his voice devastated her.

"I wish I could say yes, but I'm afraid it was pure coincidence."

Her husband made no comment, but his attractive face hardened and she could sense his despair. If only he'd leave the bedroom and end the pain for both of them, at least for tonight....

CHAPTER FOUR

"TELL ME EXACTLY HOW you came to work there."

The interrogation was far from over. Since she was married to a detective, she supposed it was inevitable.

Physically and emotionally spent, Susan looped her arms around her upraised knees beneath the covers.

"There's a woman at the shelter named Colleen Wright, who helps people find jobs. She called me into her office and said the Etoile was looking for maids because it was the most recently built hotel on the Strip.

"She volunteered to get me an interview and said she'd explain my situation to the recruiter. I was grateful because I knew I couldn't stay at the shelter much longer."

He ran agitated fingers through his hair at the temple. "It sounds like they were very kind to you there."

"You can't imagine."

"I've sent battered wives to the shelter before. It's gratifying to hear firsthand that the system is working so well." He lowered his voice. "The list of people I owe for taking care of my wife keeps growing."

One moment he was all detective. In the next instant, the husband emerged. In either role, she could tell, he was a man who was fiercely protective of the people he loved. The list of things she admired about him was also growing.

"Getting back to your CPA job for a moment, you were working on another account, too. LeBaron Fireworks. Does that name have any significance to you?"

"No," she said quietly.

"It was a company that shipped fireworks all over the U.S. The plant was located in the desert east of the city. Geoffrey LeBaron, the owner, had been put on notice that the IRS would be auditing him.

"According to you, his fear that they'd find something wrong made him unusually anxious. Both Brett and I heard you on the phone several times trying to reassure him that everything looked fine so he shouldn't worry.

"On Saturday morning, the twentieth of August, you drove out to meet with him. That was at his suggestion, because the plant was closed and you could both talk freely.

"You and I had breakfast together before you left the house. You told me you were planning to go over the areas of greatest concern to him and prove that the IRS wouldn't find anything wrong. You'd nicknamed him the 'Paranoid.'

"I walked you out to the garage and kissed you goodbye. You said you'd call me later and tell me how it went."

Susan knew what was coming next and averted her eyes. She couldn't bear to see the anguish in his while he explained what happened.

"Later in the morning there was an explosion. A lot of people in the city felt it. I thought it was the sonic boom of a jet from Nellis Air Force Base. At 8:10 the dispatcher that serves the police and fire stations received the first 911 call.

"I was just leaving the house when headquarters phoned to tell me that the LeBaron Fireworks plant had just blown up. I was to head there immediately to start an investigation."

She groaned so loudly it reverberated through the bedroom.

"We can thank God that Brett was having a sleepover at Mike's. He had no idea what happened until later in the day, when I could be with him."

Unable to stay still another second, Susan threw off the covers and got out of bed.

Now her husband was on his feet. Even after six months, his face had lost its color in the retelling. That alone gave her a glimpse of the agony he'd suffered on that fateful day.

"There was a mushroom cloud of smoke in the sky. When I got there, nothing was left but a pile of rubble still on fire."

Racked with pain for him, she hugged her arms to her waist.

"The team uncovered parts of both your car and LeBaron's in the debris, but neither your bodies nor those of the Doberman pinschers guarding the plant were found."

She listened to one ghastly revelation after another, trying to put herself in his place. Convinced she would have died from the shock, Susan didn't know how he and Brett had survived.

"At first it was assumed to be an accident, but I wasn't convinced. Not when we couldn't find your bodies. And then, after we sent material to the ATF lab for examination, the proof came back that someone had planted two bombs to trigger the explosion.

"One was placed in the plant where a lot of flash explosives had been stored. The other was in the main office, probably taped under the computer table where the two of you would've been working. That would have explained the reason there were no tissue samples found.

"The damage to the plant was so severe, I assumed the firefighters had probably destroyed any bone remnants just putting out the fire, moving material around, cutting holes for ventilation. No matter how careful they are, vital evidence can be lost while the men are trying to prevent the fire from spreading."

He reached for the chair back and clutched it so tightly, his knuckles stood out white.

"When I gave the FBI the material and disks concerning the LeBaron account you kept at your desk in the den, they went over all of it very thoroughly. But like you, their people couldn't find anything that could get him into trouble with the IRS.

"It validated your expert opinion that LeBaron didn't have anything to worry about. Yet there was a consensus among the detectives in the department that his paranoia had caused him to commit murder-suicide by sabotaging his own plant in order to avoid facing IRS scrutiny.

"I never did buy that explanation. But then it was *my* wife who'd died in the explosion. I'm afraid I wasn't in any shape to be philosophical when it came to LeBaron's state of mind."

His gaze locked with hers. "Nothing about your death made sense. And then you walked out of your apartment a little while ago...."

There was a pause before he added, "Knowing you weren't anywhere near the blast changes everything about this case.

"Obviously someone wanted it to look like you died at LeBaron's hands. Maybe LeBaron was so convinced something was wrong, he decided to get rid of you himself. It's possible he's alive somewhere and believes he's committed the perfect crime."

Her fingers tortured the belt of her robe as she tried to comprehend what he was telling her.

"Even if he didn't have a knowledge of explosives, in his business he could've hired someone who knew exactly what he was doing in order to blow up the plant that way. It took an expert to make the blast powerful enough to obliterate bodies.

"But if LeBaron *wasn't* the culprit, then whoever masterminded this plot was very cunning."

Susan moved closer to him. "In what way?"

"First they had to tranquilize or kill the dogs before placing the explosives. Yet no matter how carefully something's planned, things can always go wrong. The greatest bomb expert in the world couldn't be certain the blast would kill you—not if you and LeBaron happened to move away from the bombs at the wrong moment.

"For instance, you might've used the rest room, or walked outside for some unknown reason.

"Whatever the case, this criminal wasn't willing to take any chances. He purposely left your cars there, knowing the rescue people would believe you were inside the plant when it blew up.

"In the meantime, he took you and LeBaron to the desert to be killed. Maybe LeBaron wasn't as fortunate as you and is lying dead somewhere out there."

When she happened to glance at her husband, his eyes had darkened until their hazel color was barely visible.

"Of course, there's the remote possibility that you were the victim of a crime totally unassociated with the explosion. That would mean two separate crimes were being committed at the same time.

"It's conceivable that an assailant followed you to the plant and kidnapped you from your car. If LeBaron was inside his office, he wouldn't have had any idea that you'd been dragged off to a nearby reservation."

The working of his mind chilled and fascinated her.

"Your attacker could've been a pervert looking for a woman to rape that morning and you happened to be his unlucky victim. But there's a problem with that theory because LeBaron's body was never found.

"Unless, of course, he too was attacked, and you were both taken out to the desert for disposal."

"I—I wasn't raped," she stammered. "The clinic on the reservation examined me. Except for the blow to my head, they said they could find no evidence of anything else."

His chest rose and fell sharply. "Thank God for that."

"I did." Her voice shook. "Over and over again."

"What you've just told me has helped eliminate one possibility. I'm beginning to think your work on the Drummond account made you a target. But unlike the culprit's first victim, you're not dead."

"What do you mean, *first* victim?"

"David Beck, the accountant you replaced at the Lytie firm. I'm not so certain the accident that took his life wasn't planned. He'd been working on that account before you acquired it.

"If he'd found something wrong and started asking questions, the culprit might've had so much at stake, he felt he didn't have any choice but to wipe out Beck. When you were hired to pick up where Beck had left off, that placed you in jeopardy."

Susan had to admit his theory was sound. "Did I ever tell you I'd discovered discrepancies?"

"No. You didn't discuss that account with me."

"Why? After telling you about Mr. LeBaron, I'd assume I talked over all my business with you."

"I have to admit it was uncharacteristic of you."

His voice had gone so quiet, she had to know why.

"Maybe I shouldn't ask this next question, but if we're not honest with each other, it's going to make things more difficult than they already are."

"I agree."

"Why did I go to work in the first place? With such a beautiful home, I can't believe we needed the money."

His unsmiling glance flicked to hers. "We didn't.

Between my salary and the investments we made with the sale of my grandparents' home, we had no money worries.''

"Why do I get the feeling you weren't happy about my decision?"

"The idea of your going to work never bothered me. If a job would bring you pleasure, then I was behind you a hundred percent."

"But..."

He stared at her for a long moment. "One morning at breakfast you told us you'd already applied for an accountant's position at the Lytie Group and been accepted. It was the first I'd heard of it."

"So it came as a complete surprise."

"Yes."

"Did I have a habit of presenting things as a fait accompli rather than talking them over with you first?"

Even from the short distance separating them, she could feel his body tense.

"No. It was the one and only time in our lives. Later I learned from Brett that you'd already discussed it with him."

"That must have hurt you a lot."

"You meant no offense," he said. "Your nature is such that you wouldn't knowingly injure anyone. According to our son, you wanted to prove you could earn an adequate living in case anything ever happened to me.

"For Brett's sake you were very careful to say you'd probably do most of your work at home. If you had to go into the office, it would only be while he was at school.''

She looked away. ''Did my decision affect—I mean, were we…?''

''Intimate after that?'' He supplied what she couldn't say. ''Yes. Maybe even more so.''

But he was still holding something back. Something she could feel. Whatever it was, the hurt had gone bone-deep.

''I wish I could remember so I could explain my actions,'' she whispered.

''Right now I'm so thankful you're alive, none of that matters. The important thing here is that whoever tried to kill you is still running around loose. But not for long.''

What made his vow sound so deadly was the fact that it wasn't just her husband talking. She was married to a police detective whose only business was to track down hardened criminals and arrest them.

She shuddered because she knew he was willing to put himself in grave danger for her sake.

He must have noticed because he said, ''I'm sorry to have burdened you with all this tonight. But I wanted you to understand how complicated and dangerous the situation is.''

''You've convinced me.''

''Then we'll talk more in the morning. Try to get some sleep.''

''Wait,'' she called to him after he'd put the chair back and was ready to leave the bedroom.

He paused at the door.

''I haven't even thanked you yet. I hardly know

where to begin. It still feels like I'm in a dream, that nothing's real. Please forgive me.''

"There's nothing to forgive. How could there be?'' he asked sharply. ''You've been living a nightmare.''

"So have you.''

"I didn't lose my memory. You must feel very helpless. Under the circumstances, I admire your courage in getting a job at the Etoile and making new friends.''

"Please don't give me any credit. You do what you have to in order to survive, and I had a lot of help.''

"Susan? I hope you don't mind me calling you that. After seventeen years, I find it impossible to call you Martha.''

"I want you to call me by my real name,'' she assured him. ''It'll help me get used to it.''

"Then call me Grady. I need to hear it.''

I know you do.

She nodded.

"Do you think you'd be up to a drive out to the reservation tomorrow afternoon?''

"Yes!''

"I want to meet the Benns and take a look around. It might also jog your memory.''

"I'd give anything in the world to have it back....''

"So would I.'' His whisper sounded husky. ''Then it's settled about tomorrow.''

"Yes. I'd like to do something really wonderful for them, but I don't know if they'd accept it.''

"We could pick up some candy and a fruit basket for starters.''

"And some flowers?''

"Good idea. After we get out there, we'll determine what else we could do that would be of real use to them."

"They saved my life. There isn't a way to really repay them." She bit her lip. "Do I have any money of my own?"

"Yes. The money you earned was put in an interest-bearing account. I'd decided to leave it there for Brett's future. Naturally it's yours to do with as you please.

"However, if you're thinking of getting the Benns something more substantial, rest assured I can more than afford to do whatever you have in mind without touching your savings."

Her husband was a proud man. Had her decision to go to work—without discussing it with him—made him feel he wasn't all things to her anymore? Was that it? She sensed there was a great deal he was concealing.

"Thank you, Grady," she murmured.

"You already have."

"The words don't seem adequate. All I'm doing is taking."

"No. This is your rightful home. You made it what it is today. No one ever worked harder to turn a house into a showplace. No son ever had a better mother. No husband ever had a better wife. We've missed you."

The longing in his voice intensified her pain. She lowered her head. "I'm so sorry I don't remember. What if I never do?" she cried in anguish.

"Then we'll face that like we've done everything else in our lives."

Her head came up. She stared at him. "Have there been a lot of things—to face, I mean?"

"Some."

"Like what?"

"You got pregnant on our honeymoon. Two months before the birth, your father died of a massive heart attack in California. It hit your family hard, especially your mother."

Susan suffered over her inability to remember anything at all.

"You were still mourning his death when you had our baby daughter a month later. It was a stillbirth due to a fatal heart condition."

"No," she whispered in shock.

"The doctor said it was a blessing in disguise. If she'd survived the delivery, she wouldn't have lived more than a few weeks, but that was small consolation at the time."

To lose a child must have been devastating! Such a tragedy had to be hard on her husband, too.

"When I brought you home from the hospital, your mother came to spend time with us. The two of you were able to comfort each other. After she went back to her house in Oceanside, we decided to look for property and build this house.

"We did a lot of the painting and landscaping ourselves. It was therapeutic for both of us. We tried for another baby, but your obstetrician felt the stress of my high-risk career probably prevented you from relaxing enough to get pregnant.

"So I went from being a street cop to a detective, where there was less chance of getting injured on the job. It was a move I'd been contemplating, anyway."

Susan could hardly absorb it all. "It took three years before Brett came along?"

"Yes."

She was almost afraid to ask the next question. "Did we try for any more children after that?"

"Yes, but before you could conceive, I got shot."

She gasped. "Where?"

"It was only a flesh wound to my shoulder, but you were inconsolable for a long time and never got pregnant again."

"I'm sorry I couldn't give you more children."

"Don't say that!" he blurted angrily. "I don't want to hear the word *sorry* again. We were completely happy with Brett. If we'd had more children, we would've welcomed them. But it didn't take away our joy in him or each other."

His fierce defense of their marriage made her wonder if he was trying to convince himself. Had she let her sorrow over her inability to conceive after Brett come between them? Maybe that was why she'd gone to work. Was that the reason he'd sounded so emotional just now?

"Have you stayed close to my family, Grady?"

He cleared his throat. "After the explosion, your mother, Muriel, came to live with us for the first month. I don't know what I would've done without her. Todd, your only sibling, has been to visit us three times since the memorial service."

"How old is he?"

"Thirty-four, fifteen months younger than you. He's married to Beverly. They have two girls. Lizzy's seven. Karin is four.

"Brett's closer than ever to his uncle Todd because he reminds him so much of you. You and your brother bear a strong resemblance to each other and possess a lot of the same mannerisms."

How many nights had she lain awake in her bed at the apartment wondering about her past life? Learning all this background was almost overwhelming, yet now that they'd started, she couldn't seem to stop asking questions.

"What about your family?"

"I was an only child, born and reared here in Las Vegas. My grandparents raised me after my parents were killed in a car accident when I was a small child. Brett would have loved them. Unfortunately my grandfather died of cancer in my teens.

"You and I met before pneumonia took my grandmother, who was bedridden, so you got to know her. After we made plans to get married, I suggested we start looking for an apartment. But you took me aside and said you'd overheard my grandmother offer us a home with her.

"Then you surprised me by saying you wanted to move in with her because she needed help and obviously adored me. Your willingness to sacrifice for her made me realize I'd fallen in love with an exceptional woman.

"We got married at the house so she could participate. There was a small reception afterward. About a week later, we drove to California for another reception at your parents' home. You got your college credits transferred to the University of Nevada at Las Vegas. Once you finished up your accounting degree, you obtained your CPA license.

"I urged you to get a job if you wanted, but at the time you insisted you preferred to stay home and take care of me and my grandmother. You said and did all the things that made this man ecstatically happy."

Until thirteen months ago...

"It doesn't seem possible that I can't remember any of this. Thank you for answering so many questions. It's helped me get my bearings."

"I've probably said too much. For that, *I* apologize. Good night, Susan."

"Good night."

"DAD?"

Grady rolled over on his back. He'd barely left his wife's room and had been expecting a visit from his son. It didn't appear that anyone in this house was going to get much sleep tonight.

"Shut the door and lie down with me."

Brett made his way through the dark to stretch out on top of the king-size bed. His deep sigh wasn't long in coming.

"You know that documentary I saw?"

"Yes?"

"I didn't really believe there was such a thing as amnesia." Brett began to cry.

"I know." Grady reached out to rub his shoulder.

"It's worse than bringing a stranger in off the streets," Brett said between sobs.

Grady murmured reassurance, meaningless though it was.

"When I said good-night to her—to my *mother*— s-she just stood there at the bedroom door, like she couldn't wait for me to l-leave."

Moisture beaded Grady's eyelashes as he held Brett for a moment.

"I couldn't figure out why losing your m-memory would make the soldiers and their families not w-want to be together. I didn't u-understand."

Grady rocked him in his arms. Even though he'd seen accident victims who suffered temporary memory loss, he wasn't any better prepared to handle this situation than his son.

"If she never remembers us, then I want her to go away," Brett said in a strangled tone.

Part of Grady felt the same way. All he could do was hold his son tighter while they both tried to deal with their individual pain. It didn't help that the sobs he'd heard from the guest bedroom as he closed the door revealed that she was in the same state of agony.

He'd insisted on calling her Susan, yet it meant nothing to her. *He* meant nothing to her. How well he understood his son's anguish.

"Can I stay in here tonight?"

"I wouldn't want you anywhere else," Grady whispered. They needed each other now more than ever.

His body felt like lead. It took all his strength to turn away from Brett while praying oblivion would end their pain for tonight.

In a few minutes, he felt his son get under the

covers. "Dad? I don't think we should tell Uncle Todd and Grandma yet. It would kill them."

In one night, his son had been forced to grow up in as brutal a fashion as Grady could imagine. He decided it was time for Brett to hear all of the truth. Grady needed his son's cooperation, because their family was in danger.

"Brett?" he said, turning back to lift himself on one elbow.

"Yes?"

"What I'm going to say now can't go beyond this room."

His son turned toward him. "If you're going to tell me somebody tried to kill Mom, I already figured it out."

Grady shook his head. "How come you're so smart?"

"That's not it. About a week after the memorial service, I heard you on the phone with Detective Ross. You told him you didn't believe Mr. LeBaron set those bombs. So I realized someone else did."

Grady's head fell back against the pillow. "I'm sorry you happened to overhear that conversation. I'm even sorrier I was in such a bad way that you couldn't have talked to me about it. Instead you've had to hold in all your fears. I was wrong, Brett. When you needed me most, I failed you."

"No, you didn't, Dad." His earnestness touched Grady. "I knew how much you loved Mom. In the beginning I was angry, but not at you."

"At God, then?" he prodded.

"Him, too." Brett confessed. "But I was upset even before Mom died."

Susan was in the next room, yet his son was still referring to her in the past tense.

A few hours ago, he'd heard Brett's voice ring out loud and clear, "I knew it was Mom! Let's go get her and bring her home." It felt like a lifetime since they'd done that.

Filled with curiosity over Brett's admission, he asked, "Why were you upset?"

"Because after she got a job, everything seemed…different. She promised it wouldn't change anything. But it did, because you two weren't as happy after that, and in the end it cost Mom her life. Or so I thought," he said in a tremulous voice.

Grady had underestimated his son's awareness of what had gone on during that period of their marriage.

"You're right that things were different, Brett. I felt fine about her going to work, but it hurt to think she wouldn't talk it over with me first. We'd always been so close, it seemed out of character for her to keep anything from me. I began to question her love."

"You never said that before." He sounded faintly accusing. Grady couldn't blame him.

"I know. I was trying to support her in her decision. You'd already told me the reason she'd given you."

"It was really lame what she said about wanting to find out if she could take care of us in case you died. I thought the *real* reason was because you guys were going to get a divorce."

Dear Lord.

"Brett, I worshipped your mother. However, I can't speak for her, or know what was going on in her mind at the time. If she entertained thoughts of divorcing me, she never said the words."

He sighed. "Merrill Wilson's mom got a job before she and his dad separated. It messed him up so bad, he used to stay at his grandma's after school. That made it harder for him to be with me and Mike."

"I didn't know that was the reason he didn't come around as much."

"He made us swear to keep quiet about it, 'cause he hoped his parents wouldn't go through with their divorce, but they did." After a silence, he whispered, "Dad? What's going to happen to our family?"

Grady's breath caught. "Well—I can tell you one thing we're *not* going to do."

"What's that?"

"Fall apart. We've got to look at your mother as if she has an illness."

"You mean like Alzheimer's?"

"I suppose that's as good an analogy as any."

"Jack Openshaw's grandpa has it. He didn't recognize Jack or me the last time we went over to his grandparents' house."

"That has to be hard on Jack. Still, it doesn't change his love for his grandfather, any more than your mom's memory loss affects our love for her. Unlike his condition, however, your mother's may be reversible. Her memory could come back."

"Do you think it will?"

"We can hope. When it's safe, I'm making an appointment for her to see a neurosurgeon. We'll see what he or she has to say. If it turns out her memory loss is permanent, then we'll have to deal with it in our own time and our own way. For now, she needs our love and protection without us expecting anything in return. That's the hard part.''

"I know. I felt like a fool standing there tonight waiting for her to hug me and tell me how much she loved me.''

"Then we were both fools," Grady confessed. "I was hoping she'd ask me to come to bed and hold her.''

Another period of quiet ensued before Brett spoke again. "Dad? If the person who tried to kill Mom finds out she's alive…''

"Are you absolutely certain Mike's in the dark about the real reason you got sick tonight?'' Grady demanded.

"Positive!''

"Then our secret is safe. I've thought everything through. With Mrs. Harmon's help, we'll be able to keep your mother here for the next week without anyone knowing.''

"Mrs. Harmon?''

"Yes. We can't do this alone, and she's one of the few people I trust right now. Early tomorrow morning I'll drive over to her house. When she hears what's happened, she'll do everything she can to assist us while I get started on my investigation.''

"What are you going to do first?''

"Drive out to the reservation and talk to the couple who found your mother. When I've pieced together a few things, I'll know whether or not she needs to go into hiding for an extended period.''

''You mean like the witness protection program?''

''Yes. But it may not come to that. We'll just have to wait and see. The hardest part after next week will be for you and me to act natural around our family and friends.''

''I know. One mistake could give everything away.''

''Exactly.''

''Mike'll be dropping over tomorrow. So will some of my other friends.''

''Call them in the morning. Tell them we're leaving on vacation for Florida and won't be back until school starts.''

''Okay. What about your work?''

''I'm off duty for the next two weeks, so we're set.''

''Uh-oh. What about Mom's job at the hotel? She *can't* go back.''

Brett's quick mind gave Grady the confidence to involve his son, knowing he could trust him to say and do the things that would keep Susan safe.

''I already have an idea that should satisfy her boss as well as her roommates. I'll tell you about it tomorrow.'' He glanced at the bedside clock. ''It already *is* tomorrow.''

''You sound tired, Dad. I'll let you get some sleep.''

Grady felt the mattress give as Brett slid off the bed. When he reached the door, he paused.

''Thanks for the talk, Dad. I feel a lot better.''

"So do I."

"If Mom never remembers us," he whispered, "just know I love you, Dad."

Tears filled Grady's eyes. "I love you, too. We'll make it, Brett. One way or another, all three of us are going to make it as a family."

Grady *had* to believe that.

CHAPTER FIVE

"MOM? DO YOU WANT me to show you one of your favorite outfits?" Brett had just come into her bedroom to tell her Grady was making a big welcome-home breakfast and expected them downstairs in a few minutes.

Her son's motive for asking the question was heartbreakingly transparent. He wanted her to turn into his mother again.

Susan had spent most of the night looking through the photo album he'd left on the table. She couldn't recall seeing herself in anything remotely resembling the pink dress she was wearing.

Whoever said a picture was worth a thousand words was right.

So many birthdays, parties with friends, vacations at the beach—everything recorded there. Dozens of groupings of her parents, her brother and his family, her husband and son. She belonged to a beautiful family. They all looked happy in every photograph.

Brett was a darling boy. The kind every mother dreamed of. One day, he would mature into an attractive man. A man like his father...

But there were shadows in her son's eyes now that shouldn't be there. Shadows she hadn't seen in the pictures. The tragedy that had struck their family had blighted Brett's world. Like Grady, he was holding back his grief and confusion.

He was so careful in the way he phrased his questions, and he obviously resisted pushing too hard if he thought it would upset her. All the joy and enthusiasm for life she'd seen in his photographs had been diminished by the loss of his mother.

What exquisite irony that it was Brett who'd found her again. Brett who'd seen through the brown hairdo and bargain-store clothes to the mother he loved. A woman who had no memory of the past. A stranger who'd only hurt him further by not acknowledging him on the stairs when he'd called out to her.

Susan had to do something quick to rectify the situation. She had no idea what the future held. If she never got her memory back, it might mean they wouldn't end up living together as a family.

But she'd given birth to this boy. He needed his mother. That reality transcended all barriers, even amnesia. Now that he knew she was alive—now that she knew she had a son—there wasn't anything she wouldn't do to help him recover.

"I'll tell you what," she said. "Why don't you bring it in here and I'll wear it."

His eyes widened in disbelief. "You mean it?" he cried, running out of the bedroom backward.

His excitement gave her a jolt because it showed how starved he was for her nurturing.

While he was gone, she pulled the phone book out of the drawer and looked for a beauty salon that would take walk-in customers. She found several, writing them down on a piece of paper, which she put in her purse.

"Here you are!"

Brett had returned with a pair of pleated cotton pants in a tan color with a matching short-sleeved top. He'd also brought a pair of leather sandals in the same shade, and a scarf with a tan, cream, turquoise and blue design.

"While you get dressed, I've got to get one more thing."

Humbled by this young teen who knew his mother's taste so well, she hurried into the bathroom. Off came the pink dress. A few minutes later, she scarcely recognized the woman staring back at her in the mirror.

The clothes looked stylish and feminine, yet Susan would never have chosen them for herself, even if she could've afforded them. It was incredible that amnesia could affect her down to her preference in decor and clothes. How many more changes would she discover before the morning was out?

When she emerged, Brett was waiting for her. She didn't know what reaction she'd get, but his silence was a dead giveaway that she'd fallen short of his expectations.

"It's the brown hair, isn't it?" she asked. "After breakfast, let's talk your father into driving us to a beauty salon."

His expression brightened. "You mean you're going to dye it back?"

"I sure am. As for the length, it's shorter than you're used to, but it'll grow."

"Oh, Mom!"

The next thing she knew, he was hugging her around the waist. His shoulders shook. She wrapped her arms around him and absorbed his sobs.

Please, God. Let me remember.

She heard a noise and looked up. There was her husband in the doorway. He wore a burgundy T-shirt and jeans that made her newly aware of his masculinity.

He didn't move a muscle. Susan got the impression that he was taking in the sight of his son being reunited with his mother.

"Brett told me you were cooking up a storm downstairs," she said, hoping to lessen his intensity.

As soon as she spoke, his eyes grew haunted.

Alarmed, she cried out, "What's wrong?"

Her son had let go of her and stared at her with the same expression as his father.

Grady shook his head. "It's nothing."

"Don't tell me that. I can see it on your face."

"You used to say that a lot," Brett finally said.

"You mean 'cooking up a storm'?"

"Yeah. Did you remember something just now?"

Susan would sell her soul to be able to tell him yes, but there could be no lies between them.

"I'm sorry. I have no idea why I said it."

Her husband eyed her frankly. "There'll probably be dozens of times when you'll say or do things like the old Susan for no particular reason. It's something we'll just have to get used to."

Brett's face fell.

She tucked a finger under his chin and lifted it.

"I'll make you a promise. The second I remember anything, I'll shout it to the skies and you'll know all about it."

That brought a ghost of a smile to his lips.

"Here, Mom. I forgot."

He handed her a smooth gold bracelet. Susan slipped it onto her wrist. "I love it."

"You used to say that a lot, too." But this time he said it without looking as though he was ready to break down again.

"Did you give it to me?"

He nodded. "For your birthday."

"When was that?"

"The Fourth of July."

"You're kidding!"

He smiled. "Nope. Grampa used to call you his favorite firecracker."

"I can just imagine all the creative names people have thought up for me over the years."

"Dad has one for you."

Susan had already seen a definite gleam in Grady's eyes.

"What's that? Screaming Mimi?"

Her husband chuckled deep in his throat. It was a purely male sound that sent an odd shiver of delight over her skin.

"I see I was right."

She could tell he was about to say something when the doorbell rang.

Brett stared at his father. "I bet that's Mike."

"You know what to do."

He nodded before taking off at a run.

Grady shut the door, then turned to her. "We'll stay in here until Brett gives the all-clear."

She slid her hands into her pockets. "By the way, what have you decided I should tell my boss? I'm supposed to work on Monday."

"I've already talked to Carlos."

Somehow she wasn't surprised by anything her husband did. Susan had the impression he could move mountains if he had to. "What did you say?"

"That for months your family's been trying to find you. When they finally caught up with you last night, they were overjoyed. After I told him you wanted to quit your job and go home to Oregon with them, he said he understood.

"I conveyed your regrets for leaving without giving two weeks' notice, but he said not to worry because he has dozens of applicants waiting for a housekeeping job."

"That was very nice of him."

"I agree."

"Obviously, I'm going to have to tell my roommates the same thing."

He nodded. "Do you want to do it now and get it over with?"

"I think I'd better. Paquita generally goes out to breakfast with her boyfriend before we leave for work, and she's the only one with a cell phone."

"Did you sign a lease?"

"Yes. For a year."

"So you've got six more months to go."

She nodded.

"Tell your friends you'll be sending a money order

for your share of the rent. Let them know they can keep or throw away whatever you left behind.''

"All right. But it's going to be hard to say good-bye. Those girls saved me from falling into a severe depression. One day, when there's no more danger, I want to get in touch with them again, because I consider them my friends for life.''

"I feel the same way. They helped keep my wife safe. For that, your friends have my undying gratitude.''

My wife. He'd said it with a possessive ring. By the time she grasped the receiver, her fingers were trembling.

MIKE SCUFFED THE TOE of his tennis shoe against the cement. "How come you didn't tell me you were going to Florida today?''

"'Cause I didn't know. Dad got up this morning and said we were leaving.''

"How soon?''

"After breakfast.''

"Heck. You're going to miss swim-team tryouts.''

"No, I'm not. Dad called and found out I can do it when I get back.''

"How long will you be gone?''

"Till a week from Sunday night.''

"I bet I could come with you. Do you want me to?''

"Ah…sure, but Dad's got this idea about how we should be alone and make some new memories. You know. Since Mom died, we haven't been anywhere together. It's going to be cool.''

"Yeah? Well, I guess I'll see you when you're back, then. Call me as soon as you get home."

"I will."

Mike got on his bike and pedaled for home. Twenty minutes later, he rode up the circular driveway.

"Hey, Mike," his father called from the garage. "Where's Brett? I thought he wanted to earn some money this weekend helping us weed."

"He couldn't come." Mike jumped off his bike and rested it against the wall inside the garage.

"Is he still sick?"

"No. He's going to Florida with his dad in a few minutes."

His father threw him a pair of gardening gloves. "Are you sure? When I invited Grady to dinner last night, he didn't say anything about it."

"I guess he wanted to keep it a surprise until this morning. This spring vacation's going to suck."

"Will they be gone the whole time?"

"Yup. They're taking a cruise. Brett says they're going to snorkel and stuff."

"Well, what do you know."

"What do you mean?"

"Grady's been in a real depression. I didn't think he would ever pull out of it."

"Brett sounded pretty excited. I wish I could've gone with them, but he said it was a father-and-son thing."

"Who's going to look after their yard while they're gone?"

"I don't know."

"I'm surprised Grady didn't ask you, but maybe

he had too many things on his mind. I'll ask your
mom to give the housekeeper a call. If she'd like the
help, we could do it a couple of times so he won't
have to worry about it when they first get back."

"Great," Mike muttered, kicking the ground with
his toe. Not only was it going to be a boring vacation,
but his dad would probably make him weed the Corbitts' flower beds, too.

GRADY HAD SET THE WALNUT table in the dining
room for their first breakfast together. Again Susan
found herself admiring the decor, especially the an-
tique French breakfront.

According to Brett, the display of the six-sided yellow plates—which were decorated with a famous folk
design she didn't recognize, from Quimper, France—
had been a special Christmas present to her from
Grady.

"I've never had steak and eggs before. That was
delicious."

She saw a secret message flash between father and
son.

"Don't tell me. It used to be my favorite meal."

Grady's lips twitched. "It's everyone's around
here."

"What did you eat at the apartment, Mom?"

"I usually had an English muffin and orange juice.
We ate our big meal at the hotel on our break because
it was free."

"You don't have to worry about that anymore,"
Brett declared. "I wish we really were going to Florida this morning."

"As soon as we find out who did this to your mother and he's put away for good, we're going to do a lot things we haven't done before."

Susan hurriedly swallowed the rest of her orange juice. For the moment, her husband had quieted her fears that he might not want a future with a wife who was a complete stranger to him.

But she had to remember this was only the second day. If she never recovered her memory, he might not feel the same way later on. Then what?

Not wanting to think about that right now, she finished looking at the pictures in another album Brett had brought to the table. Throughout breakfast the three of them had pored over the rest of their family photos. She'd hoped to experience a flashback, but nothing had happened.

"Hey, Dad, when I told Mike we were going on vacation, he tried to invite himself along."

Grady sat back in his chair. "What did you tell him?"

"That this trip was a father-and-son thing. He got kind of upset. I had to pretend I was, too. But it wasn't hard to fake because we can't let anybody find out Mom's alive yet."

"You're right about *that*," Grady said. "Have you called your other friends so they won't come over?"

"I'll do it now." He pushed himself away from the table. Before he ran out of the dining room, he gave Susan a hug. She kissed his cheek and hugged him back while her husband looked on with anxious eyes.

"I know what you're thinking," she said as soon as Brett had disappeared. "It's true that I don't remember being his mother, but all my natural instincts are there to love him. He is my son. Our son. I can feel how much he needs me. I—I'm hoping that in the loving, some memory will come back to me."

"We're all hoping for that." He got up from the table and started clearing it. She shut the album and worked alongside him, loading the dishwasher in the kitchen.

"Before we buy the flowers and other things for the Benns, there's something I'd like to do first." She told Grady the reasons she wanted to get her hair dyed back to its original color. "Besides pleasing Brett, it'll reassure the Benns. They won't be so shocked if I show up looking like the blond woman they rescued."

He studied her for a moment. "It's a good idea. I think we can find a salon in the north end of town that'll be safe. As a precaution, I'm going to ask that you hide in the back seat of the car."

"All right." She opened her purse. "Here are some addresses I wrote down. What do you think?"

"That one," he said, pointing to the last on the list. "Dyeing your hair could take a while. We need to get a move on if we plan to do that and track down the Benns all in one day."

"I'm ready."

"I want to close the rest of our shutters and sheers so no one can see in." He clasped her upper arms and dropped a brief kiss on her mouth. The gesture of affection was made with such thoughtless ease, she guessed it had been spontaneous.

When he suddenly let go of her as if he'd been scorched, she *knew* it had been.

He looked at her with pleading in his eyes. "I'm sorry, Susan. For a moment everything seemed so norm—"

"I understand," she broke in. "I didn't mind, if that's what you're worried about."

"You mean that?"

"Our situation has no precedent, Grady. All I know is that when I woke up this morning, I was thankful I belonged to this family. The only thing we can do is continue to feel our way and see what happens."

She felt the tension leave his body.

"I don't think I ever realized what extraordinary courage you have. I'm in awe of it." With that remark, he left the kitchen.

I could say the same thing about you.

He was a man whose life was in danger twenty-four hours a day. He had a job most people could never handle. Grady belonged to that unique world of cops and firefighters. The best of the best.

Was the old Susan terrified of what could happen to him every time he left the house in the morning? Did that fear drive her to get a job so she wouldn't dwell on the negative aspects of his work as a detective?

Had she been afraid to tell him the real reason she'd resumed her career—that she couldn't be home all day with her secret fears? Because she knew he'd worry and possibly offer to resign from the force if that would have made her happy?

No doubt she'd kept quiet because she knew such

a sacrifice would have meant the end of happiness for him.

Even the *new* Susan knew that.

Reaching for her purse, she started to leave the kitchen, then paused on her way out the door to look at a calendar of the French Impressionists hanging on the wall. It had reproductions of French Impressionist paintings and was large enough to write notes in each day's box.

She noted that the month and date were wrong. Without conscious thought she took it off the wall to turn it to the right page.

Then her hands stilled as she realized it was last year's calendar.

Earlier that morning, when Susan had commented to Brett what an immaculate house they kept, he'd informed her that his dad had hired a Mrs. Harmon to take care of everything. Brett said she was very nice, but even more meticulous than his grandmother Nilson.

From that statement, Susan deduced that there could be only one reason an out-of-date calendar still hung on the kitchen wall: Grady hadn't been able to discard it yet.

Starting with January, she leafed through each month, noting the many messages, names of people and phone numbers written in her hand. Even though the doctor at the women's shelter had told her amnesia would affect some parts of her memory and not others, she was surprised to see that her handwriting hadn't changed.

March showed heavier activity. That was the month

she'd gone to work. From that point on, the boxes were crammed with notations she didn't understand. When she reached August, she could see they'd tapered off after the twentieth.

The day she was supposedly blown up in the explosion.

September through December only held a minimal number of reminders for things like Brett's six-month dental exam, her mother's birthday, the detectives' wives' Thanksgiving benefit for the homeless at the Las Vegas Convention Center.

"Susan? I've set the lights I want to leave on. Let's go."

"I'm coming." She put back the calendar and hurried through the house to the garage. Later tonight she'd take it to bed with her. Finding it was like happening upon a diary. She was hungry to learn everything she could about herself.

If Grady looked it over with her, they might discover something that could help him with her case. Maybe, if she was lucky, a name or event would jog her memory.

"You're going to have to ride in the back and scrunch down, Mom."

Susan smiled at her son, who held the car door open for her. "Your dad already warned me. It's kind of exciting, isn't it?" She was hoping to lighten his fears.

"As long as nobody sees you."

She climbed inside and lay down on the floor. Two male faces looked down at her from the front seat, wearing grave expressions.

Until they'd found her, she'd been existing in a permanently frightened state. Now she had a family afraid for her. Her memory *had* to come back so she could help Grady figure out who had done this monstrous thing. Then she could be a wife and mother again.

Grady's eyes held hers. "Comfortable?"

"Yes."

"Liar." He mouthed the word. "I'll get us to the salon as fast as I can without breaking the speed limit. We can't risk a patrolman pulling us over. He'd recognize me and speculate about the woman in the back seat. Gossip would spread through the department like wildfire."

"I understand how dangerous it would be to draw attention to yourself right now. Don't worry about me."

She saw his jaw harden before he turned around and pressed the remote to open the garage door.

Since last night, certain comments she'd made had managed to break the temporary rapport with him. The trouble was, she never knew which ones would trigger a reaction. It was something she'd have to get used to. But each time it happened, it bothered her a little more.

"You have to face front, Brett."

His father's reminder galvanized him into action.

With Grady's mood altered, she didn't want to be a distraction. It was better to stay quiet and let the two of them talk while he drove.

After they'd been moving in traffic for a while, she

heard Brett say, "What if somebody sees us when we get back from the reservation?"

"They won't. For one thing, it'll be dark by then. For another, our car will be parked out of sight in Mrs. Harmon's garage. We'll hide on the floor of her car and she'll drive us home. No one will question my housekeeper bringing in the mail and the newspaper during our absence."

"That's a really cool plan, Dad!"

"Did I hear my son pay me a compliment at long last?"

"Yeah!" Brett laughed.

The happy sound delighted Susan.

Grady continued to tease. "I think you've just given your old man a heart attack."

"I was afraid you were having one when you saw mom's picture on the application."

The distress in his voice was unmistakable.

"If I'd been thirty years older, I probably would have."

"You almost fainted when you found out who we were, didn't you, Mom?"

Susan could just see the top of Brett's forehead. "Yes. If your father hadn't caught me, I would have collapsed on the stairs."

"After I saw you at the hotel and you didn't know me, I got so upset I went home and threw up."

She cringed. "I'm so sorry, Brett."

"Don't turn around, son."

"I forgot."

"We're almost there, Susan," her husband said. "What was the name of the salon?"

"Loving Hair."

"The address is the Gateway Mall. We'll park around back and follow you inside while you look for it. Once you've found the place, introduce yourself as Martha Walters. I want you to pay cash."

"All right."

A moment later, Brett dropped a hundred-dollar bill over the seat. She caught it and put it in her purse.

They drove a little longer. Grady made a few more turns, then pulled to a stop.

"Okay. We're here. You can get up now. Let's go!"

Thankful to stretch her legs, she moved to the seat and climbed out. Without looking at her family, she headed for the door, which led into a breezeway. She entered the mall and asked a female shopper for directions to Loving Hair, then walked toward it.

The mall was packed, probably because it was a Saturday. The salon might take people without appointments, but Susan still had to wait fifteen minutes. Even then, it took her another minute before she realized someone was calling for Martha Walters. Already she'd come a long way since yesterday.

Jumping to her feet, she said, "I'm right here!"

A young hairdresser with red hair told her to come on back.

Though Susan couldn't see Grady or Brett, she knew they were outside the entrance keeping guard. It was a luxury she hadn't known for six months.

It felt so good she was frightened.

All three of them were trying their hardest. All were hoping for a miracle. But if it never happened, would Grady and Brett go on wanting her the way she was now?

"What are we doing for you today?"

"I want my hair dyed back to its natural color. I'm a champagne blond. If you could bring me a sample card, I'll show you the exact shade."

"You look great as a brunette. Are you sure?"

"Very sure."

Maybe if I see myself as a blonde, the memories will come flooding back. Do it quick!

The appointment took several hours.

"There you go." After giving Susan's feather cut a wind-blown look, the hairdresser turned off the blow-dryer. "Now you can peek." She removed the apron and swiveled the chair toward the mirror.

Susan gasped softly. She'd been turned back into the woman in the Corbitt family photo album. A few months from now, her hair would reach her shoulders. Then there'd be no difference at all. At least on the outside...

"It's perfect," she whispered. "Thank you."

The hairdresser seemed pleased. "I didn't think I was going to like it as much, but I've changed my mind. You have the coloring of a blonde. But you need a lipstick with coral tones now."

"Do you sell any here?"

"Sure. We have a shade that'll look great on you. Just a minute and I'll get it."

Susan was starting to feel butterflies in anticipation of Grady's and Brett's reactions.

"Here we are. Try this." She handed Susan a tissue to wipe off her old lipstick.

With trembling fingers she applied the new one.

"See what I mean?" the other woman said when Susan had finished. "Now your eyes are a radiant blue. With your new hair and that stunning scarf around your neck, the combination is dynamite."

I hope so. I want my family to want me.

"How much do I owe you?"

"Seventy-five dollars. The lipstick's on me."

Susan reached for her purse and handed her the hundred-dollar bill.

"Thanks again. Keep the change."

"Thank *you*."

With her heart in her throat, she got up from the chair and headed for the doorway of the salon. In a way, she was even more nervous than she'd been last night when she'd had to walk out of her apartment and face a strange police officer in the hall.

CHAPTER SIX

GRADY SAT IN ONE of the chairs inside the busy salon.
He held several sacks and a big fruit basket on his
lap. The large bow and red cellophane hid his face
from view. Brett was equally camouflaged with a
huge flower arrangement. He'd kept watch over his
mother while Grady rushed around getting their shop-
ping done.

Susan's hair appointment was taking a long time.
Too long. He'd been forced to sit there, a captive of
his thoughts. They made him restless as hell.

For the last twenty-four hours, he'd been trying to
grasp the events that had restored his wife to him, but
he still couldn't quite believe it had happened.

So many nights in the last six months, she'd come
to him in dreams—but never with a changed personality that transformed her from the inside out, so that
even her hair was a different style and color.

"Oh, my gosh— Dad!"

Brett's excited voice jerked him back to the present. The moment he looked up, his heart skidded to
a stop. The blond woman he'd fallen in love with on
a beach seventeen years ago had just emerged from
the cubicle.

She was even more beautiful now. Breathtaking.

His pulse raced from emotions he couldn't contain.

Brett was already on his feet hurrying toward her. Somehow he managed to balance the flowers and hug her around the waist at the same time. "Mom— Oh, Mom" was all he could say.

Grady knew how he felt. It was a good thing his arms were full of gifts. Otherwise he wouldn't have been able to prevent himself from doing exactly what his son was doing. Only he'd be kissing the daylights out of her whether she welcomed him or not.

When Brett let her go, she lifted anxious eyes to Grady. They were as blue as the cornflowers he'd always compared them to. "D-do you like it?" She'd never sounded so vulnerable.

He couldn't swallow. "It's as if the woman who walked into this salon three hours ago never existed." Except that she still didn't look at him in the old way.

There wasn't that flicker of recognition singling him out from all other men as her husband, her lover, her companion through life.

Even when she'd gotten a job without telling him and there'd been a certain emotional distance between them, her eyes would soften with remembered feelings every time he took her in his arms.

They'd had almost two decades of loving, yet he was a stranger to her now. The knowledge cut him like a knife.

He pulled a paisley scarf and sunglasses from one of the sacks. "Put these on before we go out to the car."

When she was ready, she walked out of the salon ahead of them and started toward the breezeway. Despite the scarf and sunglasses, he could see a little of her blond hair. With that voluptuous figure of hers, she drew a lot of eyes. In their private moments, he'd always called her his California girl.

They usually vacationed at the beach where she'd been born. Her skin was the velvety kind that turned golden in the sun. While they lazed on their towels after playing in the surf, there was nothing he loved more than to bury his face in the warmth of her hair. It smelled of Coppertone, salt and her lavender shampoo.

Her hands would start to explore his chest and shoulders. Everywhere she touched, she set him on fire. Her eyes would get that glazed-over look.

Pretty soon Grady would take her home for a shower, and afterward they'd spend the hottest part of the day in bed, wide awake and hungry for each other.

"Dad, open the trunk."

Shaken by memories that were painfully vivid in a brand-new way—because she no longer shared them—he found his hand trembling as he put his key in the lock. Brett helped place the gifts inside. After shutting the lid, Grady used the remote to open the door for her.

"Shall I get on the floor again?" she asked without looking at him.

"I think it would be best until we're off the freeway."

Something was different since she'd turned back into the old Susan. Grady could tell his son had been similarly affected.

When they'd left the house, she'd been a brunette dressed up in Susan's clothes. But with the restoration of her blond hair, a new nightmare had presented itself. Not only did she look at her husband and son as strangers, her life was in danger all over again.

No one said a word.

Grady drove through the streets to the freeway and headed north. Forty-five minutes later he came to the turnoff. "I think it's safe for you to sit up now, Susan. We'll grab a bite to eat here in Glendale, then drive to Moapa."

The next time he glanced in the rearview mirror, their eyes met. Hers slid away as if she couldn't face this excruciating new tension that had sprung up between them.

He found a drive-in and pulled to a stop. A waitress came out the swinging door to their car. "What does everyone want?"

"I'll have a cheeseburger, fries and a root beer," Brett said at once.

"Me, too," Susan murmured. "Make that two of everything."

"But you didn't used to like cheeseburgers."

"She likes them now, son," Grady warned, hoping he didn't sound as out of control as he felt. He gave the young woman his own order.

Lunch was another quiet affair that couldn't end too soon for him. He ate in a hurry, then flashed his lights for the waitress to take away the window tray.

"Does any of this look familiar to you?" he asked his wife an hour or so later. They'd come to Moapa, a community of about fifteen hundred people. Grady had visited it before on police business.

"Yes," Susan said, "but I couldn't tell you which house belongs to the Benns. There are more ranch-style brick homes than I'd realized."

"No problem. I'll talk to the tribal police and get the address. Since it's a Saturday, we might be in luck and catch the Benns at home."

As it turned out, the female dispatcher was the only one around, although the two officers on duty could be back anytime. Fortunately she knew the Benns and gave him directions.

Grady thanked her and went back to the car. It didn't take long to find the right house.

"I don't see their truck."

He heard the disappointment in his wife's voice. "Maybe one of them's inside."

"I hope so. If you don't mind, I think I'd better go to the door first."

"I was going to suggest it." The Benns would open it faster to her than to a stranger.

To his relief, a woman appeared on the porch, dressed in jeans and a plaid blouse. He watched in fascination as Susan engaged her in a long conversation. Eventually he saw her put her arms around the other woman and give her a hug.

Soon she pointed to the car.

"Come on, Brett. Let's meet the woman who saved your mom's life." He climbed out of the car. After retrieving the gifts from the trunk, they walked up to the porch.

The other woman smiled. "Hello."

"Mrs. Benn? As I'm sure Susan told you, I'm her husband, Grady, and this is our son, Brett. We're indebted to you for your kindness to her. She wouldn't be with us today otherwise."

"My husband and I were happy to help. I hear your son found her in a hotel by accident."

"I did." Brett beamed. "Thanks for taking care of my mom." He put the vase of flowers on the porch and shook her hand.

Grady did the same thing with the fruit basket, then gave her the box of candy.

Her eyes widened. "What's all this?"

"It's our way of saying thank you," Grady told her.

"Joseph will be surprised when he gets back from Overton." Her keen gaze rested on Susan once more. "Let me see your head." She parted her hair to examine the place where she'd been struck. "I've seen injuries like yours before. Your memory will come back."

"Why do you say that?"

"There's no dent."

Hoping the woman's prediction was right, Grady put an arm around his son. "Do you think your husband could show me where you found Susan? I'd like to look around."

"He already did that with the police in August. They didn't find anything. No tire tracks, no clothes or jewelry. But two days ago we heard through the tribal police that a man's body showed up on the banks of the Muddy River. Nobody knew who he was, or how long he'd been there."

Grady's head reared back. "How far was it from the place where you came across Susan?"

"Maybe a mile."

"Were they able to tell if he was Caucasian?"

"Who knows? The FBI took over. The police said it couldn't have been anyone in our community because no one's missing."

Susan's eyes flicked to Grady's. He knew they were both thinking it might be LeBaron.

"What you've just told us could be vital to my wife's case. Thank you." He shook her hand again. "We're going to drive over to the clinic now to thank the doctor who examined her."

"It's too late. They close at four-thirty."

Grady glanced at his watch, surprised that it showed ten after five. The day had gotten away from them.

"If there's anything we can do for you, Mrs. Benn, please call or write. I put our name, address and phone number on the card inside the basket."

"Thank you. Come again on a Sunday when Joseph's here."

"We will," he and Susan declared at the same time.

"Bye," Brett called over his shoulder.

"She's a terrific person," Grady said as the three of them returned to the car. "Too bad her husband wasn't home to show us where they found you. I'd still like to see it—and the place where the other body was found."

"I'm sure she won't mind if we come back tomorrow."

"I might do that."

Brett frowned at him. "Why won't you bring us with you?"

"Because I want you and your mother to stay home where you'll be safe. Today's outing was an exception."

When he opened the back door for Susan, she sent him an imploring glance. "Do you think Maureen liked what we gave her?"

"She might not be as demonstrative as you, but I saw her eyes light up. Of course she was pleased."

"I appreciate your buying those things for her, Grady. I'm so grateful to them both."

"I am, too," he said abruptly.

He hadn't meant to seem harsh, but every time she thanked him, it seemed to widen the gap between them. Her stricken expression was more than he could tolerate.

"I'm sorry. I didn't mean that the way it sounded."

"Don't apologize," she begged. "Let's have an understanding that if we say and do things to put each other on edge, it isn't on purpose."

That was something the old Susan would've said. *My wife, the peacemaker.*

Grady's torment came from trying to adapt to this dual woman who was fighting a battle no one but another amnesiac could understand. She needed time, and gentleness…. It was difficult for him to restrain his impatience and his rage over what had happened to her.

"Agreed. Let's go. By the time we reach Mrs. Harmon's, it'll be dark. I don't want to arouse the neighbors' suspicion because she's dropping by our house too late.''

Grady was anxious to get home for another reason—so he could put in a call to his friend Boyd Lowry. The local FBI agent could access information about the body that had been found. Until Grady knew what he was up against with Susan's case, he didn't want anyone to learn she was alive. He decided to let Boyd believe he was working on a new investigation.

''Hey, Dad? Can we stop in Glendale and get a drink?''

''Sure.''

Once they left Moapa, they picked up speed.

''Does Mom have to scrunch down again when we reach the freeway?''

''Afraid so.''

''I don't mind, Brett.''

''Your mom's a trouper, isn't she?''

SUSAN WAS NO TROUPER. She was doing whatever it took to survive. There'd been several moments today with Grady when she'd started shivering from the tension. Emotionally exhausted, she lay on the floor of the car and let them do the talking.

Brett had dozens of questions about the Moapa-Paiute culture. She listened in fascination as her husband answered each one, exhibiting an impressive amount of knowledge on the subject. When he left off talking to phone Mrs. Harmon and let her know they were almost there, Susan was disappointed.

Before long, she felt the car turn and then they were

entering a garage. As Grady shut off the engine, she heard the door close behind them.

"Okay. We've been through the drill. You all know what to do. Introductions will come later."

Susan got out of the car and ran around to the back of Mrs. Harmon's car, where Grady had opened the trunk. With his help she climbed in. He lowered the lid until her fingers could hold on to it.

"Are you all right?"

"Yes. Of course."

"I don't like the idea of you riding in there, but I need to be in the back of the car in case there's a problem."

"Don't worry about me."

"That's like asking me to stop breathing."

It's the same for me, Grady.

"Poor Mrs. Harmon. She has to drive us."

"She's so happy for us, she wants to do everything she can to help. This will be over in a few minutes. Our house is only two miles from here." His hand reached out to grasp hers for a moment. The contact sent unexpected warmth through her body. "See you at home."

What was it Tina had said? *He's the kind of man you want to take home and keep forever.*

The ride to Green Valley was uncomfortable for Susan, but it went without incident. Still, she counted the seconds until she felt the car slow down and make a turn. A moment later she heard the telltale sound of a garage door opening. She heaved a sigh of relief, knowing freedom was imminent.

Once they were enclosed in the garage, Grady was

there to lift her out. He was remarkably strong. "Home safe and sound," he whispered against her cheek before setting her on her feet.

It took every bit of self-control not to throw her arms around him....

Oblivious to her inner thoughts, he put a finger to his lips. The four of them entered the house in absolute silence.

Certain lights had been left on, including the one in the hall. This was the first opportunity for Susan to get a good look at Mrs. Harmon. She was a short, attractive widow of about sixty with light brown hair and eyes. They shook hands, then impulsively embraced.

Whispering, the older woman expressed her happiness that Susan was alive and well, and hoped her memory would come back soon. Susan in turn whispered her praise for the other woman's care of her family during such a difficult period.

They moved to the kitchen. Susan made sandwiches and cut up fruit, which they ate quickly, keeping their voices low. Afterward, Mrs. Harmon went about the business of bringing in the newspaper and the mail. When she was ready to go home, Grady walked her to the garage.

Brett helped Susan clean up the kitchen. With that accomplished, she took the calendar off the wall and they headed for the stairs. Grady wasn't far behind.

Their son disappeared into the bathroom, leaving her alone with her husband in the guest bedroom.

His eyes played over her face and figure, then settled on the calendar with a look of surprise. "What are you doing with that?"

"I thought the three of us could go through it and you could tell me what everything means."

After a prolonged silence, he said, "I could never throw it away. Your handwriting..." His voice faltered.

"I'm so glad you didn't! This will help give me a sense of myself, of our life together."

"You don't know how many times I've pored over it looking for anything that could tell me who was responsible for planting those bombs. Now that you're back, we'll go over it again and again. Maybe something will trigger your memory."

She nodded. "That's what I'm hoping. Why don't we get ready for bed, then you come in here and we'll start."

A few minutes later, he and Brett appeared in the entry wearing pajamas. Susan sat on the bed in her nightgown and robe. She patted the top of the mattress. "Come on. Let's dive in, shall we?"

For the next hour they helped her get a clear picture of the life she'd led before the explosion. Until she'd gone to work, it appeared she'd spent her days cleaning, cooking, gardening, chauffeuring Brett to his many activities. She also attended meetings for charitable committees and community organizations; Grady had told her she'd done accounting work for some of them. The many names and phone numbers were all making sense, now.

She learned that as a rule their family attended a

local church on Sundays. Their pastor had been the one to conduct her memorial service.

"I've been going to a church."

Grady couldn't hide his astonishment. "Where?"

"St. Vincent's. It's where Paquita goes. Actually, I went to confession so I could talk to the priest about my fears. He told me to keep praying and never give up hope. One day I'd like to thank him for his help."

Brett darted her a perplexed glance. "You sang in our church choir, Mom."

"Did I?"

"You're a music lover," Grady said. "We went to the symphony whenever we could."

There was so much to absorb, but she'd have to ponder everything later. "What's this notation, *bring a salad?*"

It turned out they belonged to a neighborhood swimming pool, where the three of them often swam during family hour in the early evenings. Once a month there was an outdoor barbecue around the pool.

"That's where I take swimming lessons." This came from Brett, who lay across the end of the bed with his eyes closed. "Next week I'm going to try out for the swim team."

"I'll bet you're the best one."

"Nope. There are a lot of kids faster than me."

"You're getting stronger all the time, Brett, but you know what? You've been trying to stay awake for the last fifteen minutes. It's time for bed."

With a resigned "Okay, Dad," he got up bleary-eyed and came around the side to kiss Susan good-night. Then he gave Grady a hug and disappeared.

"Thank heaven Brett had you," she whispered. "He's so wonderful."

"You're the reason why. Don't give me any credit. Since the accident, I've been the world's worst father, but that's another story."

His self-deprecation wounded her. Knowing he'd refuse comfort from her, she looked down at the calendar again.

From an earlier conversation she already knew she'd belonged to a group of detectives' wives. According to the record here, they met every two weeks and volunteered at local hospitals.

Her life sounded full and rich. If her decision to get a job stemmed from a desire to do more with her life, then why didn't she tell her husband that before she applied for work?

The excuse that she wanted to find out if she could support herself and Brett if anything happened to Grady simply didn't answer the question. There had to be a reason she'd been so secretive.

"This woman, Jennifer?" Susan tapped the calendar. "Her name appears a lot."

"She and Ellen Stevens were your two closest friends. Jennifer's a member of the Detectives' Wives Association. Her husband, Matt Ross, is a friend and colleague."

"Did we do things with them socially?"

"Not often."

His comment was a little too offhand to let go.

"Why do I get the feeling there's something you're not telling me?"

At her question, Grady's eyes narrowed on her face. "Amnesia has sharpened your ability to perceive certain things. You and I never talked about her, but the fact is, she was jealous of you."

"Why?"

"Everyone liked you. You were always friendly and got along well with people. A lot of men found you attractive. Matt was one of them."

She frowned. "Did he make a play for me or something?"

"No. Nothing like that, but Jennifer's an insecure person. I have an idea she'd built it up in her mind over a long period."

"How sad."

"I have no real proof. It's just something I sensed more and more as time went on, particularly at the association dinner with the husbands."

"You mean the one I marked down on the calendar at the beginning of March?" She flipped back to it.

He nodded.

"That was right before I went to work, wasn't it?"

"Yes."

"Why didn't you ever discuss her with me?"

"Because you liked Jennifer and appeared oblivious to her insecurities. I didn't want to say anything that could change your feelings about her."

"But you were my husband. I would've thought we shared everything, no matter what."

"Not where she was concerned." He lowered his eyes.

Susan sat up straighter. "Tell me about her. Is she attractive?"

"She's an average-looking brunette. Slim."

"How many children do they have?"

"Two. They're both in high school."

"What's she like as a person?"

He took his time answering. "She strikes me as someone driven."

"Is she home all day or does she have a job?"

"The last I knew, she was working as a part-time secretary for an office-supply company."

"Do a lot of your colleagues' wives have jobs outside the home?"

"Most of them. More often than not, you were the one called upon to fill in when someone couldn't get off work to do their part volunteering. It's my opinion that Jennifer took advantage of your good nature."

"You think she saw me as spoiled? Someone who didn't have enough to do?"

"Possibly."

"Maybe deep down she disliked me more than either of us knew."

"Enough to do you bodily harm?" he asked. "No. But in my darkest hour, the thought did cross my mind."

She fingered the edge of the calendar absently. "Was she attracted to you?"

They stared at each other for a long moment.

"I have no idea what really goes on in her mind. She's an annoying flirt, but I never paid attention."

"Did she have influence over me?"

"No. But she made the occasional jab, which I'm sure you couldn't have helped internalizing."

"Like what, for instance?"

"The night of that dinner in March, she and her husband were standing at the buffet table with a large crowd of people. You and I walked into the room. She spotted you and said to everyone within hearing distance, 'There's Susan, suntanned and beautiful as always, while the rest of us spent the day slaving away at our desks.'

"Knowing you'd been out working in the yard, I resented her remark. You laughed it off because you never take yourself seriously. We got in line to eat and that was the end of it."

Susan slid off the bed. "Maybe I felt diminished and guilty in front of you because I didn't have a job. Do you think that could be why I decided to get one first and then surprise you?"

His face darkened. "I suppose it's possible."

"Oh, why can't I remember?" she cried softly.

He got to his feet. "None of that matters now."

"Of course it does! After years of happiness, something went wrong in our marriage only a few months before the explosion. There could be a connection. But even if there isn't, I want to know what happened to us."

He grasped her upper arms, as his eyes searched hers relentlessly. "Why is that so important to you?"

Dear God. Had she misread her husband? Did the amnesia make her so undesirable to him that he planned to end their marriage once her would-be killer was caught?

"For one thing, so we can both have peace of mind."

"Have you just remembered something?" He probably had no idea he was shaking her.

"No. My loss of memory has nothing to do with this...this feeling of alarm."

"About what?"

"About the fact that there was obviously some discord between us when I drove out to the fireworks plant that morning. Don't you know I've felt your pain over this? Brett's, too?

"Help me learn the truth, Grady. I don't care how deeply we have to delve. I'll do whatever it takes to get answers. Don't hold anything back. Tell me anything and everything that's on your mind."

"I was right," he muttered. "You're the most courageous person I've ever known." His hands fell away from her and she instantly missed his touch.

"You mentioned my friendship with Ellen Stevens. What's she like?"

His hands went to his hips in a purely male stance. "Ellen is a sweetheart."

"That's high praise coming from you."

To her surprise, his expression sobered. "It was Jim's idea to move from our neighborhood. He wanted to build a bigger place for his family. Mike and Brett went into a real depression. It was hard on you and Ellen, too.

"When their family heard you'd died in the explosion, Ellen fell apart. Since the memorial service she hasn't been able to do enough for us. In her own way, she's tried her best to mother Brett, but I'm afraid he's been difficult to reach. You're an impossible act to follow.''

Tears filled her eyes. "Did she and I spend a lot of time together?''

"You probably would've spent more if she didn't work for Jim.''

"So she has a job, too.''

Grady nodded. "When she was busy, you were always here for Mike. Even their son Randy used to hang around. He had a crush on you and he liked showing off on his motorcycle.''

"I'm looking forward to meeting all of them. You haven't talked about Jim Stevens.''

"He's a workaholic.''

"Are you two close?''

"No, but he's generous and I like him well enough.''

"In other words, you don't seek his friendship.''

Grady stared at her. "You seem to have developed second sight.''

She shook her head. "Not at all. With my past life a blank, I don't know when my comments and questions will go too far or offend, but there's no other way to proceed. Who's your closest friend, Grady? The person you lean on?''

After a brief silence, he said, "You were.''

Somehow she knew he was going to say that.

"I've learned enough since last night to know I felt the same about you.'' She bowed her head. "That's why we have to probe into every aspect of our lives, no matter how uncomfortable it might be, in order to find out what went wrong.''

"And the truth will make us free?"

She caught her breath. "Yes. You can't fix something when you don't know where to start."

"Amen."

She noticed there were shadows under his eyes. "You look as tired as Brett. Maybe tomorrow you could help me decipher what I wrote on the calendar after I went to work."

"We'll do it at breakfast. Get a good sleep." As he started to walk out of the room, the phone rang. He paused.

"Our voice mail will catch all the calls this week. We'll rely on my cell phone to stay in contact with Mrs. Harmon. Good night."

"Good night," she whispered, wishing he'd stayed longer.

CHAPTER SEVEN

GRADY HAD JUST LEFT a message for Boyd Lowry to call him back on his cell phone the next day when he heard a blood-curdling scream from Brett. It was loud enough to wake every neighbor for blocks.

With his heart almost failing him, Grady bounded from the bed and raced into the hall. He saw Susan's nightgown-clad figure fly into their son's room ahead of him.

By the time Grady made it through the door, she was already rocking Brett in her arms. "Wake up, darling. You're having a bad dream."

"Mom?" he cried hysterically. He was still fighting his way out of the nightmare.

"Yes, sweetheart. I'm right here."

"I s-saw you blow u-up," he cried between sobs. "In my dream…"

Grady sat down and put his arms around both of them. "Nobody blew up. She's right here, Brett. We both are."

"Don't leave me," he begged, throwing his arms around her neck.

"I'll stay here all night," she promised him. "Lie back on your pillow."

"Dad?" His son's body was still racked with heaving sobs.

"Yes, Brett?"

"Stay here, t-too."

"I wouldn't go anywhere else." He moved around to the other side so Brett lay between him and Susan.

The double bed was a close fit for the three of them, but it didn't matter. The two people Grady loved most in this world lay within touching distance of him.

From the light in the hallway, he could see Susan's face. Her whole attention was focused on their son. She kept stroking his cheek with her finger, crooning to him the way she once did when he was a baby.

It was the gentling he needed. Soon the sobs subsided, and the mattress no longer shook.

For the first time since he'd found her at the apartment, she was behaving like the old Susan. He lifted himself on one elbow to get a better look. That was when she started to sing.

"Mr. Sandman, bring me a dream…"

His heart gave a jolt.

It was one of the songs she used to croon to Brett years ago. Her voice had a natural lyrical quality. It took him back….

He didn't dare move. He didn't dare say a word.

Something earthshaking was happening. A breakthrough. He didn't know what to do.

When she'd finished the song, Brett was fast asleep.

So was she.

Grady broke out in a cold sweat. He couldn't afford

to make a wrong move now. When she woke up, would they have their wife and mother back with her memory intact? Could it happen that easily?

A neurosurgeon had answers to such questions, but it meant phoning a total stranger whose answering service would probably suggest he take his wife to the nearest emergency room.

That wasn't good enough. Grady needed advice right now. With great stealth he got out of bed and hurried to the master bedroom. Their family doctor was a man he knew he could trust. Gordon Perry would keep everything confidential once Grady explained the situation. He picked up the receiver and called.

After Dr. Perry had recovered from the astounding news that Susan was alive, he addressed Grady's concerns.

"If two different doctors have seen her since the accident and they didn't suggest hospitalization, I have to assume she escaped critical injury to the brain and her memory is starting to return.

"It can come back all at once, but in the few cases I've dealt with personally, it returns in increments, usually in moments of emotional stress."

Brett's nightmare fit into that category.

"These experiences might be accompanied by brief bouts of nausea or dizziness. She may or may not talk to you about the experience. If she says nothing, then tell her what happened. This will encourage her in case she was afraid to admit she remembered something."

"But she *wants* to remember! It's all she can think about."

"Of course. Her whole life's at stake, which is the reason she might hold back. She might be confused, wondering if it was a false memory. Now that she's home where she's being forced to deal with her past, the lines are getting blurred. The point is, this is a very good sign, Grady. I couldn't be happier for you."

He let go of the breath he'd been holding. "Thank you, Dr. Perry. I needed to hear that."

"Just remember, I'm not a neurosurgeon. I'll give you the name of an excellent one at the health center. If you have any more questions, phone him and tell him I referred you."

After they'd finished their conversation, Grady stole back to Brett's room. For the rest of the night he lay on his side, waiting feverishly for morning when Susan would open her eyes.

The next time he was cognizant of anything, he felt movement. It was Brett disturbing the covers. The motion brought Grady out of a deep sleep. Though the shutters were closed, he could tell the sun had been up for hours.

"Mom?"

"Yes, darling?" Susan sounded wide awake. It should have been the other way around. Out of the corner of his eye he saw her lean toward Brett. "Are you having another bad dream?"

"No. Can we talk?"

"Of course."

"You sang to me last night."

"I hoped it would soothe you."

"Mom—it was the same song you used to sing to Lizzy and Karin when we looked after them. Your memory's coming back!"

Out of the mouths of babes.

"Then I w-wasn't imagining it?" Her voice was incredulous.

Grady threw off the covers and hurried around to her side of the bed. "Imagining what?"

She glanced at him, startled. "When I heard Brett scream for me in the night, I seemed to remember hearing him do that before."

His heart started to pound. There *had* been another incident with Brett. "Do you recall anything else?"

"H-he was lying next to me. Something to do with a bear."

"Dad!" Brett cried out excitedly. "Remember that trip?"

Grady hunkered down beside her. "When Brett was eight, you and I took him camping at Glacier National Park. We saw bears and moose. One of those nights, while we were all cozy in our tent sound asleep, he had a bad dream about a bear eating his toes.

"I think everything got mixed up in his mind because of his favorite movie in which a bear licks honey off the feet of a woman while she's sleeping. He screamed for you and probably terrified every animal for miles around.

"You settled him down, then sang 'Mr. Sandman' to him. It's the way you'd get him to go to sleep when he was a baby."

Susan's eyes seemed to pierce through to his soul. "That means—"

"It means exactly what Brett said. You're starting to get flashbacks from the past. Last night after you both fell asleep, I phoned our family doctor and told him what happened. He said most people with amnesia recover their memory in spurts. Do you remember anything else?"

A pained expression crossed her face. She shook her head.

"Maybe you would if you saw pictures of our trip. I'll get the album!" Brett scrambled off the bed and disappeared from the room.

SUSAN COULDN'T LOOK at her husband. He'd been waiting for her to say that *he* had been a part of her memory. It killed her to dash his hopes.

"I'm sorry, Grady." Tears rolled down her cheeks. "You don't know how badly I want my life back."

"Shh." He reached for the hand closest to him. "Let's be thankful for this much progress." Grasping it between both of his, he kissed her fingertips, sending tingles of awareness through her body.

"Look, Mom. Here we all are!"

Brett got back on the bed and set an album in front of her, one she hadn't seen yet. It forced Grady to let go of her.

She wiped her eyes to see the pictures clearly. The first photo showed the three of them at the gateway to Glacier. Five years had made little difference to Grady's appearance. If anything, he was more attractive now.

Though she couldn't be objective, Susan thought she weighed about the same. It was Brett who'd changed the most. Their cute eight-year-old towhead had grown into a young teen whose hair was going darker with time.

As she leafed through the pages, he gave her a detailed account of their trip. She sensed that both her husband and son were waiting for her to recognize something in these pictures.

Brett rested his head on her shoulder. "Don't you see *anything* about the trip that looks familiar?"

"These things can't be rushed," his father admonished him.

Desperate not to disappoint them, she searched from the beginning of the album, where she'd documented other family trips to the Redwoods, Yosemite, Yellowstone. She scrutinized every photo, trying not to panic when nothing triggered a memory.

It looked as if they went to Oceanside at least three times a year to be with her family. There were other side trips to beaches up and down the Southern California coastline.

As she studied the captions beneath the pictures, she came across one that caught her attention. *The Vincent Farrell Art Gallery, Laguna.*

"I know this painting!"

Brett's smile faded just as fast as it had appeared. "That's because Dad bought it for you last year. It's hanging in the bedroom."

Grady closed the album and put it on the bedside table. He was as disappointed as Brett that the photos hadn't helped her to remember anything else.

"I'll bet you guys are as hungry as I am," he said with feigned cheer. "As soon as I'm dressed, I'll go downstairs and make us breakfast."

"Wait, Grady…"

He paused in the doorway. "What is it?"

Her heart began to pound so hard, she felt suffocated by it. "I haven't been in our bedroom yet."

A stunned expression broke out on his face. "But the clothes you were wearing yesterday—"

Brett jumped out of bed. "I brought them to her. That means you've remembered something else!"

By this time she was on her feet. Grady waited until she caught up to him, then took her hand in a firm grip that revealed his exhilaration. "Come and look at it."

The three of them went down the hall to the master bedroom. When they entered, she gazed around and saw the large, beautiful painting hanging over the dresser.

It was a scene of a garden room overflowing with flowers. A pair of French doors were open, overlooking the ocean. The stroke work in blues, purples and pinks delighted her.

"Do you remember being in that gallery, Mom?"

"No, but the painting reminds me of the Impressionists' work. That must explain why I was drawn to the calendar in the kitchen."

While she was standing there studying it, she suddenly felt unsteady and clung to Grady for support.

"What's the matter?"

"I'm just a little dizzy."

He walked her the short distance to the bed. "Lie down until it passes."

"I think I'd rather sit."

"Mom?" Brett looked at her in fear. "Are you going to be okay?"

"She's going to be fine," Grady declared. "Dr. Perry said it was normal to experience brief episodes of dizziness or nausea with the return of her memory. Why don't you bring your mother a glass of water?"

As her son dashed to the bathroom, she stared at her husband. "It's really happening. Things are coming back to me."

"Thank God," Grady murmured.

"I've been so afraid it would never happen."

"Here you go, Mom."

Susan took the glass from him and drained it. "I'm feeling much better now."

"You mean it?"

"I wouldn't lie to you. Thanks, darling."

"You're welcome."

It seemed the most natural thing in the world to hug him around the waist. That action brought her face against his pajama top. She eyed the image of the football player before lifting her head.

"Since when did you become a Denver Broncos fan over the 49ers?"

"I didn't!" he cried. "But Mike's mom brought me these after their family went to an NFL game in Denver. Oh, Mom—you're starting to remember everything!"

She hugged him again. Over Brett's shoulder, she could see Grady standing there, smiling, but when she looked into his eyes she glimpsed a flash of pain. It was only for a second, but her heart almost stopped beating.

He was waiting for her to remember him. *Them.*

Was her mind blocking memories of Grady because of the problem between them before the explosion?

He was such a wonderful man, she was convinced that whatever went wrong in their marriage had to do with her, not him. If she didn't learn the answer soon, she was afraid she'd fall apart. The tension was overwhelming her.

When Grady's cell phone rang, Brett released her. She watched her husband answer it and turn his back on them.

"Come on, Brett," she whispered. "Let's fix breakfast and surprise your father."

Empty glass in hand, she made a detour to the guest room to put on her robe. Then she grabbed the calendar. "What else does your dad like besides steak and eggs?"

"Anything."

"That's easy, but I'll bet you love cold cereal with milk the best," she said as they entered the kitchen.

"Did you just remember that?"

"No. It was a guess. That's all my brother ever wanted in the morning before we left for school."

Suddenly she could see her brother. He was sitting on a bar stool at the kitchen counter of her parents' home, shoveling in mouthfuls of Apple Jacks.

"Todd…"

The things she'd been holding slipped from her hands. The glass shattered against the tile.

"Don't either of you move," Grady said directly behind them. "You'll cut yourselves otherwise."

Susan turned her head in time to see him get a broom from the closet. His phone call had been a short one.

"Be careful," she urged because he was barefoot, too. He quickly swept up the broken glass, checking carefully for any pieces he might have missed. Susan feared that if he got cut in the process, he'd never tell her.

"I'm sorry I was so clumsy."

Grady emptied the contents of the dustpan in the wastebasket. "As far as I'm concerned, you can break every damn glass in the house if it means you've remembered something."

Her pulse raced. "While Brett and I were talking about breakfast, this picture came into my mind of my brother wolfing down cereal when we were kids."

"Do you have full recall of him now?"

"No."

"Nevertheless, the past is falling into place faster than I would have dreamed," Grady said before putting the broom and dustpan away.

"Do you feel sick again, Mom?"

"No, darling." Not physically. Emotionally it was painful to remember things in front of her husband because none of them were personal memories of him. Every time she opened her mouth, it hurt him. She could tell by the remote look in his eyes.

"H-how do omelets sound?"

"Good."

"I'll set the table," Brett offered.

She took eggs and cheese from the fridge. Grady followed with an onion, a green pepper and some ham.

"Who was that on the phone?" she asked as he began chopping.

"Last night I put in a call to a colleague in the FBI about the body Maureen Benn said was found on the reservation."

"Did you have to tell him you're not on vacation?" She grated cheese as she spoke.

"No. He assumes I'm in Florida with Brett, but like most detectives I still take my work with me. As soon as he has any information, he'll get back to me.

"I've asked him to contact LeBaron's family so he can procure the man's dental records. If there's a match, then we'll know you and LeBaron were both victims. If they're *not* the same, I'm going to assume he's still alive and I'll have an APB put out on him.

"In the meantime, you and I are going to attack this case from another angle."

He found the frying pan and melted butter in it. She combined all the ingredients, then poured in the egg mixture to cook.

"You're talking about the Drummond account."

"It's the only other one you handled."

"Grady?" She could no longer conceal her anxiety. "I don't have any recollection of being a CPA. It sounds as foreign to me as ancient Greek."

"Don't worry. We'll open the file and try to make sense of it together. After the things you've remembered since last night, I'm convinced that given time and patience, something's going to cli—"

He stopped talking as they heard the sound of the garage door opening. Susan eyed her husband in surprise.

"Something must be wrong," he muttered. "Mrs. Harmon wasn't due here until six this evening."

The three of them waited for the housekeeper to come into the house. When they heard footsteps in the hall, Grady called out to her.

She entered the kitchen looking apprehensive. Her eyes swerved from Susan to Grady. "Forgive me for barging in, but you didn't answer your cell phone."

Grady made a strange sound in his throat. "That's my fault, Mrs. Harmon. I forgot to bring it downstairs. From now on, I'll keep it with me at all times. What's wrong?"

"I had a call from Ellen Stevens this morning. She said she was thrilled that you and Brett were having a wonderful vacation in Florida. In the next breath, she wanted to know if you'd made arrangements for someone to mow your lawn while you were gone.

"Off the top of my head, I told her you'd decided not to worry about it until you got back from your trip. But you know Ellen. Before we hung up she said that was all she wanted to know.

"There's no doubt in my mind that Mike will be over sometime today. Most likely one of the Stevenses will bring him with their mower.

"But on the outside chance that Mike comes on his bicycle, he knows where Brett's hidden a key to get into the house in case he's ever locked out. I was afraid he'd let himself in, and I couldn't risk that happening.''

If Grady hadn't put an arm around the housekeeper's shoulders, Susan would have.

"With that kind of thinking, you should be on the police department's payroll. If I could give you a medal of commendation, I would.''

She laughed off the compliment, but Susan could tell his comment had pleased her.

"I actually removed that key yesterday in the event of just such a thing,'' he was saying. "No one will be getting into the house unless they break in. If that happens, I'll be ready for them.''

"Would you like to stay and have breakfast with us?'' Susan asked.

"Thank you, but no. After what you three have been through, you're entitled to enjoy your reunion in private. Besides, I'm on my way to church.'' She took a deep breath, and Susan realized that the older woman had been genuinely fearful.

"Let me bring in the newspaper,'' she continued, "then I'll leave and see you tomorrow evening around six. If you need anything, call me and I'll pick it up for you.''

Susan moved the pan off the burner and gave her a hug. "Thank you, Mrs. Harmon. We couldn't do this without your help.''

"It's my pleasure.''

"That was smart thinking,'' their son put in. He'd taken on the job of making the toast.

A smile crept over the housekeeper's face. "Why, thank you, Brett.''

"Sure."

The warmth in his cheeks led Susan to believe that his pain hadn't allowed him to get close to the other woman. But all of that seemed to be changing now.

Grady waited to walk her back to the garage. When she'd gone, he joined them at the kitchen table. This time he'd brought his cell phone with him.

After Susan had served him, she said, "How did you ever find her?"

"I went through a reputable job agency. She was one of about a half-dozen applicants for the house-keeping position. It didn't take me long to realize she was the person we needed."

"I like her very much."

"She took good care of us, didn't she, Brett?"

"Yeah. But now we've got Mom."

"You're right about that. I think this would be a good time to give thanks."

That was all Susan had been doing since she'd found out she belonged to Grady and Brett.

Closing her eyes, she listened to his prayer. It touched her so deeply, she was half crying by the time he'd finished.

After he'd said amen, no one seemed inclined to talk. That was good, because she couldn't have said a word if she'd wanted to. Eating breakfast helped get her emotions under control. Grady finished off the last of the omelet.

"That was delicious. My compliments to the chef." He got up and started clearing the table.

Brett followed suit. "It was really good, Mom."

"Thank you."

When she stood up to help, her husband turned to her. "This is a day for you to relax and do whatever you want. The newspaper's on the table in the foyer."

"I thought you were anxious to work on the Drummond account."

"Only when you're ready. I don't want you to feel pushed. We've got a whole week of uninterrupted time ahead of us."

He was saying that for her benefit, not his. She knew he was counting the seconds until he discovered who'd done this horrible thing to their family. She was desperate for answers, too.

"We might need every bit of it to come up with some clues. As soon as I've showered, let's look over the rest of the calendar and then get down to business. I can't promise anything but to try my hardest."

She saw Grady's eyes ignite with satisfaction, and on her way up the stairs, she heard Brett tell his dad he wanted to help, too.

Susan felt no qualms about entering the master bedroom now. After finding a change of clothes, she hurried into her bathroom and got ready for the day.

She'd just slid her feet into a pair of navy sandals when she picked up the sound of a mower coming from the backyard. Mrs. Harmon hadn't warned them any too soon.

Grady met her in the upstairs hallway. He put a finger to her lips.

Until the last few days, she'd thought of herself as sexually dead. Now the combination of his touch and the scent of the soap he'd used produced a distinctly erotic sensation. If her mind couldn't remember, her body did. She felt alive in a brand-new way.

"Jim drove Mike over in the truck," he whispered before taking his hand away. "They're both mowing."

She blinked. "Is this what you meant by Jim's generosity?"

"No. He does a lot of nice things for Brett, but he's never taken it upon himself to do my yard work before."

"Not even when you and I went on vacation with Brett?"

He shook his head. "When we go out of town, there's a lawn-care company I call."

"Ellen probably asked Mike to do it as a favor. Maybe he didn't want to, so she enlisted her husband's help."

"Maybe."

Susan had been around Grady long enough now to know when he hadn't told her everything he was thinking.

"It's obvious you're the kind of man who prefers taking total care of his own family, his own business. Sometimes it's harder to receive than to give? Isn't it?"

He seemed to pale. "You've said that to me before."

"I'm not surprised. A man who lights his own fires can't abide the idea of anyone else putting them out."

"Susan," he blurted.

"Yes?"

His eyes closed tightly. "I've missed you."

He wanted his wife.

Though she had no memory of him, it didn't diminish the fact that she wanted him, too.

"Grady... I can't tell you the same thing. There's no way to predict whether or not I'll ever have total recall. But if it helps, please know that I'm strongly attracted to you. I have been from the moment we met.

"What I'm trying to say is, if you want me to sleep with you, I will."

CHAPTER EIGHT

GRADY REELED.

What man would turn down an offer like that, especially from his wife of seventeen years?

Except that it *wouldn't* be his wife in bed with him. Her body, yes, but not her mind or her emotions.

He didn't doubt her desire for him. When she'd first called herself Martha, the chemistry had been there for both of them. But even in the total intimacy of bed, he wouldn't be her Grady. She wouldn't be his Susan.

Was half a loaf better than none?

If she never remembered him, could he deal with it? Could he grow to love her as much as the wife he'd lost?

Would the striving to find the old Susan eventually tear them apart so that he lost both of them?

"The truck's gone now, Dad!"

At their son's remark, Susan moved past Grady. To his horror, he detected a glint of pain in her eyes.

"That was a nice thing for the Stevenses to do." She sounded as if nothing had happened. Grady knew differently.

"I'll bet Mike hated it."

"You think so?" Susan asked.

"His dad's always finding him extra jobs. Mike works harder than any of my other friends."

"Mr. Stevens probably had a father who made him slave," she said.

"He did. Mike said his grandfather was dirt-poor, so his dad had to earn money for everything."

"Then you have your explanation. Some patterns are hard to break."

"Don't get mad, Mom, but you've told me the same thing before."

"Why would I get mad?"

"Because I keep telling you 'you said that before,' and you probably hate it."

"Not at all. It makes me feel like I'm getting closer to being myself again."

"I love you, Mom."

"I love you, too, darling. Shall we go downstairs?"

"Yeah. Are you coming, Dad?"

"In a minute. First I need to finish talking to your mother. Why don't you go to the den and boot up the computer for us?"

"Okay."

Susan turned in Grady's direction. She was wearing a pale blue knit top with a pair of denim cutoffs. He was sure that if he'd seen those same clothes on another woman, his heart wouldn't have begun this frantic pounding.

"When I brought you home from the apartment," he said in a low voice, "my fear of frightening you off was the only reason I didn't ask you to come to bed with me. Your honesty now has let me know that's not a problem."

"But there *are* other problems." She'd anticipated his thoughts. "I know all about them. Maybe if we just got used to holding each other again?"

She wanted comforting.

So did he.

Reaching blindly for her, he whispered, "Tonight will be a new beginning."

She clung to him, trembling. He held her tight until she relaxed in his arms. Lord—to feel her like this again...

"Oh, no," she cried softly. "I've wet the front of the T-shirt you just put on. I'm too emotional for my own good." She pulled away from him before he was ready to release her.

Six months ago, he hadn't been able to accept the fact that he would never embrace his wife again. Maybe something had made him sense that she was still out there, waiting for him to come and find her.

Whatever force was at work, she'd been returned to him. Though she'd been robbed of the memories they'd shared, she *felt* like the old Susan. Tonight she'd be back in their bed.

After half a year's deprivation, his biggest concern at the moment was figuring out a way to quell the frantic beat of his heart until then. If Brett hadn't been downstairs waiting for them...

"Don't you know these tears mean you're alive? Do you honestly think I mind?"

"You might if I drown you," she murmured, wiping her eyes.

Right now she was behaving very much like the

wife he'd lost. It was those quicksilver appearances that haunted and captivated him.

Until she had a full recovery, they always would.

Grady slid his hand to the back of her neck. Together they walked through the hall and down the stairs to the den.

Brett looked up, his gaze lingering on them. "I've put in the first disk. Here's the calendar."

The glow of happiness was back in his eyes. It wasn't something his son could control. No doubt Grady's face had undergone a similar change. Susan was the heart and soul of their lives.

If her mother or brother were to see him and Brett just now, they'd realize something extraordinary had happened. No one deserved to know the truth more than they did. They loved her, too, and they'd suffered terribly after her apparent death.

The person responsible for so much unhappiness was going to pay.

"Susan? Why don't you sit at the desk and look at the spreadsheets. See what you think of them, and then Brett and I will help you make sense of the notations on the calendar."

She gave him an exaggerated look of desperation. It was so typical of the old Susan, he had difficulty believing she had amnesia. But that impression was quickly quashed when she started shaking her head.

He pulled his chair closer to her. "What's wrong?"

"I can't do this."

"You haven't given yourself any time yet."

"It's not just what's on the screen. I don't remember how to work a computer." She sounded panicked.

"That's okay, Mom. I'll show you." Brett moved his chair around to her other side.

"Who taught you?"

"You did."

"You're kidding!"

"Nope. There's nothing to it. That's what you used to tell me."

"Then I lied."

"No, you didn't," Brett insisted. "You began my lessons when I was in first grade so I'd be ahead of the other kids."

"So I was a helicopter mother?" That had always been Susan's disapproving term for parents who swooped in to save their children from every situation instead of letting them learn by making mistakes.

Grady didn't know whether to laugh or cry. This was another of those defining moments when the woman who'd given birth to their son was in full evidence.

"Mom…you weren't like *that*."

"I'm afraid to hear any more."

"You're a lot smarter than Rich Dunn's mom, and she's a heart surgeon."

"Honest? You really think I'm smart?"

"*Mom*," he said in exasperation. "See these arrow keys? They make the screen scroll up and down. If you press the page-down key, it'll go all the way to the end of the file. When you hold down the page-up key, it'll take you back to the beginning. Try it."

In about two minutes, Brett had her more confident than before. She turned to Grady. "All right. Now what am I supposed to be looking for?"

"You went to work in March, but you didn't take over the Drummond account until the end of July. I backed up all twelve disks before the FBI took the originals. Unfortunately, your notebook was destroyed with your car. Your first calendar entry reads 'File one. Check *F, P, S.*' I'd assumed those letters referred to various companies, but that doesn't seem to be the case.

"From August through to the week of the explosion, most of the boxes on your calendar contain a file number with a note to check certain items. But I don't know what they are because you had a system of using letters of the alphabet to designate everything."

"Did I always bring the calendar in here?"

"No. You'd go to the kitchen and jot down a reminder to yourself."

"That seems like a strange system." She scrolled down and back. Then she shook her head. "Grady, I don't have the faintest idea what I'm doing."

"I know that." On a burst of inspiration, he got up and walked over to the bookcase. She kept all her old textbooks there. He pulled out the one she'd always referred to and put it next to the keyboard.

"This was your bible. You've written in the margins. Maybe something in here will help you make sense of what's on the screen."

He felt her hesitate. "I'll try."

"I'll help you, Mom," Brett said earnestly.

"Thanks, darling."

"While you guys do that, I'll be in the kitchen on the phone."

Susan was glad he'd left them alone. She couldn't possibly work with him watching. He wanted answers. So did she. But he exuded an intense energy that made her far too aware of him and made it difficult for her to concentrate.

Her gaze wandered to an unlabeled envelope sitting on the desk. "What's this?"

"It's information about the CPA firm. You know, phone numbers and stuff. Dad hoped you'd remember something from looking at it."

"Oh, Brett, I think I know how Noah felt when he was told to build an ark and didn't have the faintest idea what one looked like."

"You remember who Noah was?"

"Yes. It's strange, isn't it? The doctor at the shelter told me amnesiacs remember all kinds of information like that, yet they don't remember really important personal things."

"You'll remember Dad one of these days. As for accounting, I don't think it could be as hard as building an ark."

"Don't forget Noah got a lot of help."

"You'll get help, too, Mom."

Her son's faith was humbling. She gave him a hug. "Especially with you around. Okay." Reaching for the accounting book, she said, "Let's see what's in the table of contents." After scanning the list she came to a topic and read it aloud. "'Uncovering fraud.'"

"Dad thinks someone committed fraud against Mr. Drummond and you found out."

"Assuming that's true, it would be like looking for one grain of sand in a bucketful."

"How come?"

The house phone rang just then. They both ignored it.

"Think of all the things that go into the creation of a hotel like the Etoile—the design, the funding, the construction, just to name a few."

"Yeah, except that it's built now and Dad said there hasn't been any trouble. He'd know if there was."

"I'm sure he would. So if I *did* find something wrong—"

"Then it's still hidden, because they killed you before you could tell anyone."

"It must've been something really big for them to plant bombs."

"Dad's positive the man you replaced was murdered."

"I know. Just think, Brett. If I could stay dead long enough to figure this out…"

"Do it, Mom!"

Oh, why couldn't she remember?

In angry frustration, she turned to the section on fraud. "Let's take a look at the different kinds of fraud. Tax, commercial business, construction."

"Do you think it could be one of those three?"

"Probably. I need to read about them."

"I just got an idea. Can I try something on the computer while you do that?"

"Sure. We'll change seats."

Before she began, she watched her son in fascination. "What are you doing?"

"If you want to find a word, you click on Edit, type in the word you're looking for, and the computer will scroll down to highlight it."

"What word are you going to put in?"

"Those letters *F, P, S.*"

"Do it," she urged him.

After a minute, he frowned. "Heck. It didn't find that combination."

"How about just doing the *F?*"

"It'll stop on every word with an *F* in it."

"Let me see."

He did about ten of them. "Some are in the middle, some at the end."

"Try scrolling to the top of the file, Brett. I want to see which ones begin with *F.*"

There were dozens, most of them verbs. "Too bad there's no device to pick out nouns," she murmured.

"I know what those are. A person, place or thing."

"Good for you." She squeezed his arm. "Okay. I'm going to read for a few minutes."

Susan sat back to immerse herself in actual landmark fraud cases from the past. In the margins she saw notes written in her hand, indicating why one or the other was especially interesting or important. Surprised to find the cases intriguing, she lost track of time. The phone rang again. She was hardly aware of it.

When she'd finished the last case, she shut the book and looked over at Brett, who was printing a number of pages. She saw in the corner of the computer that it was ten after three. Susan couldn't believe how long they'd been sitting there.

She jumped to her feet. "Your father's probably wondering what's happened to us. Let's go find him and fix some lunch."

"When he looked in a little while ago, he was eating a sandwich."

No doubt Grady hadn't wanted to break her concentration. "Well, I'm hungry. Do you want a sandwich, too?"

"Yeah."

"Yes, please." The minute she corrected him, she realized her error. "Forgive me, Brett. I didn't mean to say that. It just came out."

But she needn't have worried about offending him. He had a smile on his face. "For someone who doesn't remember everything, you sounded just like you used to."

She smiled back. "Then I guess it's something you still have to work on."

"Yeah. I mean, yes."

Susan couldn't resist hugging him again. "What did you print?"

"I went through the file, hunting for all the nouns that start with an *F, P* or *S*. Then I copied and pasted them to make a list."

"You're kidding! Let me see."

"I'd like a look myself."

Her heart turned over at the sound of her husband's voice. He walked toward them, carrying a bag of potato chips, drinks and a plate piled with sandwiches.

His rugged features were so attractive beneath that

dark hair, she couldn't help staring at him. "I would've made lunch for all of us."

"You were doing something much more important. Besides, I like waiting on my family."

"Thank you, Grady." Susan reached for a ham sandwich with cheese and lettuce.

Brett took a couple with peanut butter and jelly. "Yea-yes, Dad. Thanks."

"You're welcome."

While Grady gave his attention to the list, Brett shared the chips with her. They were both hungry and finished their meal in record time. Susan was about to open her soda when the front doorbell rang, startling her.

Grady put the paper on the desk, then he walked over to the shutters and peered through a crack.

When he finally left the window, she thought he was coming back to sit down—until she saw the forbidding expression on his face. A thrill of fear ran through her body as he unlocked the bottom drawer of the desk with a key he took from his pocket and retrieved a gun.

"Don't move." He mouthed the words before stealing from the den.

Susan exchanged shocked glances with Brett. By now her heart was racing so fast it was almost painful. In an instinctive gesture, she put her arm around her son's shoulders while they waited.

"Dad must think somebody's trying to break in. That'd be a dumb thing to do, because we have a sign by the door that says our house is protected by an alarm.

"Any idiot knows it'll go off at the police station. Not only that, after you died, Dad set up a minicamera that snaps a picture when a person rings the bell."

She shivered. "Unfortunately some idiots are still willing to take risks if they're desperate enough." No matter how infallible Grady seemed, bad things happened to the best police officers.

They both jumped when they heard the back doorbell ring. Susan hugged her son tighter.

It felt like an eternity before Grady returned. She thought the look on his face would strike fear in the heart of anyone who made the mistake of tangling with him. He locked the gun back in the drawer.

"What's going on, Dad?"

"Two men just cased our house," he said. "They carried Bibles and they wore white shirts and ties. They were trying to pass themselves off as Mormon missionaries."

"How do you know they weren't?"

"On closer inspection, they looked too old. Plus they weren't wearing the usual identification tags. It's common knowledge at the station that missionaries adhere to strict proselyting rules and only do front-door approaches. When this pair walked around the back to ring the other bell, they gave themselves away."

"Did they come on bikes?"

"No. That was another clue. I watched from an upstairs window. After a short wait, they took off over the back fence and worked their way through the Hanes's yard to the next street. They kept walking until I eventually lost sight of them."

Susan let go of Brett and got up from the chair. "If ours was the only house they picked on the street, do you thi—"

"No." Grady cut her off. "I'm convinced the person who tried to kill you still believes you're dead. The two thugs who came to our door were after something specific in the house."

"It's what I told you, Mom—our alarm sign scared them away."

"If they hadn't gone around back, I'd agree with you, Brett."

He eyed his dad in confusion. "Why do you think they did that?"

"To find out if Mrs. Harmon was inside. You can't see into the garage to know if her car was parked there or not. They needed her to open the door so they wouldn't set off the alarm."

Susan was as perplexed as Brett. "If they know a detective lives here, how would they dare try anything?"

"I've been asking myself the same question. The only answer that makes sense is they knew Brett and I have supposedly gone on vacation. They figured it was safe to make their move."

"But you must have taken other trips with Brett in the past six months. Why didn't they overpower Mrs. Harmon the last time you went away? Or the time before that?"

She thought Grady would answer, but it was their son who spoke up. "After the explosion, Dad and I didn't go on any trips."

Susan stared at her husband in surprise. "Not even to see his cousins in California?"

"No."

"You mean the house has never been left unattended?"

"No," he declared a second time. "I told you I haven't been the best father for the past six months."

"That's not true, Dad."

Anger raged inside her. "Don't, Grady. You can't blame yourself like this. Our lives were blown apart that day. What frightens me is the possibility that someone's been monitoring your movements, just waiting for an opportunity like this."

Smoothing the hair away from her face, she said, "I don't want to think it, but what if you're right, and an escaped convict or ex-felon with a vendetta against you intends to plant a bomb in here in order to get rid of you?

"Maybe it's a copycat bomber who knew what happened to me and has decided to get rid of you and Brett the same way. You told me that's what happened to a judge's family in Reno."

He stared at her flushed cheeks. "Anyone who hated me that much would have found another way to blow us up long before now. No—my instincts tell me that isn't what this is about."

"Dad, even if they'd been watching the house, they couldn't have known we planned to go away. We didn't decide until yesterday. The only people who think we left town are my friends."

Susan waited for Grady to say something. When he drew the cell phone from his pocket without responding to Brett, the significance of the moment sent chills through her body.

She heard him ask for Captain Willis.

"Who's that?" she whispered to Brett as Grady turned his back and walked away from them.

"Dad's boss."

The conversation went on for a long time, increasing her anxiety. She could only admire Brett, whose composure allowed him to play solitaire on the computer while they waited.

Needing something to calm her nerves, she reached for the paper Brett had printed, curious to see all the nouns he'd found.

It pleased her to discover their son had a good grasp of English grammar. Todd never did know an adjective from a preposition.

Todd.

She reached for Brett's arm. "I just remembered something else about my brother."

"Mom!" With that jubilant cry, he abandoned the computer game. "What is it?"

After she told him, he said, "Wait till Dad hears this."

They both looked in his direction, but he was still deep in conversation.

Between her worry over her husband and son, and now this latest flashback, she was an emotional disaster. Until she could talk to Grady, she would force herself to concentrate on the list Brett had made.

There weren't as many nouns as she would've supposed. She studied them several times. She eventually came up with three items having to do with building construction: fans, plywood, stain.

Was that what the letters stood for? If so, why had she made a note to check them in particular?

"Brett? Go to the top of the file and find the word *plywood.*"

"Okay."

He did something that got rid of the solitaire game, then they were back to the account. The word came right up. "It just says *plywood.*"

"Now go to *stain.*"

He did it. "*Stain. Maple* is in parentheses."

"All right—try the last one. *Fans.*"

She waited until he found it. "*Fans. Lcfpm* is in parentheses."

The three items were buried among so many dozens of others in the file, Susan couldn't be sure the letters had anything to do with them.

"I appreciate your going to all the trouble of making those lists for me, darling."

"Do you think it'll help you?"

"Maybe. Thanks to you, we have a place to start. I don't remember being an accountant, but I do know it means keeping track of costs to make certain everything balances."

She looked at the calendar again. Out of curiosity she said, "Brett? How do you get to file two? I made a note to look at the *E*s."

After he showed her, she asked him to search every *E*.

Since it was a vowel, this was an endless process. The first noun in the search highlighted *elevator.* Who knew how many more nouns relating to construction were in this file alone?

"Brett?"

Grady shut off his phone just then, and they both turned in his direction.

"The disks will have to wait. Would you turn off the computer, please? We have to talk."

That sounded ominous. In a fit of nervousness Susan cleared up the remains of their lunch and put the potato chip bag in the wastebasket.

"Okay, Dad. It's done. What's going on?"

Grady sat down in the chair he'd occupied earlier. His arms rested on his thighs, with his hands clasped between his knees. "We have to send both of you to a secure place."

"No!" they cried at the same time.

Brett's face had grown red. "I'm not going!"

"Neither am I," Susan said, dry-eyed. "We were separated once before by someone evil. I refuse to let that happen again. This family's been through hell. Now that we're together, we're going to stay together."

Her husband's mouth looked white around the edges. "I can't risk losing the two of you."

He was close enough that Susan simply fell on her knees in front of him. She gripped his hands. "As long as we can be with you to fight this, nobody's going to lose anybody. We're not leaving you, Grady."

"Yeah, Dad! I'm a teenager, not a baby. I can handle whatever happens. You've even taught me how to use a gun."

At that remark Grady shot out of the chair. Holding on to the back of it, he studied them for what seemed like an eternity.

"If I let you stay here, you have to promise you'll do *exactly* what I say."

"We promise."

It was a good thing Brett spoke for them, because relief had left Susan feeling weak. In a clumsy effort, she got up from the floor and took her seat again.

"Guess what, Dad? Mom remembered something else about Uncle Todd."

Grady looked at her intently. "Was it when you still lived with your parents?"

Don't be crushed because I can't remember you yet, Grady. I want to, more than you know.

"I'm not sure. I just suddenly recalled that he was never good at grammar. But our son is."

She flashed him a smile, hoping he would acknowledge that remark. Instead, a bleakness entered his eyes.

"Your mind must be suppressing certain memories to protect you from remembering that horrific morning."

"That's what I'm beginning to think."

In fact, it was what she believed, but she feared that deep in his heart her husband thought it might be for another reason.

I didn't fall out of love with you, Grady. That's not the reason I got the job before telling you what I'd done. It's not the reason I can't remember you. I know that in my heart. How can I reassure you?

"Do you realize that until you and Brett found me,

not one memory had come back to me? Since being with you, I've had three or four flashbacks. In time, more will come. I *feel* it. That's another reason I couldn't bear to be separated from you again.''

A tense silence stretched between them for a moment. Then he pulled his cell phone from his pocket and made another call out of their hearing.

She exchanged smiles with Brett, her fearless co-conspirator. There was no doubt in her mind that this was one of the few times Grady had ever been over-ruled when it came to a life-and-death situation.

''All right,'' Grady said when he'd finished his conversation. ''I'd wanted to keep your existence a secret. However, circumstances have changed, making it necessary for some of my colleagues to know the whole story.

''I could be wrong, but I believe the person who thought he'd killed you is still worried about being found out. He probably sent his thugs to see if I've kept copies of your accounting records, either on the hard drive or on disks. If my hunch is correct, then they have to be caught inside the house so they can be arrested and we can find out who sent them.

''Since they need Mrs. Harmon, we're going to accommodate them. She'll be arriving soon with a couple of SWAT team members hiding in her car.

''They'll be living with us for as long as a week if that's what it takes. Should the phone ring while Mrs. Harmon's here, she'll answer it. If it's a wrong number or a hang-up, we can expect visitors.

''If I'm right and they're taking advantage of my supposed absence, they'll show up. Other SWAT team members and undercover police officers will provide backup and round-the-clock surveillance, both here and at Mrs. Harmon's home.''

Susan stood up. ''What do you want us to do?''

''You two will stay in our bedroom from here on out. Brett's room will be needed for the best view of the backyard. The officers will trade off vigils, both upstairs and down. We'll let them use the guest room to take turns sleeping.''

''Where will you be?''

''Spelling them off. When it's my turn to sleep, I'll join the two of you.''

That meant her first night alone with her husband would have to be put on hold. The idea that it might be a week or more before things returned to normal devastated her.

Only now did she realize how much she'd been counting on tonight.

I'm in love with a man I don't remember.

She turned swiftly to Brett. ''Come on, darling. We've got work to do upstairs.''

CHAPTER NINE

"DAD?"

"Shh. It's only four in the morning. You'll wake your mother."

Grady might have known he couldn't sneak into the bedroom without Brett knowing about it. His son had inflated his air mattress, which he'd placed near the door. He was stretched out comfortably on top of it, covered by his sleeping bag. It touched him that Brett was prepared to protect Susan.

"I haven't gone to sleep yet. Come to bed, Grady."

His eyes closed tightly. In the dark she sounded like the old Susan who used to wait up for him whenever he was out at night dealing with some hellish situation.

The moment he felt her arms around him, all the demons fled. It always used to happen that way. There was just this warm, soft feminine body melting into him. They'd make love and forget the world…. That seemed like a century ago.

Grady crossed the room and lay down on the covers. He wore his shoulder holster and kept his cell phone in his pocket, ready to get up at a moment's notice if the surveillance team detected any movement outside.

"I didn't hear the phone or the doorbell," she murmured.

"It's been quiet, but the guys and I feel those two men will be back sooner than later. It could happen anytime."

"How's Mrs. Harmon?"

Grady turned on his side, craving her warmth. "She says she's excited to be part of it."

"But you don't believe her."

"I hate having to use her."

"Look at it this way, Grady. She came to work for you, helpless to take away your pain. Now she's in a position to actually do something to end it. You wouldn't deny her that privilege, would you?"

The woman lying next to him reasoned the same way as the old Susan. Before the explosion, she always knew how to comfort, how to say the right thing at the right time. Right here and now, he couldn't tell the difference between the two of them.

He slid his hand to her shoulder. "No," he murmured as he kneaded her satiny skin covered by the thin sleeve of her nightgown. His heart almost failed him when she nestled her head in the crook of his arm. The fragrance of her freshly washed blond hair assailed him.

His breath caught. His emotions bordered on the primitive. It was providential that Brett was in the room; otherwise Grady would've started making love to her instead of being ready to deal with whatever lurked outside.

Six months ago, he'd lost all sense of being a sexual entity. After her memorial service, he'd come back to this room with the sure knowledge that he would never love again, never know sexual pleasure again. Brett had been his only reason for drawing another breath.

If he hadn't had a son who'd needed him...

"Everything's going to be fine," she whispered. In the next instant he felt her fingers brush the moisture from his cheek. "Go to sleep for a little while. I'll listen for your phone."

"Maybe just a few minutes."

Those words haunted him when he awakened at eleven to the smell of coffee.

He jackknifed into a sitting position and discovered his wife and son seated at a card table enjoying breakfast a short distance from the bed.

"Whoa, Dad!" Brett grinned.

"Good morning, Grady. Come and eat while your food is hot." It looked as if she'd made his favorite, steak and eggs.

He rubbed his jaw.

"You can shave after," she said, obviously reading his mind. "Officer Dutton said you're supposed to relieve him downstairs in twenty minutes. We let you sleep as long as we dared."

Grady needed no urging to join them. Evidently nothing had gone on while he'd been out for the count. The respite from all his cares had done wonders for him. He was starving and ate quickly, and then, after his second cup of coffee, got up from the table.

On the way to the bathroom, he kissed Susan on the side of her neck. "*That* food hit the spot."

"I'm glad."

A few minutes later he reentered the bedroom to discover Brett watching television while his wife made the bed. She was wearing a pair of white shorts with a violet top he particularly liked on her.

Seventeen years might have passed, but she didn't look much older than the day he'd first seen her, noticing her curvaceous figure and long legs as she raced for the volleyball. With her gossamer hair waving in the ocean breeze, the combination of brilliant blue eyes and radiant smile had stopped him dead in his tracks.

Looking at her now, he felt exactly the same way.

She stood up to catch him staring at her. "I made breakfast for the officers. They said it would be all right because everything was still quiet."

"You can be sure they appreciated it."

"More than anything I think they were in shock. Both of them attended my memorial service."

He picked up the breakfast tray to take downstairs. "A lot of people are going to be in shock when they find out you're alive." He ground his teeth just thinking about the murderer who'd blown their world apart.

When Grady got hold of him…

"Dad?"

"Yes, Brett?"

"Are you okay?"

"I couldn't be better. How about you?"

"Great."

"Thanks for guarding your mother. I can always depend on you."

Brett smiled at him. "Thanks, Dad."

Grady looked over at Susan one more time. By now she was lying facedown on the bed with the accounting book open in front of her. She darted him a glance.

"Take care, Grady. See you later."

He sensed there was an implicit message in those words. A surge of raw desire shot through him.

"You can count on it."

As he started down the stairs, it hit him again how thankful he was that she and Brett had refused to be sent away. Heaven knew he hadn't wanted to let them out of his sight.

After he'd returned the tray to the kitchen, he headed for the den to take Bob Dutton's place at the window. The burly officer got to his feet.

"Your wife makes one delicious breakfast. You must be the happiest son of a gun around."

"That doesn't even begin to cover it." He knew what Bob was saying—what everyone in the department would be saying before long—Grady Corbitt's wife had come back from the dead. Things like that just didn't happen....

Yet Grady had proof they did.

His gorgeous wife was upstairs. She might not remember him, but she *wanted* to. After last night he knew that with everything inside him.

Tonight—

"There's the phone."

Bob's voice brought him back to the present. He

waited until the ringing stopped, then picked up the receiver to hear the message.

He nodded at Bob. "It's a hang-up."

"*All right!* Someone's gone hunting. We'll get Mrs. Harmon over here on the double and take care of these wackos."

"I'll let my family know what's in store, then I'll be back so you can get some shut-eye before things start to happen."

Taking the stairs three at a time, Grady hurried to Brett's bedroom first, to inform Tony Garcia of the latest development.

The other man lifted his hand in greeting. "I'm ready for them. When you have the chance, tell your wife thanks for the conversation and the meal. On top of everything else, she makes great coffee. I envy you, you know?" His eyes twinkled.

Grady felt for Tony, whose marriage had failed because his wife couldn't handle his line of work. She'd given him an ultimatum. When he'd explained that he loved what he did and wouldn't be happy doing anything else, she'd divorced him.

Susan had never questioned Grady's choice of profession. Although it had upset her horribly when he'd gotten shot, she'd never once asked him to quit the force. To ease her worries, he'd become a detective.

But for the first time, he was beginning to wonder if she'd decided to get a job outside the home as her way of dealing with fears she'd never expressed to him.

Maybe, like Tony's wife, she'd always hated Grady's job. Yet unlike the other woman, Susan would never force him to choose between her and his career. So she'd found the kind of work that was so consuming, she could fend off her fears for part of each day.

Had she been so determined to hide her fears from him that she hadn't come to him first to discuss taking the job?

"I'll pass your message along, Tony."

With Bob waiting downstairs, Grady couldn't do anything more than tell Susan and Brett to stay in the master bedroom until further notice.

His wife sat straight up. "You think they'll be coming this afternoon, then?" She sounded calm enough, but he saw the anxiety in her eyes.

"We're hoping."

"Be careful, Dad."

Shortly afterward, Grady was the only one in the den. He placed himself where he could see everything on the street immediately in front of the house. Twenty minutes later Mrs. Harmon pulled into the driveway. He heard the garage door open, then close.

To Grady's surprise, Matt Ross and another SWAT team member entered the house with her. The detective, his closest friend in the department, rushed over to give him a bear hug.

"I still can't believe what the captain told me. Thank God Susan didn't die in that explosion. Even if she has amnesia, I'm beyond happy for you, Grady."

He cleared his throat. "Thanks, Matt. Now, tell me what you're doing here."

"The captain called me in. When you scanned that

picture from your camera and sent it to headquarters, I ran it through the computer. Nothing came up on the one guy, but the dark blond character has a number of violations on his record.

"The name on his driver's license is Sean Mills, thirty-one-year-old Caucasian. Last known place of employment was DeBeer Tile Company in Las Vegas. He was working as a journeyman at the time of the accident."

Tile?

"Here's the important part. One of his violations resulted in an arrest for alleged vehicular homicide, but the prosecution couldn't prove its case for lack of evidence. It was thrown out of court." He paused significantly. "I followed up on your suggestion to check the name of the person whose car ran into that accountant, Beck, last April."

The hair lifted on the back of Grady's neck. "They were a match," he muttered. "I *knew* it!"

Matt nodded. "The man was driving a DeBeer van. It's Mills, all right. Captain Willis said your instincts panned out. There's no doubt in his mind of a relationship between that homicide and the explosion at the fireworks plant. Your wife is the link."

Grady nodded. "I knew they were after Susan's disks," he muttered. "We've got to take these guys alive and force them to spill their guts. Someone else is the brains behind all this. Every damn person involved is looking at a life sentence."

Matt started to say something when the phone rang. The line was tapped so they could trace the call. So far, the others had been out of area.

Grady turned to Mrs. Harmon, who sat at the desk. When he nodded to her, she picked up the receiver and said, "Corbitt residence."

"HI, MRS. HARMON! It's Mike Stevens."

"Hello, Mike. How are you doing?"

He shrugged his shoulders. "Not that great. This vacation has been pretty boring without Brett around."

"Are you one of the good elves who mowed the lawn when I wasn't here?"

"Yeah. Dad and I did it."

"That was such a nice thing to do. I can't wait to tell them when they get back."

Mike jumped off the corner of his dad's desk. "Do you know which hotel Brett's staying at so I can call him?"

"They went on one of those four-day cruises first."

"Heck."

"I'm sure they'll check in with me when they get to Disney World. I'll find out where they're staying and give you their phone number."

He frowned. "We're going to Mexico this afternoon and we won't be back till Sunday. I guess I'll have to wait until we're both home."

This was just great. School would be starting the day after they got back.

"I'm sorry, Mike."

"Me, too."

"I hope you have a wonderful time on your trip."

"Thanks. Bye, Mrs. Harmon."

"Bad news?" His dad was finishing up business

so they could leave. He always had last-minute stuff to do.

"Yeah. They went on the cruise first, so I can't talk to him."

"Well, it was worth a try."

"Yeah. Thanks for the suggestion, Dad."

"You're welcome. I'm about through here. Why don't you go in the house and help your mom with the rest of the packing?"

"I don't want to go to Mexico."

"You'll be happy you went. I'm planning on us catching a trophy, maybe a swordfish."

That would be fun, but his mom would hate it. She got seasick.

MRS. HARMON HUNG UP the receiver. "Mike wanted to get in touch with Brett."

Grady nodded. "You handled that perfectly. What I'd like you to do now is bring in the newspaper and the mail. Then come back in here and we'll see if we get another phone call."

She returned a minute later, handing Grady the paper and a stack of letters. "Sit down and make yourself comfortable," he urged as he scanned the mail. "If we haven't had visitors inside of ten minutes, then you can go."

"I'm willing to stay as long as you want."

"I know that, and I appreciate it. However, it's not your routine to be in the house more than fifteen to twenty minutes a day while we're gone. We don't want that to change and send up a red flag."

"You're right."

"Can I bring you something to eat or drink?"

"No, thank you. I'm fine. I'll just finish writing a letter to my daughter while I wait."

Grady turned to Matt. "I want to know everything there is to know about Sean Mills."

"If he doesn't show up today, I'll leave with Mrs. Harmon and get right over to DeBeer Tile. Even if Mills isn't working for them now, they'll remember him. Maybe the other guy was employed there, too. Before I'm through, I'll find out which side of the bed they sleep on at night," he vowed.

"Thanks, Matt. If I didn't have to pretend to be on vaca—"

"It's a masterful plan, Grady," he said, interrupting him. "Finding Susan the way Brett did, without anyone knowing, is a detective's dream. Your secret's safe with the department.

"Everyone involved has a personal interest in this case. We're going to help you nail the bastard who did this to her. The only difficult part in all this will be keeping it from Jennifer."

"I know what you mean. Brett's going to have a hell of a time staying in character once he goes back to school on Monday. The happiness in his eyes says it all."

"Tell him to wear sunglasses for a while."

"That isn't a bad idea."

"I could have a pair express-mailed to your house from Disney World with their logo."

"Make that two pairs. He can give one to Mike as a souvenir."

"Done."

Mrs. Harmon put the letter in her purse and got up from the desk. "It's been fifteen minutes."

"I know."

"Don't be disappointed, Grady," Matt murmured. "It'll hap—"

But he didn't finish what he was going to say because Grady's cell phone rang. He clicked on. "Yes?"

"The targets are a house away, coming on foot. We're ready to close in."

Adrenaline surged through his veins. "Thanks.

"This is it, Mrs. Harmon. When they ring the bell, call out, 'Just a minute,' then go upstairs and stay with Susan and Brett."

While Matt accompanied her to the foyer, Grady notified the other officers in the house. In a matter of minutes, everyone was in place for the takedown.

Grady left the den door open enough to see into the foyer, then he drew his gun. He planned to stay out of sight to maintain the fiction that he wasn't there, but he wouldn't hesitate to do whatever it took if more backup was needed.

It was just as well the others were handling this. The way Grady was feeling, he'd just as soon blow their heads off as look at them.

Finally the doorbell rang. Mrs. Harmon stood at the bottom of the stairs, and Grady heard her call, "Just a minute—I'm coming!"

Tony was primed by the door. Grady heard him undo the dead bolt. As he turned the knob and started to open it, the two men came crashing through in ski masks.

To Grady's joy, the SWAT team threw them to the floor. Everything was over in seconds. They'd been so unsuspecting, their Bibles fell from their hands, and their guns skidded across the tile.

More of the team poured into the house. On came the handcuffs, off came the masks.

"What the hell?"

"Holy crap!"

"He said we wouldn't have any trouble with the housekeeper!"

"Shut up, asshole!"

"You gentlemen are under arrest." Matt's calm voice cut through their invective. "A neighbor warned Mrs. Harmon you two were seen running through the backyard yesterday. It looked suspicious to them.

"Since she's in charge until Detective Corbitt returns from his trip, she called the Church of Jesus Christ of Latter-day Saints. There were no missionaries proselytizing on this street yesterday. At that point, she called the police.

"You have the right to remain silent. If you can't retain an attorney, one will be provided. Take them downtown and book them. I'll check in later."

Grady let go of the breath he'd been holding.

Only Captain Willis and Matt had known he'd pretended to go on vacation. The captain was a straight arrow if ever there was one. But until Matt was willing to show his face in front of these criminals just now, Grady hadn't been certain his partner wasn't involved in the conspiracy against his wife.

He put his gun back in his holster and stayed in

the den until the house emptied. Matt wasn't long in joining him.

"Thanks for covering for me the way you did."

Matt smiled. "Anytime. We now know they were taking orders from someone else."

Grady nodded, but his pleasure was short-lived.

"What's eating you?"

"I'm positive those thugs were sent to find out if I kept copies of Susan's disks with the accounts on them."

"Captain Willis told me as much."

"Matt—no one knew we were going on vacation except the friends Brett phoned to let them know we were leaving."

They stared at each other. "What is it we say about most rapes being committed by someone the victim knew?"

"I don't even want to think it, but there it is."

"Do you know which friends he called?"

"He told Mike Stevens first because Mike came over to the house before Brett got on the phone."

"Let's talk to Brett right now."

"I'll bring everyone down. They have to know." He paused at the door. "I've told Susan that you and Jennifer are our friends, but you're going to find it a strange experience when she looks at you as if you're a stranger."

Matt's brows furrowed. "I don't know how you've dealt with it."

"It was hell at first, but she's had some flash-backs."

"Then she'll probably have total recall one of these days."

"That's what I'm praying for."

He left the room and raced up the stairs. When he reached the bedroom, its three occupants got to their feet, wearing anxious expressions. His gaze met Susan's.

"It's over," he assured them. "The two men were caught without a problem."

"I *knew* you'd do it!" Brett shouted.

"We can thank Mrs. Harmon here for baiting the hook. The SWAT team did the rest."

Susan didn't look reassured. "Isn't there a risk that the person who sent these men will hire more thugs to harm us?"

"Possibly," Grady said. "We'll have to be extra careful from here on out. Let's go downstairs."

SUSAN WANTED TO KNOW the details of the capture, but she would have to ask Grady about them later. She was doubly thankful those men had been caught. An immediate menace had been taken care of. It also meant she and her husband would have the bedroom to themselves from now on.

"You're wonderful, Mrs. Harmon."

The older woman laughed. "I've read thrillers for years. Now I've had a taste of the real thing."

Grady made no response to her comment, and Susan sensed something was wrong. When they followed him into the den and she discovered a brown-haired man with a tennis player's physique waiting for them, she thought she understood.

This had to be Matt Ross, the detective who'd hidden in the back of Mrs. Harmon's car to get inside the house. The man who, before the explosion, had found Susan attractive enough to add to his wife, Jennifer's, insecurity.

Grady must've had a reason for telling Susan something so unpleasant. Did he think she'd gotten a job because she was secretly in love with Matt and could meet him without anyone knowing?

Had he hoped to jar her memory with such information?

The detective might be nice-looking, but did Grady honestly think any man besides him could interest her?

Surely he didn't harbor some fear that she and Matt had been having an affair, did he?

Determined to fight for her marriage, she moved to Grady's side and slid her arm around his waist. "Who's this?"

A strong arm wrapped around her shoulder. "I'll introduce you," he murmured, hugging her close. A feeling not unlike an electric current ran through her body.

"Susan, this is an old friend of ours, Detective Matt Ross."

She extended her hand. "How do you do."

He appeared stunned before shaking it. "I'm aware you don't remember me, but I have to tell you it's absolutely incredible to see you alive. You look more beautiful than ever."

"Thank you. Your compliment reminds me of something that happened on the night Brett and Grady came to the apartment where I was rooming with some friends from work.

"For six months I'd been living with no idea of who I was or where I'd come from. My life was a blank. It terrified me. I could have been a fugitive, or a chorus girl who'd fallen on hard times. Anything." Her voice trembled.

"Then this detective came to the door, asking me to step out in the hall. He introduced me to the blond boy I'd seen on the stairs at the Etoile.

"I couldn't imagine what they wanted until Brett told me I was his mom." Tears filled her eyes. "He showed me a family album. Grady was in all the pictures with us. That's when I realized he was my husband.

"You'll never know the thrill of that moment. Not only because I found out I belonged to a family, but that I belonged to *them*, to that boy, to that wonderful man who was handsome beyond my dreams."

"Oh, Susan..." Mrs. Harmon burst into tears. "That's the most beautiful story I ever heard." The next thing she knew, they were both hugging and crying.

Matt said something, but Susan didn't hear it. She was too busy reacting to the warmth of Grady's smile as he stared at her over the housekeeper's shoulder.

I love you, Grady. You must know that.

"Why don't we all sit down," he suggested. "There's something we have to talk about. Matt needs to hear it because he's in charge of this investigation."

Susan reached for Brett, and they sat on the couch next to Mrs. Harmon.

"Brett?"

"Yes, Dad?"

"Before Matt leaves, tell him the names of the friends you phoned to let them know we were going out of town."

Brett looked at Susan before he said, "How come?"

"I'll get to that in a minute."

"I called Dave, Jack and Ken. Greg wasn't home, but I told his mom."

Grady turned to Matt. "Dave's father is Walter Thomas, a fire insurance underwriter for a lot of buildings and hotels, including the Etoile. Hank Openshaw, Jack's father, owns Openshaw Design, a company that decorates many of the hotel interiors. He designed the French restaurants for the Etoile.

"We can rule out Ken's father, Mark Gray. He's a vet. Greg's father, Spencer Crowley, is vice-president of Southern Nevada Bank and Trust. It has major dealings with the Etoile. Mike's father, Jim Stevens, is the owner of Stevens Construction. His company has done a lot of building in Las Vegas, including the Etoile."

Matt wrote down everything Grady dictated.

"What's going on, Dad?"

"I think I'll let Matt tell you." He moved behind the couch and put a hand on their shoulders.

In a matter-of-fact voice, Matt said, "We have proof that one of the men who broke in this afternoon was the same man who drove the van that killed David Beck. He was the accountant whose place your mother took at the CPA firm."

Susan gasped.

"Someone who gives the orders was so afraid of what your mother would find, he had her killed—or so he thought. It's your father's theory, and I agree with him, that since the explosion this person has been waiting for the opportunity to get into your house to see if there's any evidence that could still be used against him.

"He couldn't try earlier because you didn't go away until this week. Plus your father's work schedule is somewhat erratic and sometimes he's home during the day. Now we come to the hard part.''

"What is it?" Brett asked.

"The person responsible for the explosion that supposedly killed your mother has to be one of the people who knew you were going out of town. That would be Captain Willis, me, the SWAT team, Mrs. Harmon or the parent of one of your friends.''

Susan glanced at her son. When the significance of the detective's words sank in, Brett's face blanched. She bowed her head, heartsick for him and ill at the knowledge that someone who knew their family well had been willing to murder her.

Grady squeezed her shoulder gently.

Matt drew closer to Brett. "What I'd like you to do for me is try to remember if any of your friends' parents have been particularly interested in your life since your mom supposedly died. Have any of them asked specific questions about you and your dad? About your mother's work?

"I don't mean you have to do that right now. During the rest of the week, something may come to your mind. Let your dad know and he'll get in touch with me.''

The tension had been building in Brett. Susan could feel his body go rigid. Suddenly he got to his feet. The torment in his eyes shattered her.

"It *couldn't* be any of them!" He shook his head wildly. "It just couldn't!''

He ran out of the den.

"Excuse me.'' Susan patted Mrs. Harmon's hand, flashed Grady a signal of distress, then hurried after her son.

Thankful there wasn't a lock on Brett's bedroom

door, she opened it and walked over to the bed where he lay sobbing. She sat down next to him and rubbed his back.

"Darling? There's one other explanation Detective Ross didn't mention. Maybe the person who tried to kill me saw me in the car when you were driving me home from the apartment. It's possible, if he'd been tailing your father since the explosion.

"In that case, he could've seen you and your dad drive away the day we went to the mall and never come back. With them gone, he had those two men get into the house while Mrs. Harmon was here."

Ten minutes must have passed before Brett muttered, "You don't really believe that."

"I wouldn't have said it if I didn't think it was a possibility."

"I'm not a child, Mom. You're only saying that to try to make me feel better when we both know it had to be one of my friends' dads. There's no other explanation."

CHAPTER TEN

YOUR DAD'S NOT ON DUTY tonight?

No.

I thought he told me he was, and that's why he couldn't come to dinner with us. I guess I was mistaken.

Dad doesn't like going places anymore, not without Mom.

I've noticed. He hasn't come to any parties at our house. Ellen and I have missed him. What a shame. It must be tough on you. Maybe you guys should sleep over at our place.

It's okay, Mr. Stevens. Dad wants Mike to come. It's just that when he gets home from work, he doesn't feel like leaving the house again.

Eventually, that'll change.

"Darling? What is it? Where's the son who used to talk to me about everything?"

The hairs on Brett's arms stood on end. What the heck?

"*Mom?*" He sat straight up and stared at her. There was a look in her eyes that hadn't been there before....

"I remember you," she cried. "Oh, Brett, darling, I remember you!"

She crushed him in her arms so hard it hurt. "I

remember our last talk. You were upset because Ken and Mike went to the sports-car show without you. And I told you that as your friends grew older, that would happen more and more because you were all becoming more independent.''

Those were his mom's exact words. She was back. *His mom was back!*

He pulled away far enough to look at her. ''Do you remember Dad?''

Her eyes glistened. ''Not yet. I don't understand it.''

Brett swallowed hard. ''Then I'm not going to tell him about this. It hurts him too much when you don't remember him. We'll keep it a secret for now.''

''Keep *what* a secret?''

Hearing his father's voice prompted Brett to roll off the bed. He stood up to face his father, who'd entered the room.

''I didn't want you to know what I just told Mom because I was afraid you'd say I was crazy. But I guess I have to tell you now.'' He could feel his mother wince.

''We can't have any secrets in this house, Brett. You know that. Not after everything you and I have been through.''

Brett nodded. ''I think I know who did this to Mom.''

''Who?''

''I never really liked him, anyway.''

''Just tell me.''

''Mr. Stevens.''

The room went quiet.

''Mrs. Harmon said the same thing before she drove Matt to her house, where he parked his car,'' his dad murmured. "Before I tell you what she told me, I'd like to hear why *you* think Jim did it. Don't forget there are three other fathers we know personally who have business connections to the Etoile. They would've had equal opportunity to commit fraud."

"I know, but I was thinking about what Detective Ross said. None of the parents except Mike's ever ask me questions or bring up stuff that makes me uncomfortable."

His dad pulled the chair away from Brett's desk and sat down in front of him. "Like what?"

"A whole bunch of things. After the memorial service for Mom, he kept saying you and I ought to go away on a vacation and try to forget the pain.

"I knew he was trying to be nice, but when he kept it up and kept it up, it started to make me mad because I knew you didn't want to go anywhere, not even to Grandma's or Uncle Todd's.

"The thing is, I don't think Mr. Stevens loves Mrs. Stevens the way you love Mom. If he's not working, he always has to be going somewhere or having parties, taking business trips. Mike used to complain that he never saw his dad do private stuff with his mom. I mean—"

"I know what you mean, Brett."

"Well, anyway, I bet if Mrs. Stevens died, he'd feel bad, but he'd still go on doing all those things. It seemed to bug him that you never wanted to go over to their house for parties or do anything after work like swim at family hour.

"The other night when he took me and Mike to dinner at the Etoile, it was like he was giving me the third degree or something."

"Tell me exactly what he said."

His dad's voice only got that scary tone when he was working on a case he was about to crack.

Without hesitation Brett relayed the whole conversation. When he'd finished, he saw his parents exchange solemn glances.

"You know what Mrs. Harmon thinks?"

"What?"

"Over the months she's noticed a pattern of Ellen phoning to try and get us to spend time at their house. The other parents have extended invitations now and then, but not with the same persistent regularity. Mrs. Harmon believes Jim mowed the lawn with Mike to make sure we really had gone away."

"I already figured that out, Dad. If you hadn't brought the key in the house, he probably would've told Mike to open the door for him with some excuse about needing to use the bathroom."

His father nodded. "Mike phoned you earlier today. He told Mrs. Harmon he wanted to call you at the hotel in Disney World."

"What did she say?"

"That we were on a cruise."

"I bet his dad put him up to it. Mr. Stevens is evil!" he cried angrily. "He tried to kill Mom!"

Before Brett could credit it, both his parents had their arms around him. "Darling," his mother said, "it sounds like Mike's father *could* be the one, but we don't have proof. What if it isn't Mr. Stevens?"

"Your mother's right. Too many people jump to conclusions based on circumstantial evidence. That's all this is until the Drummond account leads us to the culprit."

Brett eased away from them and wiped his eyes.

"Until Mom finds proof, I've got an idea. Let's give a big party next week for all the people who've been nice to us since she died.

"When they've arrived, Dad can tell them he has a surprise. Then you come out, Mom. Dad's detective friends will be watching to see Mr. Stevens's first reaction. I hope he has a heart attack and dies!"

His father smiled. "That's a great plan. If you were thinking of becoming a detective some day, you've got the intelligence and imagination for it. But until we get some hard evidence pointing in Jim's direction, it would put you and your mother at unnecessary risk.

"Don't forget that before this day is out, the culprit's going to learn his two thugs are in jail. When he hears they never got the chance to search for the disks, he'll send someone else to do it."

"If that's true, then I think Brett's idea is inspired," Susan interjected. "We could—"

"No, Susan." He cut her off. "I've already arranged for twenty-four-hour protection of the house to keep you safe. The last thing I'm going to do is offer you up as a feast to a cold-blooded killer. That's final."

The veins stood out in his father's neck. He was really upset.

"All right." She turned to Brett. "Come on, darling. Let's go downstairs and make some chicken stir-fry for dinner. Then we'll get busy on that account."

He sent his father a furtive glance. Had his dad noticed her slip about the stir-fry? She wouldn't have known it was Brett's favorite meal if she hadn't recovered more of her memory

"Okay. I'm coming, Mom."

GRADY WATCHED THEM LEAVE. When Mrs. Harmon was upstairs with Susan earlier, she must have mentioned that she'd bought the necessary groceries to make Brett's favorite dinner. Grady couldn't remember the last time they'd had it.

He waited until he was alone before taking out his cell phone to call Captain Willis. His boss needed to hear what Brett had just confided.

It was funny how you thought you knew everything your child was thinking. All these months, his son had been forced to deal with Jim Stevens, whose questions could be viewed as sinister rather than friendly, yet Grady had been oblivious.

"Captain Willis here."

"Captain? It's Grady."

"Perfect timing. I just got off the phone with Boyd Lowry. We can put the LeBaron case to bed for good. The dental record came out a perfect match with the teeth of the corpse."

"You'll never know what that news means to me, Captain. Have you informed the LeBaron family?"

"I'm going to do that now. They'll be relieved to hear he was an innocent victim. It'll end the nasty rumors floating around. But they have to understand this is an ongoing murder investigation, so nothing will go out to the press until the case is solved."

"Thanks, Captain. What was the coroner's verdict on the manner of death?"

"A massive wound to the back of the skull, probably made by a pipe. Your wife must have had guardian angels protecting her."

"There's no other explanation." His throat had almost closed up. "With LeBaron out of the equation, the field has narrowed to four men I know personally.''

''Matt's already filled me in.''

''Except that he didn't hear what Brett told me after Matt left with Mrs. Harmon.'' For the next few minutes Grady confided the information about Jim Stevens.

''Your son's instincts are probably right. We'll find out soon enough. Just in case your wife doesn't recover her memory, I've asked Boyd to find a new expert CPA to get to work on the Drummond account.''

Grady lowered his head. The captain was only being practical, but the mere possibility that Susan would never remember him, her own husband, was taking a piece out of his heart with every passing minute.

''Let's hope this expert finds the problem ASAP.''

''Boyd's looking into it now. As for the two who were arrested, I've already turned that over to the district attorney's office. Who knows, Grady? Maybe with a plea bargain we'll get a name and a motive.''

''Thanks for all your help, Captain.''

''We're family. Talk to you later.''

He clicked off. Although he was elated over the news that LeBaron had turned out to be a victim and not the perpetrator, another thought invaded his mind. It made him break out in a cold sweat.

Thank God Brett hadn't told Mike he'd seen his mother that night at the hotel. Mike would have told his father....

If Jim was the fiend who'd destroyed so many lives, he would've made a second attempt to murder Susan. This time, he'd make sure he succeeded.

And Grady would never have known about it.

Unable to deal with that nightmare, he dashed from the room and down the stairs to the kitchen. Making a beeline for Brett, who was chopping green pepper and mushrooms, he gave him a quick hug.

"Dad!" He pretended to choke and cough. "What was that for?"

"For being the greatest son who ever lived."

"He's that, all right." Susan stood at the stove browning chunks of chicken.

Needing to do something with his excess energy, Grady started setting the table.

"You're a lot happier than you were a little while ago, Dad. How come?"

He told them the news about Geoffrey LeBaron.

"How sad for him," Susan murmured.

"I agree, but it's wonderful news in terms of the investigation. Knowing he had nothing to do with the crime has unfogged the picture to a great extent."

She started cooking the rice. "I read a lot of my textbook today. After we eat, I'm going to dig into the account again. This time it'll probably make more sense."

"When you're through, let's watch home movies, Mom."

"I'd love that!"

So would I, Grady mused. Seeing their family together had to jog *something* in her mind.

"WHILE YOUR DAD'S IN the shower, I thought I'd come in and say good-night."

Brett's troubled gaze sought hers. "You didn't remember anything tonight. Not even your wedding video helped."

"No, darling. But we won't let that discourage us, because I've remembered *you*. I've recalled certain memories of my brother, and that painting. The rest is eventually going to return. I believe that in my heart. You have to believe it, too."

"I do. I just hope Dad can last that long."

"If it hasn't all come back by the time I don't have to hide anymore, I'm going to see a psychiatrist. Maybe I could be put under hypnosis to discover what's blocking it."

"Dad thinks your mind is scared of finding out what happened the day you disappeared."

"I thought that at first. Now I'm not so sure."

"What do you mean?"

"After you brought me home and I found out there'd been trouble in our marriage, I was afraid it had to do with your father falling out of love with me. But I've been with him long enough to know that's not true.

"He *did* love me, right up until the morning of the explosion. I can tell he hasn't hidden anything from me. I've never met a more straightforward, honest person in my life."

"It can be kind of scary if you're keeping something from him."

"That's what I'm talking about, Brett. Maybe I am keeping something from him. Something I don't want to face about myself, and it's hurting him."

"You mean like another man?"

"I don't know. I can't imagine it, not when I love him so much."

His eyes searched hers. "I thought you'd been pretending to like Dad all this time to make him feel better. Especially in front of Detective Ross."

"No, darling." She hugged him for a moment. "Amnesia doesn't work that way. Let's assume for the moment that you're the one who can't remember anything. Mike comes over to the house to see you. You've been told he was your best friend for years and years. How do you think you'd react?"

"Like I do at school when a new student sits next to me in class."

"What happens then?"

"I might like him, but I might not."

"Supposing that new student was Mike. Until you'd lost your memory, you knew you'd been best buddies since you were little kids. Would you pretend to like him, even if you didn't?"

He blinked. "No."

"How come?"

"Because I wouldn't know him. I guess if he wanted me to hang out with him for a while I would, until he did stuff I didn't like, or we didn't get along and started to fight or something."

"What if you liked him right off and got along great?"

"Then I guess we'd keep hanging out together."

"And maybe even become best friends again?"

"Maybe."

"That's how it happened with your father. I couldn't pretend with him. I still can't. But he was so kind and understanding and protective and wonderful, I was immediately attracted to him.

"Do you realize that during the last six months, no other man has interested me at all? I met dozens of them working at the hotel. Businessmen, tourists. I could've had a date every night.

"There was one employee at the hotel who pestered me constantly to go out with him. He was good-looking, and a lot of the single women would've liked to get to know him.''

''Dad was afraid you might have met someone.''

''Like I said, I did meet a lot of men, but I had absolutely no desire to be with any of them. My roommates couldn't understand it. Then one night out of the clear blue, Tina told me there was this handsome police detective at the door asking for me.

''As I walked past her she said, 'He's the kind you want to take home and keep forever.' So you see, even Tina was smitten by your father, who was a total stranger to her!

''When I saw him standing there, I swear my heart went crazy, Brett. I can't explain it, but it happened. Then you let me look at the photo album. As soon as I realized he was my husband, I almost collapsed a second time.''

Brett broke into a smile. ''That's probably the way you felt when you first met him in California.''

''I have no doubt of it. The point is, I didn't have to pretend anything. The more I was around him, the more I knew I wanted to be with him for as long as he'd have me. The truth is, I—I've fallen in love with your dad.''

''When are you going to tell him?''

''Tonight. But I have to admit I'm scared.''

''Why? He *loves* you.''

She put a hand on his shoulder. ''He loves the *old* me. And I believe he *likes* the new me. But he's not in love.''

''I don't get it.''

''Look, darling, I don't remember him from before,

so for me it's a matter of falling in love for the first time. But that's not true for your father.

"Don't you see? He remembers seventeen years of loving someone else. My body looks like the old me, much of my personality is probably the same, but my mind is unknown to him. If my memory doesn't fully return, I have no way of knowing if he'll ever be able to fall in love with me as I am today."

"He acts like he is," Brett grumbled.

"That's because he's in love with the part of me that's familiar, the part he recognizes. But there's another part missing. The most important part for him. I know it's complicated. I don't even pretend to understand it."

He averted his eyes. "The night we brought you home, I said something to him I wish I hadn't."

"What was that?"

"I told him that if you didn't remember us, I wanted you to go away. But I didn't really mean it, Mom."

"I know you didn't, darling. That was a difficult time for everyone. It seems like a hundred years ago now, doesn't it?"

"Yeah." Silence. "Yes."

They both chuckled.

"You two sound happy."

Grady.

She got up from the bed, aware of his intent gaze. "The movie of our son taking his first steps was hilarious. I didn't say it while we were downstairs, but he reminded me of a really drunk man trying to walk a straight line for the police officer."

Brett laughed. She thought she'd get a similar response from her husband. Once again she was wrong.

"That's what you said while we were filming him." His voice sounded far away. "Does this mean you've remembered something else?"

Her eyes caught the pained look in Brett's. He knew as well as she did that they couldn't lie to Grady.

"Yes. While I was comforting him before dinner, I had a flashback of recent memories of him. I was waiting until we were alone to tell you."

"That's fantastic." He said the words as if he were in a trance. She knew he was happy, and yet...

"Pretty soon Mom's going to remember everything." Brett filled in the gap.

"I'm sure she is."

Susan stole from the room to give them some time alone. She'd already showered, so there was nothing to do but take off her robe and get into bed.

Grady didn't come. While she counted the minutes, she suspected that he'd decided to stay with Brett for the rest of the night to sleep off his grief. Whether he acknowledged it or not, grief was what he felt.

Her inability to remember him had become such a serious issue, they needed to talk about it. She was on the verge of going back to Brett's room to get him when she saw his silhouette in the doorway.

"Susan?"

"I'm awake."

"We have to talk."

"I know. I've been waiting for you."

He closed the door. She couldn't tell if he wore anything beneath his robe. She doubted he was thinking about that right now, but she'd been living for the moment they'd finally be alone.

To her surprise, he turned off the lamp and got in

the other side of the bed. She'd hoped they could look at each other while they talked. Susan needed to see his eyes when she told him how she felt. Those beautiful hazel eyes that revealed so many emotions.

"You don't need to hide anything from me," he began without preamble. "I'm a big boy. I can handle the fact that your mind won't allow you to remember me.

"The important person here is Brett. He's got his mother back. His world is whole once more. Everything that's happened so far has been a miracle, and I'd be ungrateful to expect another one."

Keep talking tough, Detective Corbitt.

"Grady? What if we decided that when we're in the bedroom, we'll live in the present," she whispered.

"I don't follow."

His guard had gone up. The old Susan would've known how to get through. The new one had to feel her way by instinct.

"I don't like secrets any more than you do. If I didn't immediately tell you about remembering Brett, it was because I couldn't bear the thought of hurting you again by not remembering *you*."

"Susan—"

"Let me finish while I have the courage. You were right when you said it's imperative we live in an atmosphere of truth. What I'm going to say next may shock you."

"Go on," he said quietly.

"I want you to make love to me. I want it more than you can possibly imagine. However, I recognize that you're still in mourning. It may be a long time before you're ready to have a relationship with a woman other than your wife.''

"You *are* my wife." He sounded furious.

"No. You had a seventeen-year love affair with a woman who looks like me. In reality, I'm a stranger. The you and I who are together at this moment have only had a four-day history.''

If she was doing this wrong, she couldn't stop now.

"In six months, I've gotten to know myself very well. If I hadn't been attracted to you at the apartment, I would've taken you up on your offer to let my roommates come with me. They could have told you I'd never met a man I wanted to be with, so maybe that gives you some idea of the strength of my initial attraction to you.

"The more time we've spent together, the more that attraction has grown. When you said you were going to see about putting me in a protection program, I was so horrified at the thought of us being separated, I realized I'd fallen in love with you.

"I have no idea what I was like at nineteen. According to you, we were attracted from the very first day. So maybe that's my true nature. When I fall, I fall hard.

"The point is, I think I finally made Brett understand that just because I'm in love with a man I've only known four days, it doesn't mean he feels the same way about me.

"For one thing, I get the feeling that the old Susan wasn't as aggressive as I am. But maybe *aggressive* isn't the right word. Help me, Grady.''

After a moment, he said, "You're more decisive.''

"That probably comes from having to forge my

own way since the Benns found me. Is that quality repugnant to you?''

"Of course not.''

"Unappealing, then?''

"No. Just…unexpected," he said with gut-wrenching honesty.

"That's what I mean. I'm not the person you loved. Our son admitted to me tonight that in the first day or two, he wanted me to go away if I didn't get my memory back. I assume you felt the same way and still do.

"But I know you well enough to understand that you wouldn't dream of tearing this family apart for your own needs. At least not until Brett's grown.''

"You talk as if you've given up on trying to remember," he said quietly.

"No, Grady!" she cried in frustration. "Haven't you heard anything I've been saying? I'm in love with you! You could have no comprehension how much I want to be the woman you married. Don't forget, I sat through an evening of films about our life together.

"Even though I don't have an explanation for why the old Susan didn't tell you the reason she wanted to go to work, I could see that, in every other way, she knew how to make you happy, how to satisfy you.

"What I'm trying to convey is that I'm under no illusion that you're in love with *me*. If my memory doesn't come back, then all I can do is hope that one day you'll stop making comparisons and fall in love with the person I am now.''

"That would be impossible.''

It was as if he'd just plunged a knife in her heart. "I'll move back to the guest bedroom.''

Before she could throw off the covers, his arm slipped around her waist. With amazing strength he pulled her against his body.

"You misunderstood me," he whispered. "There's no way I can be objective about you. Most of the time you *are* Susan, even if you don't know it. It's only when you talk like this that you force me to try and separate the two of you.

"A little while ago, you made the suggestion that we live in the present when we're in this bedroom. I have a much better idea. Why don't we stop analyzing everything and just go with our feelings from now on. If you remember something, fine. If you don't, we won't worry about it."

"You honestly think you can do that?"

"You're lying here next to me, aren't you?"

"Yes."

"Life holds wonders man can barely imagine. Your return is a wonder I can't explain. I'm tired of trying. All I want to do is celebrate this gift.

"For the first time in six months, I don't have to remember what it was like to make love to you. Not when the real you is filling my arms. Come here."

That was all Susan needed to hear. She pressed her mouth to his with a hunger he reciprocated.

He didn't take things slow and easy out of deference to her lack of memory. She knew he was kissing the old Susan. After seventeen years of learning how to please his wife, he was doing everything by instinct. This man was loving her like she'd never dreamed of being loved.

"You feel so wonderful. I can't believe you're alive. I can't believe it" came his emotional cry. His lips roved feverishly over her face and hair. "I want to love you all night long, so I'll know this is real."

Susan responded with spiraling passion. "I want the same thing," she whispered against his lips.

Mutual desire drove their need, their passion. If they slept, she didn't remember.

CHAPTER ELEVEN

"PROFESSOR SEEDALL?"

"Yes?"

"My name is Susan Nilson. I'm calling long distance. Eighteen years ago, I was an accounting student of yours. In fact, I have your autograph on the first page of the accounting textbook you wrote, the one we used in your class. This morning I took a chance and found out you were still teaching at the university."

"Susan Nilson? The name isn't familiar, but go ahead. What can I do for you?"

"I became a CPA, but six months ago I was in an accident and I've been suffering from amnesia."

"That must be frightening."

"In the beginning it was, but I'm getting a lot of help. Right now I'm trying to rebuild my life, but I'm afraid the memory of being a CPA has been erased. Unfortunately I was working on a problem with one of my accounts when I was injured.

"It's my belief that a certain construction contractor didn't want me to report the problem to the owner of the building he was working on, and that's the reason I was injured. Now I need to be able to prove fraud."

"How can I help?"

"I'd be grateful if you could answer a couple of questions for me. In the section of your book on construction fraud, I jotted down some phrases in the margins while I was taking notes during your lecture. Could you tell me what they mean?"

"If I can."

"The first is *bonded warehouse*. The second is *schedule of values*."

"Oh, yes. I probably gave you the example of a contractor who works with the architect to make a schedule of values for the items he's planning to order for a given project.

"When he makes an actual purchase order far ahead of the time it'll be needed, he has to have a warehouse in which to store the item. Therefore the warehouse has to be bonded."

Susan was trying to understand. "So what does that have to do with fraud?"

"One doesn't necessarily have to do with the other. Say the contractor is ordering wood for a trim. The architect designates maple on the schedule of values. However, the contractor makes a purchase order for poplar, which is a cheaper wood. After the construction is done, he'll put a maple stain on it."

Maple stain... That was one of the items on the list Brett had made.

"When the architect makes the inspection, he probably won't catch the difference because it's all installed and looks like maple, so he signs the pay request for the maple wood specified. It's unfortunate, because the architect is supposed to protect the owner.

"Let's say the contractor gets paid by the bank. He in turn sends a check to the supplier for the poplar wood and stain. The extra cash goes in his pocket."

"I get it. Now, tell me about the fraud example you gave us using the bonded warehouse."

"Let's assume the architect specifies a cast-iron tub on the schedule of values. The contractor orders it ahead of time. So it sits in the bonded warehouse. In the meantime, he orders a steel tub which he installs right away.

"It's likely that neither the architect nor the building inspector will notice the difference in tubs, so the contractor submits the pay request for the cast-iron tub to the bank. With the money, he pays for the steel tub, and sends the cast-iron tub back to the supplier. That way he pockets the extra two hundred or so for himself."

"Does this go on a lot in the construction business?"

"More than it should. What you need to do is check the schedule of values against the purchase orders and bank lien waivers. All three should match for every given item.

"If they don't, then you know something's wrong. Find an independent building inspector who will do an on-site inspection of the finished product to prove the contractor shortchanged the owner.

"For that, I'd get hold of an architect who writes a lot of specifications. He'll be able to recommend an inspector and answer questions about the construction business I couldn't possibly answer."

She was starting to get excited. "Professor Seedall,

I can't thank you enough for your help. You've done more for me than you'll ever know.''

"I'm glad to be of assistance.''

"My husband tells me I've used your textbook and notes like a bible.''

"Well, I'm flattered. Good luck to you, my dear. If you solve your problem, I'd like to hear about it.''

"I promise I'll give you a call. Thank you again, and goodbye.''

Armed with that information, Susan turned on the computer the way Brett had shown her. It didn't take long to bring up the index file on disk one.

After a study of the various headings, she came to the conclusion that other accountants must be handling the financial records of the Etoile's casino, restaurants and shops.

It appeared Johnny Drummond had put the Lytie Group in charge of his accounts dealing with the erection of the building, the grounds and the swimming pool.

There were headings for general landscape artist, design group and general contractor. Under *contractor* she discovered sixteen sections. In each one, she found references to the terms she'd discussed with the professor.

He'd told her to make certain everything matched up. She'd start with the first item and work her way through every section. If there were discrepancies, she'd find them.

"Hi, Mom!''

She turned in the chair. "Good morning, darling. Did you just get up?''

"A little while ago. Hey, you're already working. I told you the computer was easy to run."

"At least for the things you taught me."

"How long have you been down here?"

"About an hour."

"I heard you on the phone. Who were you talking to?"

"My old accounting professor in California. He gave me some pointers so I'd know how to proceed."

"That's great! Want some help?"

"I was just going to ask if you'd show me how to print off these sheets."

"Sure." After he'd explained the steps, he asked, "Where's Dad?"

"He was sound asleep when I left him a little while ago."

Their night of lovemaking had been so satisfying, she'd awakened wanting to start all over again. Grady had become her addiction and she hoped it had been the same for him.

She'd lain there for a while, willing him to wake up so she could reach for him again, but he never stirred. After a half hour of feasting her eyes on his rugged male beauty, she finally left him to enjoy his slumber. As for Susan, she'd felt like conquering the world.

The sooner she could find the person who'd tried to kill her, the sooner their lives could return to normal. There was a whole world of living ahead of them. She couldn't wait to shout to the entire world that she was alive and happy. So happy it was almost frightening…

Not wanting to disturb her husband, she'd darted across the hall for a shower in the guest bathroom. Once dressed in another pair of shorts and a T-shirt, she'd crept downstairs to the den to make the call to Professor Seedall.

"Are you hungry, or can you wait until your father's up?" She clicked on Print.

"I already had a bowl of cereal."

Susan smiled. "I should have known. Okay. Why don't you sit next to me. Thanks to my old professor, I've found the schedule of values and the purchase orders on the disks so we can begin checking them. Here's the purchase order for the electrical items. Start at the top and read each one. I'll double-check them on the schedule of values sheet and we'll see what happens."

Brett tucked one leg beneath him and began. He read down a list of twenty items. Everything checked out on her sheets. She printed the next set of sheets and they continued. When she got to wiring, she found a problem.

"Read that again, Brett."

"Twelve-gauge wire. At fifty feet, the cost is $7. 95. The order is for twenty thousand feet, which makes $32,000."

"My sheets say ten-gauge wire. At fifty feet, the cost is sixteen dollars. For twenty thousand feet that comes to $64,000."

They looked at each other. "Mom—that's a difference of $32,000!"

Susan was trembling. "There's our first discrepancy. I've marked it. Let's go on."

They worked for another hour, reading off item after item.

"Bathroom fan, seventy cubic feet per minute, at $27 times 4,050 makes $109,350."

"My sheets say bathroom fan, 210 cubic feet per minute, at $60 times 4,050 makes $243,000! Quick, Brett. Check that list you made for me."

"Oh, yeah. Fans were on it." He pulled it out of the drawer and gave it to her.

"Those little letters meant cubic feet per minute. Brett," she cried. "That makes a difference of $133,650."

Her mind was leaping ahead. She quickly put down the papers and returned to the computer. After going to the section on interiors, she printed the sheets and found the maple stain. After what the professor had told her, she looked for the item she suspected would be there.

"Oh, boy, Brett. This is like hitting the jackpot."

"What do you mean?"

"The purchase order for poplar trim doesn't jive with the maple trim on the schedule of values. There's a difference of $222,000." She lifted her head. "I've got to tell your dad."

She grabbed all the sheets and hurried from the den to the staircase. Brett followed.

"Grady?" she called out to her husband, dashing up the steps as fast as she could. Her voice rang through the house.

He raced down the hall toward her, tying the belt of his robe. His hair was still damp from the shower.

The familiar smell of the soap he used was a potent reminder of last night.

"Easy, Susan." His hands went to her upper arms. "Did you have another breakthrough?"

Those eyes… They were begging for the right answer this time, but she still couldn't give it to him.

All the joy of the night they'd spent together instantly evaporated. He'd just presented her with incontrovertible evidence that he wanted the old Susan back. To believe anything else would be a lie.

There was no question she'd brought him pleasure. But until she'd heard the eagerness and yearning in his question, she'd refused to admit that the kind of intimate love talk and laughter a husband and wife normally shared had been missing last night.

When he'd made love to her, it had been with his body, not his heart and soul. There was no use kidding herself.

It wasn't his fault. He could no more help it than he could stop breathing. Every time she went to bed with him, she had to face the fact that he'd always be searching for the familiar, would always be waiting breathlessly for the change in her to happen.

In the meantime, Grady would honor his marriage vow to love her in sickness and in health because that was the kind of man he was. But she would never know the full measure of his love, which was reserved for the woman he'd married.

Last night shouldn't have happened.

Until then, she'd lived with the belief that everything would turn out all right. She'd imagined Grady had, too. Now they both knew differently.

Since her husband would never refuse her in his bed, Susan would have to be the one who prevented a repeat performance of last night.

Making love with Grady in the future would be like dying a little every time they did, until eventually there was nothing left. She couldn't risk it.

"No. No breakthrough. But Brett and I have found the evidence we've been looking for," she said before his expression closed. After telling him about her call to Professor Seedall, she handed him the sheets.

"The proof's on the paper, Dad!" Brett cried out. "Mr. Stevens has been stealing from Mr. Drummond."

"Brett's right, Grady. Out of the hundreds of items we've gone over so far, only three haven't matched. Yet Jim has already been overpaid by almost $400,000.

"I have a feeling this is just the tip of the iceberg. His take could be in the millions." She pointed to the items she'd checked off.

As Grady looked everything over, his face darkened. "He obviously stole on items that would pass the building code. That's how they got by the inspection.

"Most architects trust the general contractor and don't bother to check the figures that carefully. For that matter, a lot of accountants aren't as thorough as they could be.

"Jim was probably lulled into believing he could get away with anything. Winning the bid to build the Etoile must have seemed like a godsend. However, he didn't count on Drummond hiring such a superior accounting firm.''

"Yeah," Brett muttered. "He's going to find out you don't mess with Mom."

Susan smiled at her cheering section before looking at Grady once more. "Why didn't the Lytie Group handle all his taxes? Did I ever tell you?"

He nodded. "Johnny Drummond built his first hotel in Reno and used a firm there to manage his accounts. As you explained it to me, your boss told you that when Drummond built the Etoile, he decided to separate the casino and payroll end of the two hotels from the new physical plant in Las Vegas.

"Apparently he did it to have better control. As it turns out, he was right. The Lytie Group did a good job for him. So good, in fact, that Jim Stevens had to kill off their top accountants unless he wanted to be ruined."

"Did my boss give the account to someone else?"

"No. According to Boyd Lowry, Drummond grew frustrated at the idea of a third person being assigned, so he withdrew his business and put it all back in Reno."

She shook her head. "After Mr. Beck died and I was supposedly killed, wouldn't you think he'd have suspected foul play?"

"Yes, but on Geoffrey LeBaron's part. There were rumors that he'd committed a murder-suicide."

"When Mr. Drummond finds out what really happened—"

"It's going to be a shock to a lot of people," her husband said.

"Brett, thanks to you, we'll know the whole truth by the end of the day."

"How come?"

"Those lists you made with the letters I wrote on the calendar? So far, two of the items are the ones we found where he cheated the owner. Something tells me you cracked my shorthand code. It's going to make my work go a lot faster. You're brilliant, you know that?"

"You're both brilliant," Grady said in a solemn tone.

She turned to her husband. "Mr. Beck probably found the discrepancies and phoned Jim's office to discuss them."

"That was his fatal mistake." Grady's eyes held a faraway look. "Jim must have been close to a stroke when he found out you'd been given Beck's account. From that moment on, your days were numbered and we never knew."

Susan shuddered. "What I'd like to figure out is how Jim learned Mr. LeBaron was a client of mine."

"That was my fault, Mom."

"What do you mean?"

"When you got your first account, you told Dad and me that Mr. LeBaron owned a fireworks plant. I was so excited, I called Mike to tell him. We were both hoping that when you knew him better, you'd be able to get us some deals on fireworks."

She smiled. "I can understand that. What doesn't make sense is how Jim Stevens knew I'd be going to the fireworks plant on the morning of the explosion.

Those bombs had to have been set in place earlier than Saturday.''

"I know how he found out," Brett said. "When we were swimming at family hour the week before, I heard Mrs. Stevens invite all of us to the speedway on Saturday morning to watch Randy race his bike. They had free tickets for our family.

"You told her you had to meet Mr. LeBaron early for a big meeting that might go on all day, so you couldn't come. When she acted really disappointed, you explained that he was a nervous client and it would probably take you a long time to reassure him that he wasn't in trouble on his taxes.''

"That's right," Grady concurred. "I remember that conversation, too. We decided to let you sleep over, Brett, so you could go with Mike the next day. I had business downtown I couldn't get out of. It wouldn't surprise me if those men we caught yesterday were the ones Stevens hired to get rid of your mother and LeBaron.'' By now his fists were clenched.

"Grady? You said the Stevenses moved from the neighborhood about a year ago. How soon was that before the completion of the Etoile?''

"Six weeks. By then, you'd started working for the Lytie Group.''

"It all fits, doesn't it?''

"I'm afraid so.''

"I just thought of something else. Remember when you first brought me home and mentioned that I'd never discussed the Drummond account with you, and you couldn't understand why?''

His grimace spoke volumes.

"You told me Ellen worked for her husband. According to you, she's a sweetheart. Maybe when I discovered Jim was cheating Mr. Drummond out of hundreds of thousands of dollars, I thought she was part of the scheme. That would have been horrifying for me to contemplate.

"With you being a detective, I probably couldn't bring myself to discuss the case with you until I was absolutely certain of my facts. Especially considering that Mike and Brett were so close."

After a brief silence, he said, "That's as good an explanation as any I can think of."

But you're not sure. I hope it's the reason I didn't come to you immediately, my love. I want to clear away the shadows.

Susan turned to her son. "I'm so sorry it's Mike's father, of all people."

"Me, too."

"If Ellen's innocent, then this is going to devastate their family when they find out what he's done."

"He's probably been stealing money on most of his jobs over the years," Grady muttered. "No wonder he was able to build a multimillion-dollar place of his own and afford all his trips and expensive toys. I knew there was serious money to be made in construction, but I never could understand how he became that affluent."

Brett's eyes filled with angry tears. "How could he sit there in that restaurant and ask me what I thought of the Etoile when he was the one who got rid of Mom? I hate him!"

"Jim's obviously a very sick man."

Susan concurred with her husband. "When the truth comes out, Mike will need his good friend more than ever."

"Dad? Do you think Mrs. Stevens knew what he did to Mom?"

Grady was slow to answer. "I doubt it. But she might have had an idea he was stealing and pretended not to notice. That just means she's no different from a lot of spouses who either live in denial or are too needy to confront their partners.

"After his arrest, there'll be a jury trial. One way or another, the truth concerning Ellen will come out before the judge hands down his sentence."

"Will Mr. Stevens get the death penalty?"

"Nevada still has that law on the books, so it'll either be that or life imprisonment for him and his henchmen."

"What I'd give to see his face when he finds out Mom's alive…"

Yes. I'm alive. But I'm not the woman your father wants.

She took the sheets from Grady. "I'm going to fix lunch. When you two are dressed, come downstairs and we'll eat. Then I'll finish working on the account."

No longer comfortable around her husband, she avoided his eyes and hurried off.

GRADY STOOD THERE in agony. Like a fool, he'd assumed a night of lovemaking would be the catalyst to bring years of intimate memories rushing to the surface. How wrong could he have been?

Susan's capacity to face reality had been much greater than his. Last night she'd tried to warn him, but he hadn't listened. His response to her haunted him now.

A little while ago, you made the suggestion that we live in the present when we're in this bedroom. I have a much better idea. Why don't we stop analyzing everything and just go with our feelings from now on. If you remember something, fine. If you don't, we won't worry about it.

You honestly think you can do that?

You're lying here next to me, aren't you?

Yes.

A shudder racked his body. He'd meant those words at the time. That was before he'd taken her in his arms. To his shock, he'd found himself making love to a stranger.

The difference between the two women—the Susan he'd married and this one—had become markedly pronounced in the darkness. He'd thought it would be the other way around.

Maybe he was crazy, but it had felt like making love to a virgin. Not the innocent nineteen-year-old he'd married, but a thirty-six-year-old virgin. A mature, beautiful, desirable, confident woman who'd never been with a man before.

He hadn't been able to shake the guilty feeling that he'd been unfaithful to Susan with a woman who'd once called herself Martha Walters. Undoubtedly a psychiatrist had a name for what was wrong with him.

It had undeniably been an enjoyable experience, but God help him, he still missed his wife....

He pulled out his cell phone to call his boss. "Captain Willis? I've got big news."

"Did your wife regain her memory?"

Grady gripped the phone more tightly. "No, but I know for sure who planned Susan's death."

"And?"

"It's definitely Jim Stevens. I've seen the proof." For the next ten minutes, he presented the facts as he would in any murder investigation.

"What a testimonial to your wife! Even without her memory, she was able to crack this case."

"Brett helped, too. They've both done an incredible job."

"I'm more than impressed. I guess I don't have to ask how you feel about it."

"No. I'm still in shock that she's alive and back home with us."

"I'm having trouble believing it myself. Okay, Grady. This is your call all the way. How do you want to proceed?"

"By the end of the day, Susan will have gone through the entire account. If you could send Matt over with Mrs. Harmon this evening, he can wind things up and take the disks and printouts to give Boyd. We'll plan a strategy for Jim's arrest."

"All right. In the meantime, I'll get word to the D.A. Now that we know the brains behind everything, we ought to be able to get a full confession out of the suspects arrested at your house. Two murders and one attempted murder could mean the death penalty."

"Or a couple of hundred years' prison time for the bunch."

"Amen to that. Keep me posted."

"Will do."

"Grady, when this is all over, take a month or two off and enjoy a second honeymoon. Know what I mean?"

"I do," he said in a quiet voice. "Thanks, Captain."

He ended the call, but the elation he should have felt knowing the six-month nightmare was all but over just wasn't there....

Something was drastically wrong with him. He didn't want to go on another honeymoon. Not without his wife.

Tears sprang to his eyes. He shouldn't have touched her last night. Feeling the way he did now, he couldn't do it again. He didn't dare even consider what would happen if she never recovered her memory.

The last thing he wanted to do was hurt her, but they were going to have to talk about this. He couldn't pretend something that wasn't there. It wasn't in his nature.

It wasn't in hers, either. Like the old Susan, she was honest, just more direct.

Trying to put aside his personal worries for the moment, he dressed in a polo shirt and trousers.

"Dad?"

He turned his head. "Looks like you're ready. I am, too."

"Before we eat, I want to tell you something I was thinking."

"What's that?"

"Since we know Mr. Stevens was the person who did that to Mom, she's finished with her part, isn't she? I was hoping we could drive to California so she can see Grandma and Uncle Todd. Maybe if she's with the family, she'll remember something else.

"I don't have to be back at school till Monday. Mrs. Harmon could smuggle us out in her car, and then we could rent one. If we drove at night, no one would see us."

Grady stared at Brett. There were times his son was positively inspired. A little while ago, he felt as though he'd reached the depths. Now, suddenly, there was a glimmer of hope.

He grabbed Brett, holding him close for a few seconds. "What would I do without you? Let's phone your uncle Todd right now."

"Yes!" Brett let out a whoop.

"He'll be at the office."

"I know his work number. Can I tell him?"

"You found your mother on those stairs at the hotel," Grady murmured. "You should be the one to let the family know she's alive."

Grady sat on the edge of the bed while Brett picked up the receiver and punched the buttons.

"I'd like to speak to Mr. Nilson, please. Tell him it's his nephew, Brett."

After a minute, he said, "Hi, yourself! Are you sitting down?" Brett's smile filled his whole face. "How much would you give to see my mom again?"

Grady could just imagine Todd's reaction.

"What do you mean, where did that question come from? Just answer me."

His smile turned into a frown. "I know you're busy, but you can't hang up yet. I've got something important to tell you. Mom didn't die in the explosion. She's alive!"

A moment later, Brett handed the receiver to Grady. "Uncle Todd wants to talk to you. He sounds freaked."

That was a good word for it.

"I'm going to tell Mom he's on the phone so she can talk to him."

"Give me ten minutes, then bring her up."

"Okay."

He put the receiver to his ear. "Todd, it's Grady. Everything Brett told you is true. Stay seated and listen."

His brother-in-law wept while Grady gave him a detailed account of their lives since last Friday. "She remembers Brett and has had some flashbacks of you growing up, but that's it so far."

There was a long silence on the other end before Todd asked, "How the hell have you handled that?"

"Not well," Grady confessed.

"Mom's not going to believe this."

"It might be better if you broke the news to her. I was thinking if the three of us drove down tonight after dark, we—"

"I'm going home right now to tell Beverly," he interrupted Grady. "We'll get everything ready for you."

"Before you hang up, there's someone here who

wants to talk to you.'' Brett and Susan had just come into the bedroom.

Grady motioned her over to the bed. Her hand shook as she took the receiver from him.

"H-hello?"

CHAPTER TWELVE

"SUSIE Q? IT REALLY IS YOU!"

Susie Q...

"Todd!" she cried as memories of her family came flooding into her mind. But before she could talk, she got too dizzy to hold the phone. It slipped out of her hand.

"I feel sick, Grady."

Her husband caught her in time to help her onto the bed. She could hear Brett in the background, telling his uncle they'd call him back. She felt so far away.

Still looking into her eyes, Grady said, "You've had another flashback. Tell me about it."

Susan's inability to recall memories of her own husband was taking on hellish proportions.

"When he called me Susie Q, it all came back in a rush. I remember my whole family. Mom, Dad, Bev and the girls, Todd, home, the beach." Tears filled her eyes. "Grady, I don't know *why* I can't remember you and our life together."

"Don't worry about it, Mom." Brett had hung up the receiver and come to sit on her other side. "Probably what happened to you at the fireworks plant before they took you out to the desert was so awful, you're afraid to remember. Maybe you knew you were going to die and you got so scared you'd never see Dad again, you don't want to relive it.''

Did you hear that, Grady?

Thank you, my dear, dear son.

''That must be the reason, darling,'' she said.

''I agree with Brett, too,'' her husband murmured.

But he didn't! Not deep in his soul.

''Would you like to drive to California tonight and see everyone?''

''Oh, yes!'' Yes! *I'm afraid to spend another night alone with you. I couldn't bear to hear you make up a reason for not coming to bed with me.*

''Then we'll do it. How are you feeling?''

''Much better. I'd like to get up now.''

Grady guided her to her feet. ''You sure you're steady enough?''

''Yes. You can let me go.'' *I promise you don't have to touch me again.* ''Lunch has been ready for quite a while. I've already had mine, so I'm going to keep working on the account.''

''After we've eaten, Brett and I will help you. Matt will be over later with Mrs. Harmon. We'll give him everything you've found.''

''Now that I know what I'm looking for, I should be able to finish the whole thing before we leave.''

It was one-thirty; by seven in the evening, she was able to call it quits.

''We're done.'' She closed the last file, removed the disk and turned off the computer. Grady had been adding up the tally on their calculator. ''What's the grand total?''

"Would you believe Jim pocketed 5.5 million? He probably paid his cronies half a million apiece to kill everyone off and kept the rest."

She shook her head. "I'd love to see his tax return."

"No wonder Randy was able to buy that twenty-thousand-dollar motorcycle!" Brett said.

Susan glanced at Grady. "Considering how much it costs to build a four-thousand-room hotel in Las Vegas, I can't say I'm surprised his take was that high. As you pointed out, everything he cheated on still made it past the inspection."

"Except that in a few years the inferior products will have worn out faster and then there'll be problems and further costs."

"Poor Mr. Drummond."

"He probably won't miss it, Mom."

"That's where you're wrong," Grady interjected. "He may be the owner, but he has stockholders to answer to. Anyway, it doesn't matter how much money he has. He was robbed.

"Because of Jim's dishonesty, he'll have to order more repairs to be made to the hotel much sooner than he would've expected. Everyone loses on this deal."

Brett looked suitably chastened. Susan got to her feet. "Come on, darling. Matt and Mrs. Harmon will be here any second. While your dad talks to them, let's go upstairs and start packing. You can show me where we keep our suitcases. I'm so thrilled about seeing the ocean again! As soon as you can smell it, you know you're almost home."

"Did you know Uncle Todd got a new dog?"

"What happened to Lumpy?"

"They had to put him to sleep."

"Oh, no— Did they buy another terrier?"

"No. Aunt Beverly loved Lumpy too much, so they got a black Lab puppy and sent pictures. I can't wait to play with her."

"How long ago was that?"

"About three months."

"Then she'll be a lot bigger. What's her name?"

"Susie Q."

GRADY WANDERED OVER to the doorway and listened to their conversation until they'd gone upstairs. He'd been waiting to see if Susan remembered his grandmother's pug, Gypsy. The dog had lived six years beyond his grandmother's death.

When Gypsy had finally died of old age, Susan had grown so attached to her, she couldn't bear the thought of getting another dog.

"With that adorable little pug face of hers, no other dog could replace her, Grady."

By then Brett was a toddler, and the subject of getting a new dog didn't come up again. Since most of the work would fall on Susan if they got one, he didn't push it. Her thoughts had been centered on having another baby.

He wondered now if losing their first child was such a traumatic experience, she couldn't face getting another dog, only to lose it one day, too.

The sound of the garage door opening broke his concentration. He waited until it closed again, then went to welcome Mrs. Harmon and Matt into the house.

"So I was right about Mr. Stevens." Mrs. Harmon spoke up at once before going about her duties.

Grady's gaze flicked to Matt. "He took 5.5 million off the top."

The other man whistled. "Sean Mills made a phone call. It was to the same attorney who represented him in court during the Beck trial. The other guy's name is Sykes. He's using Mills's attorney, too."

"Have they done any talking?"

"Not yet."

"So—" Grady handed Matt a large envelope with all the disks and printouts. "It looks like Jim's bought himself an attorney as well."

"No doubt about it."

"Which means he knows they've been arrested by now."

"It was a stroke of genius to pretend you're in Florida. As long as those birds don't sing, he can't be implicated, so he won't do anything unexpected. He'll assume that when you hear about it, you'll figure it was a failed burglary attempt in your neighborhood."

"That's the way we've got to keep it for now. According to Mrs. Harmon, the Stevenses are in Mexico and won't be back until Sunday. As it happens, I'm taking my family to California tonight. We'll be back sometime Sunday evening."

"How are you getting there?"

"A rental car. I'll ask Mrs. Harmon to help me."

"I've got a better idea. Let me give you the key to

my car." He reached in his pocket and gave it to him. "It's parked in her garage. Go home with Mrs. Harmon and take mine. She can come back for me. I'll tell Jennifer mine had to be towed, so she'll pick me up in hers."

"I don't want to leave you stuck without a car."

"I'll borrow one from the station in the morning. Don't worry about it. I know you'd do the same for me. We'll keep in touch. Let me know when you want to move in on Stevens."

As Grady put the key in his pocket, Mrs. Harmon returned. "Here's your mail." She arranged everything on the table.

"You're an angel. Do you mind making two trips to your house tonight?"

"Of course not."

"Thank you. I'll let Matt explain while I gather the family."

He hugged her before racing upstairs. Susan was in their room with Brett, and he saw three suitcases open on the bed, filled to the brim.

"We're only going to be gone for five days."

"I like to be prepared."

Brett grinned. "You always did pack too much, Mom."

"Did I?"

"It's why I have a bad back," Grady teased.

As long as she'd recovered this much of her memory, he had to believe the rest would come. The problem was, they never knew what would trigger it. But he was willing to try anything that would restore his wife to him.

He took a deep breath. It was going to be a relief to get out of the house. Neither she nor Brett had complained, but he imagined they, too, were feeling claustrophobic about being shut inside. The five-hour drive to Oceanside would provide a much-needed change for all of them.

Once again, he had his son to thank for the idea. Earlier this morning Grady's thoughts had been too black to see his way clearly.

"Let's get going, shall we?"

Everyone scurried for the last-minute items, and soon they were making their way to the garage. Matt waved them off.

Grady caught Susan's arm as she headed for the trunk. She turned to him.

"What is it? We still have to keep my presence a secret until Jim Stevens is arrested."

"That's right, but this time I'll get in the trunk."

He saw a glint of fear in her eyes. "What if someone crashes into the back of the car?"

"It's only two miles, remember?"

"I'll tell Mrs. Harmon to drive slowly."

Her anxiety for his welfare increased his guilt about not being able to accept her as she was. At least not in their bed.

Was he subconsciously rejecting her because *he'd* felt rejected when she'd made the decision to go to work without talking it over with him first? Could he really be that cruel a person?

Susan was trying so hard. He'd never seen anyone with more courage. She'd had the determination and intelligence to call her professor in order to get the help she needed to solve her own case.

How could he fault her for anything? She was a loving, giving person. Surely it hadn't come down to his being jealous of Brett and Todd.... That would be unconscionable.

Disgusted, he made a mental effort to put negative thoughts away and concentrate on the trip ahead.

Once everyone was settled, with Susan on the floor in back, Brett crouched in front and the bags on the back seat, he climbed in the trunk and lowered the lid. Mrs. Harmon pressed the remote and the garage door lifted.

The ride to her home seemed to take forever. No doubt Susan was cautioning their housekeeper to drive safely.

It was a relief to hear her garage door go up. The plan was that she'd pull in behind Grady's car, already parked in the garage next to Matt's. Then they'd all get out and put their luggage in Matt's car.

From there, they would drive to the Gas and Go service station near the last exit leaving Las Vegas, two blocks from the freeway. Mrs. Harmon would call for a taxi to take her home. Then she'd drive back to the house for Matt.

When they finally reached the service station, the older woman told Grady, "I hope you all have a wonderful time."

"We will," Grady assured her. "Thanks for helping us."

"It's been a lot of fun."

"You're great, Mrs. Harmon," Brett added.

"Why, thank you. I don't know when I've received a nicer compliment."

Within a half hour, they were driving through the desert en route to California, just like they'd done dozens of times over the years. Susan in front, Brett sprawled in back despite his seat belt. Everything seemed so normal.

Maybe it was the only normal he'd ever know. *Better get used to it, Corbitt.*

AT QUARTER TO FOUR in the morning, Susan followed her mother into the house where she'd been raised. After a joyous three-hour reunion at Todd's, she'd asked Grady if it would be all right if she went home with her mom for the rest of the night.

Though he'd acted surprised, in her heart of hearts she knew her husband was relieved. Since Brett was thrilled to be with his cousins, there was no problem.

The drive to the beach had been therapeutic, but Susan hadn't realized how much she'd needed her mother until they were finally alone on the living room couch.

Blond and blue-eyed like her children, Muriel Nilson had slowed down since Susan's father died, though she still worked part-time for the Red Cross.

Her shrewd gaze rested on Susan for a few minutes. "Want to tell me why you'd leave Grady at Todd's? Knowing how deeply you love him, I would've thought you couldn't bear to be out of his sight. Not after that horrendous six-month separation."

She felt a distinct prickling at the back of her eyes. "Oh, Mom—"

"Come here, darling."

Susan laid her head in her mother's lap and began sobbing. "H-he thinks I don't love him, and that's why I—I can't remember him. It's hurt him so much, I can't look in his eyes anymore."

"You haven't even been back a week! He's still in shock. In time he'll remember how much you've loved him the whole of your married life."

She sat up abruptly. "Did I, Mom?"

"What do you mean?"

"Did I always love him?"

The compassion in her mother's eyes melted her heart. "You never could see anyone but Grady Corbitt from the day you met him on the beach. When you brought him home to meet us, your father and I both agreed it was a love affair that was meant to be. Even Todd approved. That son-in-law of ours was so crazy about you, it was beautiful to watch."

Wiping the tears from her face, Susan said, "Well, something went wrong. He hasn't said it in so many words, but I know he thinks I fell out of love with him and that's why I went ahead and got that accounting job without telling him. Why would I do something that would hurt him so much?"

Muriel looked puzzled. "Honey, you were only trying to help him."

"What do you mean?"

"Jennifer Ross told you Grady had confided in her husband, Matt, that he'd lost money on his investments and was worried about the future. You were so upset to think he'd keep something that important from you. You phoned me to discuss it."

"Mom? Since I was a CPA, how come I didn't handle our finances?"

"From what you told me, Grady already had his arrangements in place and you saw no need to get involved. However, when you called me about his supposed financial loss, my advice was that you go to Grady and make him tell you the truth. But you said you couldn't because it would get Jennifer in trouble with her husband. You also indicated that you were married to a very proud man.

"The next thing I knew, you called me again and announced that you had a job with the Lytie Group. When I asked how Grady felt about it, you said you hadn't told him yet. You were still trying to think up a reason that wouldn't tip him off you knew about his financial problems."

"Oh, Mom." Susan's heart was racing so fast she felt sick. "What a fool I was to keep that from him!"

"It was cruel of Jennifer to tell you something her husband had revealed in strictest confidence."

"Did Grady ever admit to you or Todd he was in trouble financially?"

"No, and to be honest, I haven't seen any sign of it. If Grady was hurt because you made a decision without him, you were the only person who knew it, because he never complained to me or Todd. He wouldn't do that.

"But I have to admit I never approved of Jennifer after that. When we heard the ghastly news about the explosion, I blamed her in my heart. If it hadn't been for her, none of this would have happened to you."

"You've met her, then?"

"Several times on visits to see you. I must confess I still blame her."

"Don't," Susan cried. "The fault lay with me for not taking your advice and telling Grady what I'd learned." Susan jumped to her feet. "I've got to tell him now!" She dashed into the kitchen to call him. Muriel followed her.

"Honey, it's five in the morning. You'll wake everyone. Let him sleep. This can wait a few more hours, can't it?"

She let out a shuddering breath before putting the receiver back. "You're right. Oh, Mom—thank you." She threw her arms around her mother. "Thank you. With this knowledge, I may be able to hang on to Grady a little longer."

Her mother eased her away so she could look her in the eye. "What are you saying now?"

Susan swallowed hard. "Last night we made love for the first time. It was thrilling for me, but when he woke up I had the impression it had been a distasteful experience for him."

"In what way?"

"I don't know exactly. He hasn't treated me the same since. Oh, he's always wonderful. It's not that. I just sense that he wishes it hadn't happened."

"He was probably hoping you'd remember him. When you didn't, he retreated to protect himself from more hurt."

"You think that's it?"

Muriel nodded. "I'm positive."

The tears started again. "I'm so thankful I have you to talk to."

"I'm more thankful to have my daughter back." Now her eyes were wet, too. "My darling daughter. I thought you were in heaven with your dad all this time."

Susan laughed through the tears. "Not quite yet."

"Not for years and years. Your life with Grady has only just begun."

"If he'll let it."

"Oh, ye of little faith. You have to hope and pray and trust…."

"That's what the priest told me."

"What priest?"

They walked back into the living room and talked until nine in the morning, filling the gaps in each other's lives.

"Brett wants us to throw a huge surprise party next week. Invite all our family, friends and colleagues. When everyone's arrived, Grady will get their attention and tell them I'm back from the dead. At that point, I'll make an appearance. What do you think?"

Muriel's chuckle turned into full-blown laughter. "It's brilliant!"

"He wants to see Jim Stevens's face before Grady arrests him."

The laughter subsided. "We all would."

"So…do you think the party's a good idea, Mom?"

"I can't imagine a better way to celebrate your return to the living—and to bring all this sadness and uncertainty to an end. Trust my grandson to come up with something so creative."

"Brett's so wonderful. I wish you could've heard

him at the apartment when he said, 'Your hair's a different color and it's shorter, but you're my mom.' You'll never know.''

"You and Brett have always had a close relationship. How did you feel when you looked up at Grady and realized he was your husband?"

"Stunned. Nervous. Excited. Attracted—"

"You've fallen in love with him all over again."

"I love him desperately." She got to her feet. "It's after nine, and I know you're exhausted. But I want you to tell Grady what Jennifer said. I'm going to call him now and ask him to come over."

"Go ahead. I'll sleep later."

Susan ran into the kitchen once more and called Todd's. Bev answered and told her Grady was in the other room with Todd and the kids.

"Will you please ask him to get in the car and come over to Mom's alone?"

"Does this mean what I think?"

"No. But it's something very important."

"I'll tell him."

"Thanks, Bev."

After she got off the phone, she rushed into the bathroom to wash her face and fix herself up a little. Her mother's house was only a couple of blocks from Todd's.

By the time Grady walked through the front door wearing cutoffs and a T-shirt, she was back on the couch waiting for him.

"That was fast," Muriel commented with a smile.

"Bev said it couldn't wait."

Grady's eyes swerved to Susan's for an explanation.

"Bev was right. Mom and I have been up all night talking. I just found out a vital piece of information you should hear from her."

His expression sobered. "What is it?"

"Something that should make you happy," Muriel said. "Why don't you sit down, Grady."

As if in slow motion, he did.

Susan eyed her mother before she said, "First of all, I have to ask you a question, and you have to be totally honest with me when you answer it."

"What question?"

"How bad is our financial situation? I know we lost money on our investments. Have you had to take out a second mortgage in order to keep the house? Is that the reason you and Brett never went on any vacations or entertained after you thought I'd died?"

He leaped to his feet. "What the hell are you talking about?"

"Grady, it's all right. You don't need to hide the truth from me. I know from a reliable source that you kept certain information from me so I wouldn't worry about money."

His eyes narrowed. "There's nothing wrong with our finances. There never has been. All you have to do is call Stokes and Briarson. They'll give you a seven-digit figure to prove how well our investments have been serving us all these years. What reliable source are you referring to?"

Uh-oh. Susan's mouth went dry. "Jennifer Ross."

Grady stared at her. "Jennifer told you I was in financial trouble?"

"Your wife can't answer that because she can't remember," Muriel said. "However, I recall the incident as clearly as if it were yesterday."

For the next five minutes, Susan listened to her mother repeat what she'd just told her. But instead of looking relieved, Grady's expression turned to thunder.

"You took the word of a sick little troublemaker like Jennifer Ross instead of coming to me? What in God's name were you thinking?"

His outrage still reverberated against the walls after he'd disappeared from the house.

"Grady!" Susan called after him, devastated.

"Let him go," Muriel advised as Susan raced to the front door to stop him. "He's been holding that in since you sprang that job on him. Now he knows the truth, and he can heal. Just give him time."

"I had no idea how much I'd hurt him. What a horrible wife I was!"

"Don't beat yourself up for being you, darling. You did what you thought was best under the circumstances. You didn't know you were being lied to. Learn from this experience to always discuss everything you're thinking and feeling with your husband."

"You talk as if there's going to be a future, but there isn't! You saw him. He hates me for what I did! I'm sorry, Mom. I've got to be by myself for a while. Can I take your car?"

"Of course. The keys are on the kitchen counter. Just drive carefully."

The air was brisk; the sun hadn't burned off the morning fog yet. With the temperature in the fifties, she could have used a jacket, but she was oblivious to any discomfort as she drove toward the beach.

When she found a place to park, she noticed there were only a few people walking along the surf. Removing her shoes, she got out and started running toward the area where she and her friends used to play volleyball.

A couple of minutes later, she reached it and sank down on the sand. So much had happened since she'd come home from the Etoile last Friday, she felt as if she'd lived two lifetimes.

Physically and emotionally drained, she rested her head on her arms. The ebb and flow of the ocean could be very soothing. Right now she needed its calming effect.

Her husband had been stretched beyond his limit. So had she.

After her mother had told him everything, Susan had thought it would bring him the comfort he'd been craving for the last year. But she'd done too much damage by not confiding in him. Whether she recovered her memories of him or not, their marriage couldn't survive this kind of pain.

It was here on this beach that she'd met him. She had proof. She'd seen the photographs in one of their family albums. How sad that this couple, so deeply in love, had nothing in common with the two people who'd bolted in different directions from her mother's house a little while ago.

She was back here again—the place where it had all started. This time she was alone, all memory of the man she'd lived with for seventeen years now wiped away.

Maybe her life had been spared, not to resume her marriage, but to be there for Brett and to right a tremendous wrong.

Today her husband had received information that would make him free. Armed with the knowledge that she'd always loved him, he could move on to find happiness with someone else.

Susan would have to move on, too.

Because of Brett, she'd have to stay in Las Vegas. A CPA job was out of the question, unless she went back to college and took all her classes over. She didn't know if she wanted to do that.

If she couldn't be Grady's wife, the only other thing that appealed was the idea of working in a place like the women's shelter. So many people had been kind to her there. Images of Maureen and the girls at the apartment came into her mind.

Tears trickled out from beneath her closed lids. To be able to help people the way she'd been helped would be very fulfilling. Could she find that kind of work and make a living at the same time?

Father Salazar might know. As soon as it was safe for her to join the world again, she'd go to see him. In her time of anguish, she'd turned to him. His advice had helped her hang on. Why not again?

The thought brought her a modicum of comfort.

She finally sat up. After lying there for almost an hour, she felt a little chilly. The sun still hadn't broken through, but she could tell it was overhead. If she didn't get back to the house soon, her mother would worry.

Gathering her purse, she clambered to her feet. On the way to the car, she leaned over to brush the sand off her legs. When she straightened, she saw Grady walking toward her.

The ocean breeze had disheveled his hair, making him seem dark and dangerous. His eyes looked more green than hazel near the water. He really was a beautiful man. She'd been so lucky for so many years. But the fact remained that she'd undergone a life-changing experience and nothing would ever be the same again.

"I've been waiting for you," he said in a husky voice.

"I'm sorry. If I'd known, I would've come back to the car sooner."

"Susan—"

"It's all right, Grady. You don't have to say anything. We've both tried our very best. Sometimes that isn't enough.

"While I was lying there, it came to me that destiny had something different in mind when it preserved my life. I've come to accept that."

There was a bleakness in his eyes she'd never seen before. "What are you talking about?"

"Divorce. It's the first step to free us from a situation that's been taken out of our hands. Even if my memories of you return, our world has changed, Grady. We're no longer the same people.

"Until Jim is arrested, no one has to know. After that, I'll move out. Don't worry, I won't go far. Las Vegas is Brett's home. I intend to be his mother as long as I live."

His mouth had gone white around the edges. "You promised before God to be my wife as long as we both shall live."

"I'm not your wife. I tried to tell you that last night. Unfortunately you had to find out you were making love to a stranger before you believed me.

"It was a beautiful experience," she whispered with tears in her voice. "But that's all it was. The Susan you knew might as well have died out on the reservation."

Moisture glazed his eyes. "Don't say that."

"I have to go, Grady. Mother's waiting for me. I'll sleep there until we leave for Las Vegas."

She didn't remember the drive home.

CHAPTER THIRTEEN

"Mom?"

"I'm in the bedroom."

She heard footsteps running down the hall. "You've been asleep all day!" he blurted. "Aunt Bev has dinner ready. Dad thought you'd be over by now."

"Your grandma and I stayed up too late talking. Where is she?"

"Helping Aunt Bev fix the food."

"You're kidding! She should've awakened me. It's a good thing I showered before I went to bed. I'll hurry and get dressed."

She threw off the covers and slipped on a clean pair of shorts and a top while Brett waited out in the hall.

"Could I ask you a favor, Mom?" He followed her into the bathroom.

"What do you think?"

"I need you to talk to Dad."

She felt a surge of pain. "About what?"

"Getting a dog."

Oh, Brett.

She finished brushing her teeth. "I agree Todd's Lab is awfully cute."

"When I asked Dad a few minutes ago, he said it was out of the question right now."

It hadn't taken Grady long to recognize that a divorce was the only solution, the only thing that would bring an end to their agony.

She ran a brush through her hair, then put on lipstick. "He was right. Let's give your dad time to deal with Mr. Stevens, then I'll find a way to broach the subject to him. I think getting a dog is a wonderful idea."

If she could find an apartment or rental house that took animals, she'd keep one there. It would be Brett's dog. They'd work it out somehow.

"You're the best. Thanks, Mom."

"That's nice to hear." Susan smiled. "Have you decided what kind you want?"

"I like Labs, but Ken has a collie that's pretty cool."

"A collie? You don't see a lot of those anymore."

"Her name's Mitzie. She's really smart."

"Well, we'll have to look into it, but let's keep this to ourselves for now."

"Okay."

"I'm as ready as I'm going to be. Did you walk over here?"

"No. Karin let me ride her bike."

"I'll race you back in Grandma's car."

He grinned. "You're on. The winner has to buy the loser a frozen chocolate banana at the marina after dinner."

"I haven't had one of those in a long time. Get ready for your chocolate banana!"

Brett dashed through the house ahead of her and managed to beat her to Todd's. They were both laughing when they entered the living room, where everyone was waiting for them.

"It took you long enough, Aunt Susan," Lizzy grumbled. "Everybody's starving!"

"I'm sorry, honey." Avoiding Grady's eyes, she gave her niece a hug. "Being at the ocean always makes me sleepy for the first couple of days."

"Come on, folks," Bev called to them from the dining room.

Susan hurried ahead of the others so she could sit at the rectangular table between the two girls. Let Grady find a spot with Brett.

Todd said the blessing. It turned out to be a long, very touching prayer thanking God for bringing Susan back to them. By the time he'd finished, all the children were squirming in frustration.

Bev, a lovely brunette as Grady described her, had prepared Swedish meatballs and sour cream noodles, an old Nilson family favorite. It happened to be Susan's favorite meal. She reached around Karin to squeeze Bev's hand. "It looks wonderful, as always."

"What's wonderful is seeing you here." Bev's voice wobbled. "You have no idea."

"Speaking of ideas," Susan's mother interjected. "I think it's time Brett told everyone his plan."

Brett looked surprised. "You mean the party?"

"Don't tell me," Todd interjected. "It's going to be a surprise party and your mom will pop out of a cake."

"Hey—that's not a bad suggestion, Uncle Todd." Everyone laughed except Grady. Susan kept eating.

"Actually, I thought we'd call it a thank-you party for all the people who were so nice to us after Mom died. That way, no one'll guess what's really going on. Especially Mr. Stevens. When everyone gets there, Dad will tell them he has a surprise. That's when Mom'll walk into the living room."

Todd's smile disappeared. "That ought to be a sight to see."

"Yup. You guys have to come."

"When is this going to take place?"

"I'm hoping next Wednesday night," Susan said. "Grady wants to make the arrest as soon as possible, but we need that long to plan it and get the invitations out. I was thinking that I'd work on them tomorrow and express them to Matt Ross at the police station.

"He can put them in the mail for us so there's a Las Vegas postmark. I'll have to find a telephone directory for the addresses.

"We can go to the library for that," her mother said.

"First thing in the morning, Grady will need to contact a catering service. It'll be a big crowd. I'd like to invite the friends I made while I was away from all of you."

Todd nodded. "We want to meet them, too. Sounds like a doozy of a plan, Brett."

"Thanks."

"Are you okay, Grady?" Bev asked, with concern in her eyes.

Susan lowered her head.

"Yes. I'm simply contemplating the pleasure of taking that monster into custody at the end of the party."

"Is that when it's going to happen, Dad?"

"With Captain Willis and some of the other detectives, including Matt there, it'll be the perfect time. As soon as he and Ellen start to leave, I'll draw them aside and we'll close in."

"What if they don't come?"

"That's a possibility, Lizzy. If they don't show up for some reason, we'll drive over to their house afterward and make the arrest."

"Don't worry. Mr. Stevens will come," Brett muttered. "Trust me. He loves going to parties so he can brag about all the stuff he owns."

Bev caught Susan's eye. "That'll be horrible for Ellen."

"She might have helped him." Again Brett had spoken.

"That's why we'll only be inviting adults," Susan rushed to explain. "I don't want her children to witness anything."

Her sister-in-law nodded. "Well—does anyone feel like dessert yet?"

"Mom owes me a frozen chocolate banana."

The girls immediately chimed in that they wanted one, too. Couldn't they all go to the marina and walk around with the dog afterward?

"Looks like we'll have to eat my chocolate cake tomorrow," Bev said good-naturedly.

"As long as we're going, I might as well buy the

invitations tonight and get started on them at Mom's. After sleeping all day, I'm wide awake.''

She caught the private exchange between Bev and Todd. They'd picked up on the tension between her and Grady.

"Okay," her brother said as he stood up from the table. "Everybody grab a jacket and we'll go."

Bev began clearing the table. "Why don't you and Grady take the kids in our car? Susan and I will go with Mom in hers after we've finished here."

"Did you hear that, guys? We just got out of doing dishes," Todd teased. "Run for your lives before your mom changes her mind."

Unable to stay seated, Susan shot up from the table and ran around to hug her brother. "I've missed you, Todd."

"Ditto, Susie Q."

As soon as his dad drove them into the garage in their own car on Sunday night, Brett jumped out and opened the door for his mom. She'd been hiding on the floor of the back seat for the drive over from Mrs. Harmon's house.

Grabbing one of the suitcases, he dashed through the house to the study where Mrs. Harmon put the mail. Sure enough, there were the sunglasses Detective Ross had ordered from Disney World. Brett took them to his bedroom.

Mike ought to be home from Mexico by now. Brett couldn't wait to find out if they'd gotten their invitation yet. But first he listened to the messages. Three of his friends had already called, including Mike.

Without hesitation he phoned him.

"Stevens residence."

Brett's jaw hardened. Mr. Stevens wouldn't be answering his phone much longer.

"Hi, Mr. Stevens. It's Brett. Is Mike there?"

"He sure is, and he's dying to talk to you."

"Same here."

"Did you have a great trip?"

"It was okay." His dad had told him to downplay it.

"Just okay?"

"The snorkeling was pretty exciting, but I think Disneyland's better. How was Mexico?" he asked as his father walked into the room.

Brett made a circle with his thumb and index finger to let him know it was Mr. Stevens on the line.

"We caught ourselves a marlin. Wait till you see it stuffed!"

Wait till you see where you're going to be stuffed in about three days.

"Did Mike help catch it?"

"It took both my boys to help me."

"That sounds cool."

"Ellen tells me we got an invitation to a party at your house on Wednesday night."

"Are you going to come?" he asked, holding his breath.

"What do you think? I told you at dinner the other night that your father would start to feel better one of these days."

Brett nodded to his dad.

"I don't know about that, but he said he owed a

lot of people." *And you're going to get paid back big time.*

"How did he arrange all that and go on a trip, too?"

"You know. Mrs. Harmon. She did the invitations. Oh—guess what? She said our house almost got broken into while we were gone."

Brett was listening hard and noticed the slight hesitation before Mr. Stevens said, "What happened?"

"One of our neighbors phoned Mrs. Harmon about a couple of guys dressed up like missionaries who came to our back door and then ran away. It seemed suspicious, so she called the police. Sure enough, those guys came back and the police caught them."

"Thank goodness for that. Did she find out what they were after?"

It was getting more difficult to pretend. "No. The police told her they were probably going to steal electronic stuff."

"I'm sure that's what it was."

You evil liar.

"Yeah, but Dad felt bad that it happened while Mrs. Harmon was looking after the place. She got pretty scared. I've got to tell Mike about it."

"He's standing right here. I'll put him on."

While Brett waited, he covered the receiver with his hand and whispered to his dad, "I could tell Mr. Stevens already knew about the break-in." Then he put the phone to his ear again.

"Brett! When did you get back?"

"Just a few minutes ago."

"Am I glad! This has been the most boring vacation of my life."

"Mine was okay. I brought you a present from Disney World. You'll probably think it's kind of stupid but I didn't know what else to get."

"You want me to come over?"

"Yeah, but Dad says I have to get ready for bed. I'll ride my bike to your house right after school tomorrow and bring it."

GRADY LISTENED WHILE SUSAN emptied Brett's suitcase and left his room to do laundry.

After delivering her bombshell at the beach, she'd given him no opportunity to speak to her in private. Todd had remained a silent observer until yesterday morning, when he'd asked Grady to go to the store with him for groceries.

As soon as they'd backed out of the driveway, his brother-in-law admitted the trip was just an excuse to get Grady alone in case he wanted to talk. Todd had a way of inviting confidences. It didn't take long for Grady to break down and tell him everything.

"I blew up at her for something she couldn't even remember. She has every right to hate my guts."

"That would be impossible. I know my sister. She's in love with the man you are now, but she knows you're in love with the old Susan. I can understand how she doesn't want you to feel trapped. A divorce would solve the problem."

"I would never give her one."

"Of course not. You guys need time. One of these days she's going to remember you. As you know, we've had Lizzy in counseling since her friend was kidnapped. When you told me about Susie's amnesia, I called Lizzy's psychiatrist to ask some questions.

"He told me Susan's suffering from hysterical amnesia. That means there's no physiological problem. Her mind is protecting her from something painful, and when it's ready, it'll allow her to remember. Until then, you just have to chill."

All the other doctors had said virtually the same thing. After what Muriel had revealed about Jennifer's lie, he had even greater proof of the old Susan's love for him. Between his mother-in-law's contribution and the talk with Todd, Grady had been saved from losing his sanity.

Earlier on the beach, where he'd first met the great love of his life, Susan had struck pure terror in his heart with her talk of divorce.

Grady decided his big mistake had been making love to her too soon. Having learned from that experience, he realized that what they needed to do now was relax and take one day at a time. Tonight after Brett was asleep, he'd find a way to reach her.

"Dad?"

"I'm putting the luggage away in the closet."

His son came into their bedroom. "Did I do okay?"

Grady closed the louvered doors. "You were perfect. Jim's not going to know what hit him."

"Mike's kind of upset he wasn't invited to the party."

"Unfortunately he'll know why before that night is over."

"He probably won't want to be my friend anymore."

"We won't let that happen."

Grady lifted his head. Susan had entered the bedroom. She walked over to Brett and put her arms around him.

"When it's the appropriate time, we'll shower their family with the kind of love people showered on you after I died."

Brett's lips curved upward. "That sounds so weird when you talk about being dead."

"It's a bizarre situation."

"Maybe you should write a book to help other people who've lost their memories. In my class on the Second World War, we learned that some of the wounded British soldiers had amnesia. My teacher said nobody knew how to treat it. They had a really hard time."

"You think I could write a book?"

Grady heard the incredulity in her voice—shades of the old Susan, who'd always been self-effacing.

"After the way you solved your own case, do you even have to ask?" Grady said. Her eyes swerved to his in surprise. "There isn't anything you can't do. You've already proved that."

A delicate blush crept into her cheeks, confusing him. He hadn't thought this new version of Susan could do that. For the first time since they'd discovered she was alive, her reaction touched a place deep inside him, bringing out his protective instincts.

"It's time for bed, son. Six-thirty comes early."

"I know, but it's going to be hard to go to school."

"How come, darling?" Susan asked as they headed for his bedroom.

"Because I'm afraid you won't be here when I get back."

"Oh, Brett."

Grady could understand that feeling.

When he'd finally returned to her mother's house to apologize to his wife and discovered that she'd been gone for several hours, he'd almost lost his mind. Muriel had suggested he look for her at the place they'd met seventeen years before.

He'd needed his mother-in-law's inspiration. After the way he'd wounded Susan, he'd been too traumatized by his own guilt to think rationally.

"Good night," he said from the doorway while he waited for her to reassure their son.

"Good night, Dad. 'Night, Mom."

He waited for Susan in the hallway. She walked past him to the staircase. He followed.

"What are you going to do now?"

"You said the caterer wants you to phone her in the morning with a list of the things she'll have to bring. Dishes, glasses and so on. It'll take me a while to make an inventory of what we have on hand."

Grady wasn't about to be put off. "I'll help you."

"A little while ago you said you were tired and ready for bed."

"Not without you."

"I'm sleeping in the guest bedroom until I move out."

"Then I'll join you there, because you haven't given me the chance to tell you how sorry I am for the way I hurt you at your mother's house. I'd like to explain what I was feeling and ask your forgiveness. That explanation is likely to require some time.''

She looked directly at him. ''It's all right, Grady. You think I don't understand the kind of torment you're in, but I do. There's nothing to forgive. I'd just feel more comfortable if we slept apart.''

''After everything we've been through, are you really prepared to traumatize two members of this family all over again?''

A stricken expression crossed her face. ''What do you mean?''

''Brett's still so fragile, he's afraid to leave the house for fear you'll vanish. If he thought you and I were having trouble, it would tear him apart.

''As for me, I need my wife in our bed every night.'' He took a deep breath. ''While we were in California under separate roofs, I lay awake with the same fear as Brett. What if she's not there in the morning? It made me break out in a cold sweat.

''Over the last few days I've learned something vital. Full memory restored or not, you're the only woman I'll ever want. Don't put me through any more hell by distancing yourself from me. I couldn't take it.

''Let's not worry about the physical side of our marriage right now. I understand if you don't want me to touch you, but I have to know you're there next to me. Come to bed. I'll help you sort things out in the morning.''

"You're not going to work?" She sounded surprised.

He frowned. "No. Whatever gave you that idea?"

"I guess I just assumed that with Brett returning to school, your vacation was over, too."

He shook his head. "Far from it. I have seven weeks coming. After Jim's arrested, I thought we'd pull Brett out of school and rent a place at the beach on Maui until the end of May. It's a trip we'd always planned to take when he was old enough to appreciate Hawaii."

"What about all the class work he'll miss?"

"If necessary, he can go to summer school. At the moment, it's more important for our family to be together."

She flashed him a troubled look. "That's the kind of vacation for lovers."

"I'm not worried about that just now. After our experience in California, I've realized how precious life is and I don't want to waste another second of it. Let's be thankful for the second chance we've been given. Six weeks without worries or pressure should make new people of us and ease Brett back into his normal carefree self."

Her head was bowed. "The last thing I want to do is upset him more than he already is, so I'll stay in our bedroom. As for the trip, I don't know about that yet."

He sighed inwardly at that much progress. Once Jim Stevens was handcuffed and jailed, Grady would find a way to make her say yes. Perhaps the opportunity to face her would-be killer, knowing he could never hurt her again, would help remove that last barrier in her mind.

But if it didn't, Grady wasn't going to fall apart. During those two agonizing hours in Oceanside, when he'd feared she might have gone off for good, he'd found out he wanted her at any cost.

"Fair enough. Come to bed now. I've made a couple of decisions about our party."

She started toward him. "What?"

"First, we'll make it a garden party. And second, I won't prepare our guests for the surprise. That's why we have to decide where we'll put Jim and Ellen. When you step outside the back door, I want you to know exactly where to look. No one has a greater right to witness his shock firsthand than you."

"Wow, Mom!"

She whirled around. "Do you like this dress?"

"It's Dad's favorite."

Wear the black. Definitely the black, Grady had said, pulling it from the hanger before he'd gone downstairs. But she'd scarcely been aware of his comment. He'd just finished dressing in a new suit bought expressly for the occasion. In the charcoal weave, toned with a pearl-gray dress shirt and tie, he was so handsome, she felt stunned.

With an ache in her heart, she'd slipped on the black dress and matching heels, wondering if the day would ever come when he'd look at her in the same admiring way.

Since their conversation in the upstairs hall after their return from California, he'd treated her as if everything was normal. For the last three nights he'd given her a peck on the cheek, then proceeded to fall asleep. No pressure. No uncomfortable moments. A state of limbo. But it couldn't go on forever.

To her relief, this night had finally come. Once it was over, she would carry out her original plan to find work and get an apartment. Some place an easy biking distance from the house.

"You look pretty terrific in that suit yourself, Brett."

"Thanks."

"Where's the family?"

"Downstairs helping themselves to the punch. Mrs. Harmon's coordinating everything."

"Have other people come yet?"

"A few neighbors. Captain Willis arrived a little while ago. He's positioning the men."

"What about your dad?"

"He's greeting people at the front door." Brett's eyes searched hers. "Are you scared?"

"Yes and no." Her voice trembled despite herself.

"Don't be afraid of anything. Dad and I are here to protect you."

"I know you are. I love you so much."

"I love you, too, Mom. Just think—the next time I see you, everybody's going to know you're alive and our family's back together again."

Oh, Brett, darling… It's not that simple.

She hugged him hard before letting go. "You'd better hurry downstairs and help your father."

"I'm going."

She watched him stride from the room, then went

into the bathroom to put on her makeup and brush her hair one more time. Ten minutes later, she was ready, and walked to her assigned post at the window in Brett's bedroom.

From that vantage point she'd wait for Grady's signal, which would come after dinner.

For the next forty-five minutes, she stayed in place and looked down on people who, for the most part, were strangers to her. They wandered around the yard, to the banquet table manned by catering staff, and another table that served as a bar, and to visit with other guests. Afterward they'd returned to their places at the decorated tables, where name cards had been arranged.

Seventy people had been invited. A full house if you included her family, which brought the number close to eighty.

It was a warm, beautiful night. Grady had been working in the garden over the past few days. Everything looked perfect and festive. She'd wanted to help him, but for secrecy's sake she'd been forced to remain indoors.

Barring unforeseen circumstances, Susan couldn't imagine anything going wrong. She'd written personal letters of explanation to Colleen, Paquita, Tina, Father Salazar and the Benns—the six people she'd invited—stressing that her appearance at the party would be a surprise. If people asked, they should say they were old friends of Susan's and let it go at that.

Suddenly she saw Grady's dark head as he made his way over to the end of the banquet table where the prime rib had been served. Her heart almost tripped over itself as she realized the signal had been given.

She left the bedroom and walked to the top of the staircase. Ascertaining that no one was in the foyer, she hurried down the stairs to the kitchen. The catering staff probably thought she was a guest who'd come through the wrong part of the house, but they didn't say anything.

Susan tiptoed to the open back door and stood behind the screen. Grady was winding up his speech just a few yards away from her.

"So before we left for Florida, Brett and I decided it was long past time to say thank you by giving a party upon our return. We hope you'll stay and enjoy yourselves this evening."

Now was the moment to make her move. With a little push of the screen door, Susan walked outside toward Grady.

One second there'd been noise. In the next, shocked silence. The guests clearly didn't know whether to believe their eyes or not.

Susan couldn't worry about that right now. She had one goal in mind as she leveled her gaze on the sandy-haired man with the squarish jaw seated at the center table facing her.

Jim Stevens's reaction was no different from anyone else's, except for one thing. While she heard the sound of her name being whispered, then cried, then shouted in variations of joy and incredulity, she had the satisfaction of watching the blood drain from his face.

Maybe it was a good thing she had no memory of

him. Otherwise she wouldn't have been able to look into those cold gray eyes without flinching. This was the man who'd destroyed lives, shattered dreams.

The woman seated next to him just sat there with tears of happiness streaming down her cheeks. In that instant Susan knew Ellen Stevens had played no part in what her husband had done.

She felt deep pain for the agony about to be visited upon his wife and family. Grady must have sensed her distress, because his arm slid around her waist and he pulled her tightly against him.

"In case you were wondering, this is no clone," he began. His deep voice quieted the din. "My wife has returned from the dead. I'm going to let her explain."

CHAPTER FOURTEEN

ONCE MORE SHE TRANSFERRED her gaze to Jim Stevens. "Six months ago, a client of mine, Mr. Geoffrey LeBaron, and I were the victims of a vicious crime. On the morning of my disappearance, we were kidnapped from his fireworks plant.

"While bombs went off, blowing it to bits, we were transported miles away to the Moapa Paiute Indian Reservation, where we were struck on the back of the head, our bodies dumped into the wild grass, left for dead.

"I guess it wasn't my time to die." Her eyes sought Maureen's at the next table over. "Nevertheless, if it hadn't been for the Benn family, who found me barely alive with all traces of my memory gone, I wouldn't have survived."

Collective sounds of disbelief rippled through the crowd.

"They took me to the clinic, nursed me in their home, then drove me to the women's shelter in Las Vegas."

Susan's gaze shifted to the woman seated next to Maureen. They smiled at each other.

"It was there I made friends with a volunteer, Colleen Wright. She did everything in her power to find out who I was, but since no one knew I was missing, no one came forward. After watching the TV at the shelter, I named myself Martha Walters.''

Everyone laughed.

''Colleen helped me find a maid's job at the Etoile Hotel. That was my lucky day for many reasons. First of all, I met Tina and Paquita, who became my roommates at an apartment we rented in the north end of town.'' The two of them beamed at her. ''They became my dear friends and helped me keep body and soul together.

''Through Paquita, I met Father Salazar at the Catholic church.'' Her gaze glided to the priest, who was seated next to Colleen. He nodded to her. ''I found out I'm a Protestant, Father.''

He chuckled softly, as did the crowd.

''This wonderful priest urged me to have faith in the future, saying that one day I'd get answers to all my questions. As you can see, Father, your words came true.

''It was at the very hotel where I worked that I passed a young teen on the stairs a week ago last Friday night. He turned out to be my son, Brett, who'd been to dinner with Mike Stevens and his father.''

With one notable exception, all heads turned in her son's direction.

''I heard him call out *Mom?* But I thought he must be talking to his mother who'd gone down ahead of him. Later that night, when I returned to the apartment, I had a visitor.

''It was a police detective. A very attractive detective, according to Tina." Her friend grinned. "He introduced himself and said he was looking for a missing person.

"With him was the boy I'd seen on the stairs. He told the detective—" Susan's voice broke, and she had to make an effort to regain her composure. "He said, 'She's my mom!' Brett had recognized me, even though my hair had been dyed brown and was shorter than before."

By now she couldn't see a dry eye in the crowd, except for Jim's. He sat rigidly, staring at her as if transfixed.

"I was handed a family photo album. That's when I realized Detective Corbitt was my husband. He doesn't know this, but I almost had a heart attack knowing I was married to a man who was that gorgeous."

At that comment, everyone broke into laughter again.

"He said I'd have to go home with him and stay out of sight because my life was in danger until the person who'd tried to kill me was caught. The rest is history. I was united with my family in California.

"I've recovered part of my memory, but not all. Please don't be offended if I don't recognize some of you. I'm hoping that will change in the future."

Otherwise, I'm afraid for my marriage.

"My husband and I decided there was no good way to announce my return to the living. Under the circumstances, we thought it might be better just to get you all together at the same time. You're a glorious sight."

Grady's arm tightened around her. She heard him clear his throat. "Thank you all for coming. And thank you for being there for Brett and me during these empty, desolate months. You reached out to us in the darkest hour of our lives. We'll never forget."

One by one the guests jumped to their feet and began clapping. Then Susan was besieged. Ellen Stevens was the first person to reach her.

"I can't believe it." She wept as she flung her arms around Susan. "Thank heaven you're alive! It's so *wonderful* to see you again. I've missed you so much. I'll call you first thing in the morning."

If it hadn't been for a lot of other women crowding around to hug her, Susan wouldn't have known how to respond. Not when she knew what was awaiting Ellen and Jim when they left the party.

"Susan Corbitt—you almost gave *me* a heart attack."

Susan recognized Jennifer Ross from the photos in her album. The rather cross-sounding brunette gave her a quick hug. "I'll call you tomorrow and we'll go to lunch. We've got a lot of catching up to do.

"All the women who had hopes of becoming the second Mrs. Grady Corbitt will die of shock when they find out you're back in the picture."

For the next hour Susan hugged everyone at the party, but it was Jennifer's remarks that stayed with her. They'd been intentionally hurtful.

How had the old Susan tolerated a woman like that?

After the crowd had dispersed, she talked at length

with the friends she'd met since the accident. Finally she was able to get the priest alone.

"Can I meet with you soon, Father?"

His brown eyes were compassionate. He could tell something was bothering her.

"Of course. Call the church and make an appointment with the secretary."

"I'll do that tomorrow."

As he walked away, she was grabbed from behind.

"That was quite a performance, Susie Q."

She whirled around and hugged her brother. "Have you seen Grady?"

"He walked around the side of the house with the Stevenses."

Susan shuddered. "Ellen doesn't know what her husband did."

"She knows now. It'll be hell for her for a while. No question about that."

"Mom?"

Susan turned in the direction of Brett's voice. He came running over, with the rest of her family following.

"What happened when you looked at Mr. Stevens?"

She put a hand on his shoulder. "He went white, and sat there like a piece of petrified wood."

"I wanted him to die. But for Dad's sake, I'm glad he didn't. He's been waiting for this moment."

No one knew what Grady had experienced after the explosion better than Brett. Just now he sounded very grown-up.

"We all have, darling."

"What we must do is remember Ellen and her family in our prayers," Muriel said.

"I can see why Grady never liked Jennifer, Mom. She tried to hurt me again tonight."

"How?"

Susan repeated the conversation to her mother. "She's really quite cruel. I have no intention of being her friend again."

"Good for you."

Bev slipped her arm around Susan's waist. She whispered, "Now that this is over, you and Grady can really begin to live."

"I'm not the woman he fell in love with," Susan whispered back.

"It looked like love from where I was sitting. But if you're still left with doubts, then find ways to entice him all over again. Believe me, you've got what it takes."

Except the one part of her brain Grady wanted more than anything else.

"Susan?"

She swung around. "Yes, Mrs. Harmon?"

"Your husband's on the phone. He wants to talk to you. If you'll get it in the den, I'll hang up in the kitchen."

"Thank you. I'll be right there."

"Can I come, too, Mom?"

"Of course."

"Take all the time you need," Muriel said. "We'll help the caterer finish up."

"Thanks, Mom. What would I do without you?" Susan dashed into the house with Brett. By the time they reached the den, an adrenaline surge had made her feel as if she were jumping out of her skin.

"Grady?" she cried the second she picked up the receiver. "Brett's here with me. Are you all right?"

"Jim's in custody. I couldn't be better."

"Thank God." She smiled at their son to let him know he could stop worrying. His anxious expression changed to instant relief.

"How did it happen?"

"After Ellen hugged you, Jim found her and they started to leave. I joined them and said I'd walk them out to the car. He told me not to bother, but I insisted. That's when Jim started to look nervous.

"As I led them around the side of the house and unlocked the gate so we could pass through, four of the men were standing there talking to Captain Willis.

"Jim flashed me a look that needed no translation. It was the supreme moment for me."

Susan could imagine.

"I put my arm around Ellen to introduce her to my colleagues. When I'd finished, Matt stepped forward to arrest Jim and read him his rights. He knew it was coming and didn't put up a fight."

"Poor Ellen," she whispered.

"It was pretty bad. She went into shock. As they led him to an unmarked car, I told her I'd drive her down to headquarters in her car. Captain Willis accompanied us. En route he explained everything. Suddenly she started crying and couldn't stop. It was obvious she had no idea about Jim or the two men who were paid to do his dirty work."

Ellen's pain was just beginning. "Who's going to be there to help her?"

"Fortunately, she has a strong support group within her own family. Her sister will meet her at the station and drive her home. As I understand it, her parents will come to the house so they can tell Mike and Randy together.

"I told her our family loves her and the boys, that nothing's going to change our relationship with them. But she can't comprehend much of anything right now. Her horror over what her husband did runs too deep."

"My heart aches for her," Susan murmured.

"So does mine. It's going to be a long time before she can face people again, let alone you."

Not if Susan could help it.

"When will you be home?"

"I'm not sure."

"I forgot—you don't have a car."

"Matt'll drop me off."

"I'd be happy to come and get you."

"This could be an all-nighter."

Somehow, she was sure he wouldn't have said no to the old Susan. Still, she didn't argue.

"Our son wants to talk to you. Here he is." She handed Brett the phone and left the den. Both Mrs. Harmon and the caterer needed to be thanked and paid.

Once they'd gone home she'd tell her family the latest news before everyone went to bed. Todd had to be back in Oceanside by noon the next day, so they'd have to get up early in the morning to make the drive.

Bev was anxious to get back to the girls, who'd stayed behind with her parents. This had been a sort of experiment to see how Lizzy would handle the two-day separation after being in therapy. There'd been a few phone calls back and forth, but so far she was dealing with it.

Lizzy still suffered from extreme anxiety, even though her kidnapped friend had been found safe. Observing her behavior made Susan more aware of what Brett had gone through. When she moved to an apartment, she'd have to go out of her way to ease his fears that she might disappear from his life again. From now on, reassuring her son would be her number-one priority.

KIDS WERE WALKING to school as Matt pulled the car into the driveway. Grady had the door open before it came to a full stop.

"Thanks for the lift. I owe you."

"Forget it. See you in six weeks. Enjoy yourselves in Hawaii."

"We intend to. Take it easy, Matt."

He waved the other man off, then hurried to the front door to let himself in. With the whole ugly past behind them, all he wanted was to climb under the covers and hold on to his wife while they made plans for their trip—and their new life.

Feeling ten years younger, he entered the house and peeked in the den. Brett had given up his room to sleep on the hide-a-bed. It looked as if he'd already left for school.

Grady ran up the stairs. The empty guest room

meant Susan's family had gotten an early start for California.

Excited about having Susan to himself, he tiptoed into their bedroom, not wanting to disturb her in case she was still asleep. When he saw that the bed was already made, he felt a wave of disappointment.

Maybe she was out in the yard still cleaning up from the party. He raced down the stairs to the back door, but it was locked. Alarmed, he headed for the kitchen. It was empty, but to his relief he caught sight of a note attached to the fridge by a magnet. He reached for it.

Dear Grady,
If you return and I'm not back yet, don't be concerned. Brett and I decided to drive over to the Stevenses' and pay a surprise visit.

The sooner their family knows that we'll always love them, that we consider Jim a sick man and don't blame the rest of them for anything, the sooner Brett and Mike can resume their friendship.

I may not be back until afternoon. After I drop Brett off at school, I intend to drive to the apartment to see Tina and Paquita. I'm taking them out for breakfast before they leave for work.

Then I plan to stop at the shelter and chat with Colleen. On the way home, I have a few errands to run.

There's plenty of food in the fridge. As soon as you've eaten, why don't you go to bed and sleep around the clock. No one deserves that kind of rest more than you. Brett and I promise to be quiet as mice.

You were a mighty force to contend with last night. It must have terrified the living daylights out of Jim Stevens to know he was well and truly caught by none other than the renowned Detective Grady Corbitt.

I have it from the highest authority at the LVPD that your colleagues regard you as the best of the best. Brett and I are so proud of you we could burst.

Susan

Grady read it twice before crushing it in his hand.

Already he could feel Susan distancing herself from him. He'd hurt her too badly the weekend they were in California. Some premonition told him she hadn't changed her mind about a divorce.

Any hunger pangs he'd had earlier vanished as the bile rose in his throat. He barely made it to the guest bathroom in time to be sick.

When the house phone rang, he thought it might be Susan. He finished rinsing his mouth and hurried to the den to pick it up. In his rush to talk to her, he forgot to check the caller ID before he said hello.

"Grady? I didn't know you were home from the station yet."

Jennifer Ross.

It would be a cold day in hell before he forgave that woman for what she'd done to Susan.

"I just walked in. Your husband should be arriving at your place any minute now."

"I'd like to talk to Susan if I could."

He gritted his teeth. "Sorry. She won't be available for at least six weeks. Even when she is, don't expect a phone call. Her experience has taught her to be wary of people who purport to be her friend.

"You cold-bloodedly lied to her about us being in financial difficulty. I don't have any idea why you did that or what you expected to gain. I don't know how you sleep at night. Matt deserves better from his wife, and I hope he wakes up one day soon and realizes it."

After a silence, he heard the click.

Good. That ended the final chapter of the Corbitt family's painful history.

He put the receiver back, determined that a happy new history would begin. One that included the three of them.

No sooner had he started up the stairs for a shower than the phone rang again. He hurried into their bedroom, frowning when the caller ID indicated it was someone from St. Vincent's Church. Curious, he picked up the receiver. "Hello?"

"Good morning. This is Father Salazar's secretary returning Susan Corbitt's call. Is she there?"

He drew in a ragged breath. "Not at the moment. May I take a message for her?"

"Yes. Tell her he can meet with her tomorrow morning at eleven. If that's not convenient, ask her to call me back and we'll reschedule for another time."

"I'll do that."

"Thank you. Goodbye."

As if he'd been scorched, Grady dropped the receiver back on the hook. Letting out a curse, he jerked his tie loose and removed the clothes he'd been wearing for the past eighteen hours.

Susan had her own pastor if she needed spiritual guidance. She was up to something. Whatever it was, he intended to go with her and find out.

After his shower, he dressed in a T-shirt and jeans. While he waited for his taxi to arrive, he drank a soda to settle his stomach. Then he gave the driver the address of her girlfriends' apartment. He'd wait in his car for Susan.

Once she was free, he had plans for them. She could visit the women's shelter another day.

"I THOUGHT YOU SAID your husband would be home asleep this morning."

Tina must have seen Grady at the wheel of the car at the same time Susan did. Both women flashed her a knowing smile. Paquita said, "Obviously he can't stand to let you out of his sight, you lucky thing."

Susan was surprised he'd come looking for her. There must be something he needed to talk to her about—in all likelihood, more police business. She didn't think she could cope with it yet, not after the short visit with Ellen's sister.

She'd met Susan at the door. According to her, the boys had been so devastated, they'd gone to their grandparents' house. The doctor had given Ellen a strong sedative. She was upstairs sleeping and probably wouldn't be awake until afternoon.

Susan had left the Stevens home feeling sick at

heart. The fact that Grady was here, waiting for her, could only mean more bad news. But he didn't give off any signals she could read as he put down the newspaper to greet them. With one easy smile, he charmed her friends just as he'd done last night.

"Good morning, ladies. I have no intention of barging in on your visit. Since I'm on vacation, I thought I'd chauffeur my wife around town. Do you mind?"

Of course they didn't.

In fact, her friends appeared delighted to see him again and practically begged him to have breakfast with them at their favorite pancake house.

He declined with the excuse that he planned to catch up on some much-needed sleep while they were inside. Grady told them to take all the time they wanted. He wasn't in any hurry.

Knowing her husband was outside the restaurant distracted Susan so much that she couldn't confide her worries to her friends, let alone bring up the topic of divorce. They would tell her she was out of her mind to even consider it.

Relieved when the time came to drop them off at the apartment so they could go to work, she promised to invite them over for dinner the following week.

"Make that about seven weeks," Grady interjected before they left the car. "I'm taking my family to Hawaii for a long-overdue vacation. We'll call you as soon as we return."

When he'd driven out of the parking lot, he turned to her. "Before I left the house, Father Salazar's secretary phoned."

Susan bowed her head. She'd hoped he wouldn't find out about that.

"You're scheduled for an eleven o'clock appointment tomorrow morning. Is it so vital you talk to this priest that you can't wait until we get back from Hawaii?"

When she didn't respond, he went on. "I'd like to leave tomorrow. Not only does Brett require your continual presence to help him recover from all the trauma, he needs time away from home to figure out how he's going to deal with Mike when he gets back.

"I talked to Ellen's parents before I left headquarters. They're keeping the boys with them for a while. When Ellen's over the worst of the shock, they'll be taking her and the children on vacation, too.

"Everyone needs to heal, Susan. So do you and I. If we make our travel plans now, we can drive over to the school later and discuss a summer school program for Brett with his counselor. How does that sound?"

His reasoning made perfect sense. By June, everyone would be in much better mental shape to hear that she was moving to a nearby apartment.

Grady would fight the divorce at first, but in time he'd see it was the only solution. As for Brett, he'd realize that both parents would always be there for him.

"It sounds fine."

Despite the distance separating them, she felt him relax. "That's all I needed to hear."

"OVER THE PAST SEVERAL weeks, those of you who have been visiting Kilauea have been fortunate enough to see some incredible surface lava flows as they cascade down the *pali*. They've formed a new ocean entry, which is creating a fast-growing coastal bench.

"Most of you are unaware that Kilauea releases about one thousand to two thousand tons of noxious sulfur dioxide into the air each day. Island residents are used to the effects of this gas, a major contributor to volcanic air pollution. It's the cause of the haze you will see on the leeward side of the island.

"This week, with the southerly winds, Kilauea has produced pollution that has at times made the air nearly unbreathable."

The ranger's voice droned on and on. Susan had been feeling nauseated ever since they'd flown to the big island from Maui three days ago. Grady had made reservations at Volcano House on the Kilauea crater.

What should have been a thrilling, once-in-a-lifetime opportunity to see the world's most active volcano had, instead, been making her sick to her stomach. It was the fumes.

She hadn't said anything to Grady yet, but she longed to go back to Maui. The first three weeks of their trip had been perfect. Now they were island-hopping, but she couldn't face another flight feeling the way she did.

Perspiration broke out on her body, and her mouth filled with that salty taste. "Grady?" she whispered. "I'm going to be sick." He held her while she bent over to throw up.

"Mom!" she heard Brett cry in alarm.

"She'll be all right," Grady said, calming their son. "Come on. Let's get your mom back to the hotel."

Later, Susan scarcely remembered the journey. All she knew was that her husband carried her the whole distance while she lay limp in his arms. He didn't seem the least out of breath when he finally set her down on the bed in their room.

He didn't ask if she'd had another flashback. He'd learned his lesson too well the other times, but she knew it was what he assumed.

As Brett got her some water, she heard Grady ring for the hotel doctor.

"I don't need one," she murmured. "It's the air here. I've been bothered by it for the last few days."

He stared at her, grim-faced. "Why didn't you tell me?"

"I thought I'd get used to it. When I'm feeling a little better, can we go back to Maui?"

"Of course, but I'm going to have you checked out first. Maybe the doctor can order some oxygen until you've recovered enough to leave the hotel."

But when the doctor arrived and took her vital signs, he told her the pollution wouldn't cause the rise in her blood pressure or her accelerated pulse rate. Something else was going on.

When Grady explained about her amnesia, the doctor felt she should be driven by ambulance to the hospital in Hilo, where a neurosurgeon could examine her and take X rays if he deemed them necessary.

Susan fought the suggestion to no avail. Before long, she was being wheeled into an emergency room cubicle. Her husband and son stood at the end of the examining table as the nurse started taking her vital signs.

Soon afterward, the attending physician came in. He asked Grady and Brett to leave while he did an examination. Then he called for some lab work and X rays.

That part seemed to go on forever. The only good thing about it was that since throwing up, her stomach didn't feel as queasy.

No matter what the hotel doctor had said, the air had affected her. She felt much better away from the volcano. When she told Grady as much, he didn't act reassured. His taut features were a dead giveaway.

"You should've been checked out by a neurosurgeon before we ever came on this trip. It's my fault. I was too eager to get away."

The anguish in his eyes reminded her of another night more than a month ago when he realized she couldn't remember the explosion that had robbed him and Brett of their wife and mother. When she couldn't remember *him*.

She still couldn't. Something told her she never would.

Once again she was powerless to take away his anguish. It was still there. A wound bleeding more profusely than ever.

They'd had a wonderful holiday together, but now she needed to go back to Las Vegas and begin a new life. So did he. The sooner, the better.

With Brett gone for the moment to find a soda, she

felt this would be a good time to broach the subject of their going home.

"Grady," she whispered. "As soon as I'm released, I think it would be best if we flew back to Nevada."

That awful bleakness she sometimes saw in his gaze was visible now. "Is that what you really want?"

"Yes. I've loved the trip, bu—"

"Mrs. Corbitt?" The doctor suddenly appeared, interrupting their conversation. "The radiologist finds nothing wrong with your X rays, so we won't need to call in a neurosurgeon."

Susan had thought her husband would be relieved by that much good news, but he appeared as solemn and tight-lipped as ever.

"While we're waiting for the results from the lab, I'll order one more test that we didn't run."

"Why not?" Grady snapped.

"To save time and money in case the X rays revealed the problem," the doctor answered with unflappable calm. "This one shouldn't take long. If you'll step outside for a moment, Mr. Corbitt, I'd like to talk to your wife."

The doctor had already taken her history and knew about her amnesia. It surprised her that he had any further questions. She could tell that Grady was more upset than ever.

"Why don't you find Brett and get a drink, too?" she urged him.

He hesitated, then left the cubicle without saying

anything. The doctor sat down on the stool next to her and took her pulse.

"Your color is much better. I take it the nausea isn't as bad."

"No. It's gone. Actually, I'm hungry now."

He eyed her for a moment before taking her blood pressure. When he'd finished, he said, "Your pulse is normal, and your blood pressure has dropped. All of that's a good sign. Tell me—when was the last time you had a period?"

"I don't remember. Six or seven weeks ago."

"You don't keep track?"

"No. There's no reason."

"Are you on birth control?"

She blinked. "No. I can't have children."

His brows quirked. "You have a son who looks just like you."

Susan smiled. "After he was born, I was never able to conceive. Since my amnesia, my husband and I haven't had sex. I take that back. We did one night, about a month ago." Her eyes filled with tears. "It was a disaster."

"I see."

"Why are you asking me *these* questions?"

"Just checking for the possibility of female problems. Did you notice any pain in your ovaries when you became ill on Kilauea? Sometimes when an egg bursts, it causes a woman to faint. That might have happened to you. Especially since you'd been doing some hiking and could have been a little dehydrated."

She shook her head. "No. There was no pain. All

I could think about was how much I wanted a breath of fresh air.''

He stood up and patted her arm. ''I'll be back soon with some answers.''

''What do you mean, 'answers'?''

''If we still haven't found out what's wrong, at least the lab tests will tell us what we can rule out. Then I'll order others, but I suspect they won't be necessary.'' After a pause, he said, ''I'll send your husband back in. I don't remember the last time I saw a man this worried about his wife.''

''We've been through too much with my amnesia. Grady's in pain because I don't remember him or our life together. I can't take it anymore. Neither can he. That's why we're getting a divorce as soon as we fly home.''

''I'm sorry to hear that.''

''Don't be. It's the only way to end the pain.''

CHAPTER FIFTEEN

THE VENDING MACHINES were located at one end of the emergency waiting room. Grady felt Brett's eyes on him as they drank their sodas.

"If Mom's head is okay, then what do you think's wrong with her?"

I wish to God I knew.

"I'm sure it's nothing too serious," he lied, trying to reassure his son. "She seems better since we brought her here."

"That's what I think, too. Maybe it's what she said." Brett sounded a little brighter. "The gas from the volcano made her sick."

Somehow Grady couldn't believe it was that simple, but the thought of her suffering a debilitating or life-threatening disease was too horrifying to consider. He tossed his can in the wastebasket, needing a physical release for his anxiety.

"Let's go back to your mother."

When they entered her cubicle, the ache in his stomach was worse than ever. He moved to the head of the examining table and kissed her forehead. To his relief, the clamminess had left her skin.

"How are you feeling?"

"Much better."

"You look healthy, Mom."

"I'm sorry I gave both of you such a fright. When I'm released, why don't I stay in a hotel here in Hilo while you two go back to Kilauea and take that hike you planned?"

Grady shook his head. "If you recall, we decided to do everything on this trip together."

"Yeah, Mom. Besides, nothing's as much fun without you."

"Is that right?" she teased.

"Mrs. Corbitt?" The doctor entered the cubicle holding a cup with a straw. "Now that I know the results, you can drink this juice." As soon as he handed it to her, she sucked thirstily.

"Is my mom going to be all right?"

"More than all right. She's going to be terrific, but I'd like to talk to your parents alone first. Would you mind waiting in the lounge? They'll come for you in a few minutes."

"Okay. Sure." Brett sent both of them a nervous smile before disappearing.

"What's the verdict?" Grady demanded.

"Before I tell you, I have to say that I sincerely hope you two decide against a divorce."

Grady froze. *She'd confided that to a stranger?* He was hardly aware that the doctor was still talking.

"...not only for your son's sake, but for the baby you're going to have around mid-February."

The cup fell to the floor, disturbing the instant stillness that had pervaded the cubicle.

"What did you say?" Susan was the first to cry out.

"You're pregnant. Congratulations."

"We're going to have another child?" Grady half gasped the question in disbelief. And delight...

Now she *couldn't* leave him.

The satisfaction of that knowledge was so great, he couldn't control his emotions.

"That's right," the doctor said. "As soon as you return home, I suggest you contact your obstetrician for a complete physical. From this point on, you mustn't take any medication. You'll need to get started on a prenatal vitamin regimen right away.

"Now I'll give you two some time alone. You're welcome to leave the hospital whenever you're ready."

Grady glanced at his wife. She looked so staggered, he found himself wondering if she would've preferred hearing she had cancer or some other critical illness.

He took a shuddering breath. "You can forget about a divorce. I would never have given you one, anyway. As for getting you pregnant, I'm not about to apologize for the fact that I didn't use protection.

"It isn't as if we didn't try to have a baby after Brett was born. Even if you don't want one now, I do."

Fearing he'd explode in front of her, he left the cubicle to collect his thoughts outside before he broke the news to Brett.

GRADY? MY PERIOD CAME.

Don't worry about it, sweetheart. There's always next month.

No, there isn't. I've just turned thirty-six. The clock is running out.

Don't be ridiculous. You still have years.

Years— I'll be forty before I know it. That's too late. I was so sure I was pregnant this time. I want to have another baby so badly, but I'm afraid it's never going to happen now.

It's not important.

You're just saying that to make me feel better, but I know how you really feel.

No, you don't. I'm satisfied with my family just the way it is.

You should've married a woman who could give you a house full of children.

I didn't want another woman. Remember? I married you.

We were young and didn't know what the future would hold. For your sake I should've listened when you brought up the subject of adoption. I've been horribly selfish, but I wanted to give you another baby of our very own.

You gave me Brett. No man could ask for more.

That isn't what Jenny told me.

What are you talking about?

She said you told Matt you desperately wanted a large family because you were an only child.

I never said that to him or anyone else!

But she said—

Then she lied.

I don't think she did. You're always trying to protect me, Grady. I'm sorry I've been a disappointment to you.

That's it. Stay right where you are. I'm coming home. Get ready for a night of loving that'll convince you I'm the happiest man alive. I love you, Susan. I always have, from the moment I saw you on the beach. You know how it was with us. How it always will be. How can you possibly doubt it?

"I don't want to doubt it, Grady. I adore you."

"Mom?"

Brett's voice reached her through the myriad of memories filling her mind so fast she couldn't contain them all. She lifted wet eyes to her son.

"Mom, I've been waiting, and I finally decided to come in. That's when I heard you talking to Dad just now, but he's not here. Why are you crying? What's going on?"

Brett sounded frantic.

She jumped off the examining table and threw her arms around him.

"I remember your father!" She began sobbing, overcome with joy. "I remember everything!"

When the news registered, he pulled away, just far enough to look at her. "So *that's* why you got sick! Oh, Mom..." The light in his eyes almost blinded her.

"No, darling. That's not the reason. The doctor just told me I'm pregnant. My first bout of morning sickness hit while we were on that nature walk. I've always wanted another child so badly, the news must have removed the final block."

Brett's eyes grew two sizes.

"You're really going to have a baby?"

"Yes!" she cried out, uncaring if everyone in the

ER could hear. "I'm due next February. We'll know in a few months if it's a boy or a girl."

"Whoa— Does Dad know?"

"Yes, but he thought I was unhappy about it. He left before I could tell him I'd regained my memory."

"I've got to tell him!"

"No—wait. Let me get dressed and we'll both look for him."

She threw on her clothes in record time and then they dashed through the emergency room and out the automatic doors to the drive.

"Where's the car?"

"After we followed the ambulance, Dad parked the rental car down the street."

"If I know him, he's taken a walk to blow off steam. I have a duplicate key. We'll get in the car and cruise around until we find him. When you see him, get down so he doesn't know you're in there with me."

"How come?"

"Just do it, darling, and I'll explain later."

"Okay."

She was going to do something she hadn't done since those first two weeks after meeting him seventeen years ago. Because of her, he'd ended up staying at a friend's much longer than he'd planned.

Without transportation, he'd been forced to rely on her if they wanted to drive anywhere. Every morning she'd cruise by his friend's house in her mom's convertible and act as if she was trying to pick him up. He loved it, especially when she did it in front of all his buddies....

GRADY CHECKED HIS WATCH. He'd been gone longer than he'd realized. What kind of monster was he to blow up at her again and storm out of the hospital when she'd just learned she was pregnant with his child? Deserting her and Brett like that was unforgivable.

He picked up his pace and swung around the back side of the hospital where other people were walking. There was a considerable distance to go before he reached the entrance to the ER.

The sound of screeching tires distracted him for a moment. Some idiot had made a U-turn along the busy street. The car drew up next to the curb and began keeping pace with him. He started to jog. It still followed him.

What the hell?

The traffic behind it had been forced to slow down, or wait to pass. Horns were honking, and angry drivers were creating a scene. Everyone was staring, trying to see what was going on.

He heard a wolf whistle. "Hey, Grady Corbitt— you're looking mighty fine today! How about plunking that gorgeous bod in my car? What do you say, baby?"

Grady kept jogging until that voice and those words finally registered, triggering echoes from the past. He stopped in his tracks.

From the corner of his eye, he saw the car pull into a parking space. A knockout blonde opened the door, throwing him a beguiling smile.

"You know you want to come with me," she said in front of a dozen fascinated onlookers. "We can fool around for as long as you want. Nobody's home today. What's the matter, Grady? Don't tell me the guys in Las Vegas are chicken?''

His heart lurched out of control.

His entire body yearned toward her.

"You're flirting with danger, sweetheart."

"So far, you're all talk. Why don't you try proving it for a change? Let's see what you've got."

"I intend to."

He started for her.

"Uh-oh." She ran away from him, laughing the excited, shaky laugh that used to drive him crazy. Her beautiful long legs were driving him crazy.

She was a fast runner. The years hadn't slowed her down. But he was faster.

"You're in for it now."

"No, Grady," she screamed in frightened delight.

He caught her and whirled her around to face him.

And then he saw it for the first time since she'd come back into their lives.

Recognition.

Her blue eyes were charged by it.

This was the wife he'd been waiting for, aching for.

"Darling" was all she said before she threw her arms around his neck and sought his mouth with a voluptuous hunger that he now knew deep in his soul had always been reserved for him.

Oblivious to the whistles and shouts from passing cars, he crushed her against him. He had no idea how long they clung to each other. This was his beloved wife who'd been restored to him. Nothing else mattered.

BRETT KEPT TURNING AROUND to see if they were coming back to the car. It was embarrassing to watch his parents acting like some of the couples at school who made out by their lockers. At least they were in Hawaii where nobody knew them.

But inside he was feeling a new excitement about life. His mom was back. That meant his dad was going to be happy again. And they were going to have another baby, something his mom had always wanted.

Everything would be perfect if only he could tell Mike about it. Well, maybe he could call Uncle Todd. There was a two-hour difference between Hawaii and California. At three on a Saturday afternoon, his uncle was probably home.

He glanced back one more time. His parents didn't look like they'd be coming to the car anytime soon.

His dad's cell phone lay on the seat. He grabbed it and punched the preprogrammed button. It rang a long time.

"Hello?"

"Uncle Todd?"

"Brett, I didn't expect to hear from you. Where are you, anyway?"

"In Hilo. I just thought you'd like to know Mom's going to have another baby."

"What?" he cried out. "Hey—hang on a minute."

Brett could hear him tell his aunt Beverly to get on the other phone.

"Okay. She's listening, too. Say that again."

"Mom's having a baby in February. She just found out today. And guess what else? She got her memory back."

His uncle went real quiet. Brett could hear a couple of coughs and sniffles. His aunt was crying in the background.

"I guess I don't have to ask how your dad's feeling."

"Nope."

"Can I talk to them?"

"Not right now. They're busy."

Laughter burst out of his uncle. "Dare I ask what they're doing?"

"Kissing. I've been waiting for them to come back to the car, but I don't think that's going to happen for a while. That's why I called you."

"Where are they?"

"Out in front of the hospital where everyone can see them."

"The *hospital*," his aunt cried.

Brett launched into an explanation of what had happened at the volcano. "It was really scary. Dad still can't believe it."

"I'm surprised he didn't pass out when he found he was going to be a father again," his uncle teased. "It means middle-of-the-night feedings, changing diapers. I hope you're ready for that."

"I think it'll be fun."

"So what do you want? A brother or a sister?"

"I don't care. Mom told me about the first baby she lost. I just hope she doesn't lose this one."

"She won't," his uncle declared. "This baby has

been on order for a lot of years. Nothing's going to go wrong now."

"You're right. Mom came back from the dead."

"She sure did. It's all meant to be."

"Uh-oh. I can see them through the rearview mirror. They're walking this way. I've got to hang up. Make sure you tell Grandma everything."

"Don't worry. We will. When your parents come down to earth, tell them to call us."

"Okay. Bye for now."

He clicked off and left the phone where he'd found it, then sat back and waited. When his father opened the door for his mother, Brett caught a glimpse of their faces. The joy he saw there made him feel as if he were floating.

"Did you think we were never coming back?" his dad asked after they got into the car.

His mom turned toward him. "I'm sorry we were so long."

"That's okay, but I'm getting hungry. Do you think we could go eat?"

"Your mother just asked the same question. We'll find a hotel for the night and order room service. After what she's been through today, she needs food and an early night."

Brett could tell his parents were impatient to be alone together. He figured they'd be like this for the rest of their vacation.

As soon as they went to bed, he'd call his aunt and uncle again and tell them to come to Hawaii with his cousins so he'd have someone to do things with. Lizzy and Karin were better than nothing.

A SOFT NIGHT BREEZE WAFTED through the open doors of the hotel room balcony. The balmy air of the islands acted like an aphrodisiac on Grady's senses. An exhilaration he'd never known before kept him awake.

Susan lay in his arms with her face buried in his neck. For the last eight hours, their need for each other had been insatiable. It would be morning soon. He was afraid he'd worn her out.

Knowing she was pregnant, he should have been more careful. But tonight was like their first honeymoon, their passion so overwhelming, they couldn't get enough of each other. They'd lived through those agonizing six months of separation, and their marriage was more precious to them than ever.

"Do you have any idea how much I love you?" she whispered, pressing kisses against his jaw.

He'd thought she'd fallen asleep. Thrilled that she hadn't, he pulled her tighter against him and kissed her hair. "I think we're both pretty clear about how we feel."

"Oh, Grady," she cried softly. "What if Brett hadn't gone down those stairs when he did—"

"Then it probably would've taken you longer to recover your memory before you came back to me. It's a strange irony that the man who separated us unwittingly united us, too, when he invited Brett to have dinner at the Etoile that night."

She raised her head to look at him. "Now that I remember everything, there's so much to tell you."

He kissed the mouth that had done the most wonderful things to him all night. "We've got the rest of our lives."

"I know, but I'd rather tell you now to get it out of the way."

"This sounds serious."

"It is, because it caused you so much pain when there was no need."

Grady raised himself on one elbow. "We've already discussed Jennifer, and we don't ever need to mention her name again."

"I agree. What I'm talking about is the reason I never discussed the Drummond account with you."

"I can guess. You suspected Ellen was involved."

"Yes. I knew she handled Jim's books. But even before that, I was given Mr. Beck's notebook. In it, he'd raised some questions that bothered me, too.

"The more discrepancies I found between the schedule of values and the purchase orders, the more I realized he'd discovered some problems before he died. After some additional digging on my part, it looked to me like Jim and Ellen had been working a con for years.

"I didn't want to believe it of either of them. Anyway, the day before I was to meet with Mr. LeBaron at the plant, I checked into a room at the Etoile to do some snooping."

"*What?*"

"Yes. I took my camera and some tools with me. First I lifted the bathroom ceiling cover to see what type of fan had been installed. Sure enough, the cheapest kind had been put in, though a much better one had been specified by the architect. I took pictures before I put the cover back.''

Grady couldn't believe his ears. ''Where's the film?''

''I guess it's still in my camera on our closet shelf.''

''You mean all this time vital clues have been sitting there and I had no idea?''

''I'm sorry, darling. My whole intention in keeping quiet was to impress you if I uncovered hard evidence. The next thing I did was chip the tub with the hammer.''

''Good grief!''

''Guess what? I discovered steel, even though cast-iron tubs had been designated. After taking more pictures, I went in the other room and removed some trim from the wall. At the hardware store the man told me it was poplar, with a maple stain.

''When I returned to the hotel, I took a picture before I nailed the trim back. Later at the front desk, I told the receptionist I dropped my metal hair dryer in the tub by accident and it chipped the enamel. I offered them $400 cash to pay for a new tub.

''They were very nice about it and said the hotel carried insurance for mishaps of that type. So I paid cash for the room and checked out.''

Grady didn't know whether to laugh or cry. ''If Brett could hear this, he'd say you make a scary detective, my love.'' He rocked her in his arms. *Wait till the guys down at the station heard about this.*

''No matter how terrible I felt about the Stevenses' involvement, I was excited about my finds. My plan was to meet with Mr. LeBaron the next morning, then come home and tell you everything so you could take over from there.''

He clutched her to him. ''Never doubt that you've impressed me. What I want to know now is if you're ready to talk about what happened at the plant.''

''There's very little to tell.''

''What do you mean?'' He eased her away from him so he could see her expression.

''When I arrived there, I saw a car and presumed it was Mr. LeBaron's. As I was getting out of mine, somebody must have crept up behind me. All I remember was this hand clamping a cloth over my nose and mouth. It had a suffocating smell. My next memory was of waking up at the reservation clinic.''

Tears stung his eyes. ''Thank God you were spared the horror of knowing what went on after you passed out.''

She cupped his face in her hands and kissed his eyelids. ''I agree it was a great blessing. Until Jim's trial when it all comes out, I don't want to think about it anymore.''

''Neither do I. So, how soon do you want to go back to your job with the Lytie Group? After your brilliant handling of the account, they'll probably promote you to vice president.''

''I don't want that job, at least not in the foreseeable future.''

''Why not?''

She pressed a passionate kiss to his mouth. ''Because I'd rather stay home and take care of you and our children.''

"You don't have to say that to please me."

"I know. However, you need to understand that the only reason I went to work before was to help with our financial situation. Since I've found out that isn't necessary, I'd rather stay home and pamper myself during this pregnancy. I'm not getting any younger.

"When our child's in school, I'll probably do some work at the women's shelter. It's a place where I know I can make a meaningful contribution. In the meantime, all I want to do is luxuriate in the excitement of carrying our baby.

"We have important things to discuss, like turning the guest bedroom into a nursery and picking out names.

"If it's a girl, I was thinking Kristy Ann Corbitt after your mother and grandmother. If it's a boy, Richard Payne Corbitt in honor of your father and grandfather. We could call him R.P. for short. Brett would love it."

After a long pause, he whispered, "You won't get a dissenting vote from me."

"Good. Now that everything's settled, what do you say we fool around?"

His body quickened. "For how long?"

She slid her hand over his chest. "Poor Grady. You must be tired. There was a time when you would've gotten down to it without asking that question. I'm afraid your age is showing."

His Susan was back.

He grinned in the darkness before taking her in his arms.

Much, much later, as sunlight streamed into the

room, Grady's last thought was that the human experience didn't get better than this. A son sleeping peacefully in the adjoining room, a baby on the way, and the love of his life nestled against his heart where she'd always belonged.

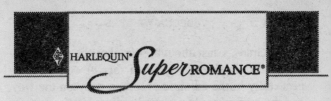

HARLEQUIN *Super* ROMANCE®

One of our most popular story themes ever...

Pregnancy is an important event in a woman's life—
and in a man's. It should be a shared experience,
a time of anticipation and excitement.
But what happens when a woman is
pregnant and on her own?

**Watch for these books in our
9 Months Later series:**

What the Heart Wants by Jean Brashear (July)

Her Baby's Father by Anne Haven (August)

A Baby of Her Own by Brenda Novak
(September)

The Baby Plan by Susan Gable (December)

Wherever Harlequin books are sold.

HARLEQUIN®

Makes any time special ®

TRUEBLOOD, TEXAS

Coming in June 2002...
THE RANCHER'S BRIDE
by
USA Today bestselling author
Tara Taylor Quinn

Lost:

His bride. Minutes before the minister was about to pronounce them married, Max Santana's bride had turned and hightailed it out of the church.

Found:

Her flesh and blood. Rachel Blair thought she'd finally put her college days behind her—but the child she'd given up for adoption haunted her still.

Could Max really understand that her future included mothering this child, no matter what?

Finders Keepers: bringing families together

HARLEQUIN®
Makes any time special ®

Visit us at www.eHarlequin.com

TBTCNM10

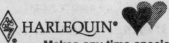

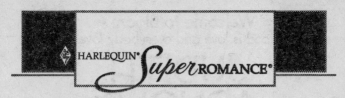

HARLEQUIN *Super*ROMANCE®

They'd grown up at Serenity House—a group home
for teenage girls in trouble. Now Paige, Darcy and
Annabelle are coming back for a special reunion,
and each has her own story to tell.

SERENITY HOUSE

An exciting new trilogy
by
Kathryn Shay

Practice Makes Perfect—June 2002

A Place to Belong—Winter 2003

Against All Odds—Spring 2003

Available wherever Harlequin books are sold.

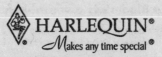

HARLEQUIN®

Makes any time special®

Visit us at www.eHarlequin.com

HSSH05